SPEAK NO EVIL

CHRISTIAN ROMANTIC SUSPENSE

THE LOST ARE FOUND
BOOK TWO

REBECCA HARTT

Edited by
JULIE SCHWARZBURG

Rise UP
PUBLICATIONS

ALSO BY REBECCA HARTT

The Acts of Valor Series

Returning to Eden

Every Secret Thing

Cry in the Wilderness

Rising From Ashes

Braving the Valley

All Things Together

The Lost Are Found

Fear No Evil

Speak No Evil

Flee From Evil

Released September 2025
ISBN: 978-1-64457-783-7

Rise UP Publications
644 Shrewsbury Commons Ave
Ste 249
Shrewsbury PA 17361
United States of America
www.riseUPpublications.com
Phone: 866-846-5123

PROLOGUE

FOURTEEN YEARS AGO, MIAMI, FLORIDA

Gabriel Villalobos, eighteen years old, blew out a nervous breath as he waited in the visitation room. His stomach growled. Sitting behind a window of Lexan glass, wearing an orange jumpsuit and wringing his hands, he pondered who might be coming to see him. Only Felix, his stepfather, had visited him days earlier, promising he would "fix the situation." Mamá couldn't afford to take time off from work, so Felix had to be the reason why Gabe had been summoned here.

The awful food he was served wasn't enough to feed his growing body. It sickened him anyway. How long had he been here? At least a week. All the days ran together into one big blur of confusion and dread. How could his decision to help a young woman in distress have backfired so badly?

Pricking his ears, Gabe overheard his visitor enter the sterile space. But it wasn't Felix. The mid-forties man helping himself to the chair on the other side of the glass partition and wearing a suit that strained to cover his midsection was a stranger. He set a brief-case on the countertop between them and popped it open.

"You're Gabriel Villalobos?" He eyed Gabe through the lenses of his glasses as his voice came through the slit in the window.

"Yes, sir."

"I'm John de Silva. I'm your lawyer."

Confused, Gabe watched the man take a stapled packet of papers and a pen from his briefcase before he shut it and placed it by his feet.

"But I already have a court-appointed lawyer."

That earned him a dispassionate glance. "Felix Suarez hired me to represent you. Trust me, if your court-appointed lawyer couldn't get you a bond, you don't want him working on your case."

So, Gabe's stepfather had *hired* this man? How could he afford him? Felix worked as a night custodian, making twenty an hour, which barely covered the rent for him, Mamá, and Isiris. Gabe swallowed the sudden lump in his throat. Felix had gone to bat for him.

"So," the lawyer was frowning at the packet of papers, "you're being charged with attempted rape and malicious wounding. Why don't you describe to me what happened?"

Gabe scrubbed a hand over his eyes. He'd hardly slept since being thrown into this place. "On May 28th, I went to a graduation party at Wendie Pheifer's house."

"Pheifer?" The lawyer's sparse eyebrows rose before he searched the printout, looking for the name. "As in Pheifer Pharmaceuticals?"

Gabe shrugged. "I guess."

"Is she a friend of yours?"

"No. I went to the party 'cause I wanted to see how the other half lived. The whole school was invited."

"Did any of your friends go with you?"

"Yeah. Danny Fry, but he left before I did, so he didn't see anything."

"You didn't have any other friends there?"

"I don't have time for lots of friends. I work after school."

"Okay… so you went to this party and then what?"

Gabe pictured the ill-fated event. "Danny and I swam for a while. Most of the party was out on the deck, where they have a pool and a hot tub. After we swam, we had pizza—"

"Was there alcohol? Were you drinking?"

"Oh, there was plenty of alcohol, but I don't drink." Memories of his real father screaming, hitting, always with a beer can in his hand, flashed through his head.

The lawyer raised a disbelieving eyebrow. He looked back at the paperwork. "That's not what the field officer reported." His gaze dropped. "*But* your blood alcohol shows zero, so I guess you weren't. Hmph." He looked back up. "So, then what?"

"Danny and I went inside to play foosball. They have a big game room off the deck with a pool table and pinball machines. After Danny left, I decided to leave too. But first I used the hallway bathroom, and that's when I heard Wendie screaming, '*Stop it!*' in a room above me."

"How'd you know it was her?"

Gabe shrugged. "I just recognized her voice. I heard it all the time at school. I wanted to mind my own business, but…" The cries had triggered memories of his mother in distress.

"So, you went to investigate."

"Yes." He'd taken the stairs three at a time. "Finding the right room was easy. She's a loud person. The door was locked, so I used my debit card to get it open—"

"You broke in with a debit card?"

Why did people always act like that was such a crime? "Yes."

"Huh." De Silva held a finger up, telling him to wait a minute while he examined the document. He looked back up. "And what did you see after you broke in?"

"Wendie was on the bed being held down by two guys, Chad Simkins and Wes Bosman. They were… forcing her."

"You knew who they were?"

"They're baseball players; everyone knows who they are. What's weird is they're also Wendie's friends. I saw them by her locker all the time. She would flirt with them." Not that she deserved what they were doing to her.

"What happened then?"

"They wouldn't get off her, so I got them off."

The lawyer frowned down at the stapled printout. "Says here, both boys were bleeding when the police showed up. One had a broken nose. The other had a broken jaw. That's the basis for the malicious wounding charge. Are you willing to admit you're responsible?"

The satisfaction of hearing their bones crack under his knuckles hadn't waned. "They deserved it." He described what they were doing to Wendie.

De Silva winced, then studied his report again. He seemed to read the same paragraph three times. "Says here that the victim pointed to you as her attacker. She stated that you'd asked to see her bedroom, and when she took you to it, you locked the door and attacked her. Her two friends heard her screaming, broke into the locked door to pull you off her, but then you beat *them* up."

Gabe's temples throbbed, *woosh, woosh, woosh.* "She's lying. I would never do that to a woman—*ever.*"

De Silva shook his head, clearly confused. "But what does she gain by lying?"

"If I knew that, I wouldn't be sitting in here." Realizing he was talking through his teeth, Gabe flexed his jaw muscles. An idea sparked in his head. He sat forward. "Look, you just said they broke into the room? If they forced the lock, then the door frame should be damaged. But I didn't damage the door because I used a debit card to get in. There's the proof right there."

The lawyer had probably never been told how to argue a case, let alone by an eighteen-year-old Puerto Rican. Gabe didn't care. He was past caring. "Wendy's lying. For whatever reason, she's throwing *me* under the bus instead of two guys who are supposedly her friends. Maybe she doesn't want them getting into trouble—I don't know. All I know is I can't afford to sit in here any longer. Felix needs my help putting food on the table. But because of that"—he caught back the vulgar word he was about to call Wendie—"that lying, privileged little princess, I'm locked up in here for no reason!"

Shaking with righteous anger, Gabe reined himself in. Now he had a full-blown headache.

De Silva sent him a slow nod. "All right. I believe you, Gabe. And don't you worry. I'm going to get you out of here. I've set another bond hearing for tomorrow morning. With any luck, you'll be home by lunchtime. I'll see you then."

Sagging back into his chair, Gabe watched the man put everything back in his briefcase before he stood. "See you tomorrow."

"Thank you."

"You bet." With another nod, the lawyer walked away.

Gabe heard the door open and close. Somebody would come for him shortly, taking him back to the chaotic rec room where the inmates all hung out for the day, where, as the youngest, he'd had to use his mallet-like fists to protect himself and establish his rank in the pecking order.

Helplessness swirled in him. Felix was going into debt because of Gabe. His advice when he'd visited the last time replayed in Gabe's head. *"God's not going to let you serve time for a crime you didn't commit, Gabriel. Pray to Him. He will comfort you."*

Blowing out a breath, Gabe tried to pray, but he gave up without much effort. God hadn't heard him when he'd prayed as a boy for his father to change. Why would God listen now?

CHAPTER 1

PRESENT TIME

At zero-two-hundred hours, the Special Operations Craft-Riverine slid with a hiss onto a deserted strip of rain-soaked shore. When it stopped, Lieutenant Gabe Villalobos, call sign Lobo—"wolf" in Spanish—shook off his night ops jacket and stuffed it into the gunwale locker. The Riverine had just delivered the four-man firing squad to their insertion point on the Mexican side of the Rio Grande River, ten miles from Matamoros.

Beneath their night ops jackets, Gabe and his men were dressed to resemble civilians. Oversized T-shirts disguised their pistols and backup blades. A light rain dampened Gabe's black wavy hair as he shouldered his lightweight pack. He'd filled it with the same items all four of them carried: a SIG Sauer mini assault rifle, a three-day supply of Meals Ready to Eat, night-vision monoculars, baby wipes for hygiene, climbing gear, and a fresh T-shirt. Gabe, being the officer in charge, also carried a LEO satellite phone.

Giving his squad the go-signal, he vaulted off the craft into several inches of mud. It sucked at his boots as he high stepped to firmer ground, followed immediately by his men. Vulnerability assailed Gabe in the absence of his night ops attire and camo paint. At least with his swarthy coloring, he could pass for a tall Mexican, while two of his teammates had to wear floppy hats and bronzing lotion.

Despite the cooling rain, a sweat filmed Gabe's skin as he jogged along the humid curve of the river, skirting brambles and hedges, while counting on his men to keep up with him. Over the lapping water and the squish of the mud, he never heard the Riverine retreat on its journey back to the aircraft carrier sitting in the Gulf. In just another hundred yards, they would arrive at a prearranged location, where they would rendezvous with an OGA—other government agency—rep who would drive them to Matamoros proper.

Gabe swept his gaze over the scrubby terrain for potential hostiles before he glanced at his wristwatch. They'd almost reached the coordinates for the meetup. At the edge of a scrubby field, he hunkered in tall grass and waited, followed shortly by his squad members: Rodeo, the blue-eyed cowboy from Montana; Doc, the empathic medic from Maryland; and Zen, a Japanese American from California.

As they rallied around him, scarcely breathing hard, Gabe shrugged off his pack and pulled out his sat phone. A simple three-digit combination put him in touch with his superior.

"Home plate." The operations officer, Lieutenant Commander Strong, was monitoring their every move from the Team building on Dam Neck Naval Annex in Virginia Beach.

"Heads up, Home plate." Gabe tended to encode his comms with baseball jargon—he loved the sport that much. "Miami Marlins are at first base now, waiting for the ump to show up, over."

Rodeo, who was peering through the high-powered scope on his sniper rifle announced, "Here he comes now."

Over the patter of rain, Gabe heard the car coming before he saw it. Twin beams shot over a rise and then sheared the tops of the scrub grass as the car barreled closer.

Their so-called umpire was an undercover DEA officer liaising with the SEALs. Agent Cruz would deliver them to Matamoros and hover nearby as they undertook a forty-eight-hour reconnaissance. Once the target was recovered, Cruz would then speed them to a remote location outside of town to be extracted by helicopter.

"Umpire has arrived, Home plate," Gabe relayed. "We'll check back after the first inning, over."

"Good luck, Marlins. Play ball."

With a scowl, Gabe put his phone away. Strong's words reminded him he'd missed the Marlin's most recent home game because he'd been heading out on an operation that wouldn't be necessary if the daughter of Clark Petroleum's CEO had left Mata- moros when the State Department issued a mandatory evacuation. In her honor, Gabe had dubbed this mission "Operation Dumb Blonde."

"That's our OGA," Rodeo confirmed, lowering his rifle.

A yellow taxi, complete with a lit sign, came to a squeaky stop and dimmed its lights.

"Let's go. Doc, you first."

The lanky medic with psychic abilities darted out of hiding first. He sprinted fifty yards before dropping and providing cover for the rest of them. They reached the cab just as the trunk popped open, inviting them to stow their packs inside it. Zen then covered for Doc, who did the same. As three men crammed into the back seat, grunting at the tight fit, Gabe took shotgun, as was his due as OIC. Cigarette smoke filled the car's interior, which came with plastic seat covers and a working meter.

"Evening." He sized up the undercover agent.

From his thick mustache to the big, shiny buckle on his belt, Cruz resembled a local. "Welcome to hell," he grated, tossing his Marlboro out the window. After engaging the meter like he intended to charge them for every mile, he hammered the accelerator, flinging them all back in their seats as the taxi took off.

Gabe frowned at the man's foreboding words. Beyond the crucifix swinging from the rearview mirror and the slapping wind- shield wipers that ticked like a time bomb, the silhouette of Mata- moros, where rival drug cartels had turned its streets into cemeteries, beckoned them into danger.

The spitting sky, the time of year—late spring—and the circumstances of this op all called to mind what had happened to Gabe at Wendie Pheifer's graduation party. Privileged daddy's girls were nothing but trouble.

Here he was, putting himself and his teammates into peril for what? To extricate the precious daughter of an oil magnate from troubles of her own making? Was she looking for attention? Or was she just so accustomed to being treated like a princess that she didn't realize what could happen to her if a member of the Zeta or Gulf Cartels got to her before the SEALs did?

One thing Gabe was sure of: If anything went wrong, he would take the blame. He felt it in his bones. After all, given the SEALs' agenda, the recovery target's father had friends in high places. Everything Gabe had accomplished since high school would count for nothing if the CEO of Clark Petroleum didn't get his daughter back without a hair on her head harmed.

His mouth turned dry at the thought. *No pressure,* he assured himself. *We got this.*

Peering from her third-story window at El Instituto Para La Salud Ambiental, Libby Clark searched the dark campus below her. Once a convent in the heart of Matamoros, the lovely campus comprised colonial-style buildings and graced with centuries-old tulip trees. The fragrance of their blossoms filled her nostrils as she pulled the shutters closed on another stressful day.

By the grace of God, the cartel members who clashed in the streets of Matamoros by day hadn't tried climbing over the ten-foot walls that enclosed the institute. No doubt, the glass shards glimmering wetly atop the walls provided some deterrence, as did the thick wooden gates, all bolted from the inside.

But how long would Libby's luck hold out?

With the first window shuttered, she reclosed the screen from the inside, then moved through her darkening bedchamber to repeat the process on the second and third windows, all located on the topmost floor of the old dormitory building. Given the endless clatter of gunfire by day, the precariousness of her situation wasn't lost on her. Daddy had been right to insist she leave Matamoros days ago. If only it were that easy.

With the dark, drizzling sky now blocked by the shutters, Libby felt her way across the room to the four-poster bed she'd been given. The power had gone out yesterday, not that she would have turned on a light and advertised herself to the outside world. She wasn't that stupid. But her phone, which she'd powered down to save what was left of her battery, only had a 14-percent charge.

After slipping off her wrapper, Libby ducked under the netting in just her thin cotton nightgown. The damp quality of the sheets made her grimace. Northern Mexico was as hot and humid in April as her hometown of Austin was in August. Hot and far more dangerous.

A week ago, she would never have believed the events that were about to unfold. When her employer, International Water Institute, sent her here to teach future scientists how to test water for chemical pollutants, El Instituto was a thriving school of higher education, with twenty-two environmental science professors and two hundred students from all over Mexico.

Just days into her course, an unexpected clash between the Gulf and Zeta cartels escalated into a full-blown war, turning the streets of Matamoros into a battleground. The director had bolted the gates, canceled classes, and ordered all students to leave.

Most of them had scattered immediately. Libby's employer, IWI, had secured her a ride to the airport. She was about to depart when she witnessed the director of El Instituto jumping into a blacked-out car and taking off, leaving two remaining students still in the school with no way home. Both were young women, only eighteen and nineteen years of age.

How could Libby abandon them knowing the horrors that awaited them if they fell into the hands of the clashing cartels? She couldn't. She had told as much to her father after he heard from IWI that she hadn't left.

He had pleaded with her. *"Libby, think of your own safety. The U.S.*

State Department just issued a mandatory evacuation for all Americans. You can't stay." But she had, throwing herself into helping the girls find a way home. Alas, neither of their families nor any of their friends owned a running vehicle. Public transportation had ground to a halt. There wasn't a taxi driver in all of Matamoros willing to give them a ride—not for the meager five thousand pesos Libby had on hand. And no one in these parts had even heard of Cash App, PayPal, or Venmo.

Libby's father could have hired some mercenaries to help her get the girls home—not to mention herself—but turning to Daddy would only prove what he had insisted ever since IWI had hired her back in January. She'd heard him fret at least a dozen times: "*A young, pretty woman in a Third-World country is going to end up getting kidnapped or killed.*"

Libby closed her eyes and clasped her hands together. *Please, Lord, don't let that happen. You know how dire my situation is becoming. I think I need Your help to get out of this.*

Agent Cruz delivered the SEALs to an abandoned office building where a large corner office on the third floor could be used as their command center. Not only was it situated in the heart of Matamoros, but their hideout sat catty-corner to their recovery target's last confirmed location—the Institute for Environmental Health when translated from Spanish.

They arrived at dawn, tossing their packs onto the office's linoleum floor where they slept, rotating watch every hour until daylight shone through the windows and roused them.

With rain still dappling the street below, Gabe and his men studied their surroundings through the four glass windows, each cracked to admit the warm, wet air. Their hideout put them at the intersection of Avenida Juárez, lined with colorful, flat-roofed, three-story buildings like this one, and Calle Reforma, where El Instituto sat across from a shuttered municipal monstrosity.

From what Gabe could see, the former convent was

surrounded by a high stone wall that cloistered a sandstone chapel and several rectangular buildings, all painted salmon pink and surrounded by gnarled, old trees blooming with pink and white flowers, the scent of which floated across the street and into their command center.

It was still early morning when movement on the third story of one of the colonial-era buildings caught his notice. A woman leaned out of the window as she opened the wooden shutters. Having seen a photo of his recovery target, Gabe's stomach lurched with recognition—and with something else he couldn't put a finger on. "There she is! One o'clock, third story."

His men all scrambled for a look.

Rodeo gave a low whistle as she came into view opening the second set of shutters. "Well, hello, darlin'."

Elizabeth Clark was somebody's darling all right—her daddy's. Honey-blonde hair cascaded over her shoulder as she peered warily out at the sleeping city.

Gabe turned to the medic, whose different-colored eyes, one blue, one brown, made his gift of knowing things before they happened seem twice as cool. "Picking up on anything, Doc?"

"Yeah. She's scared."

No kidding. Even Gabe, whose sister accused him of being a numbskull, could tell that much.

The disturbing thing was that Miss Clark was about to get the fright of her life because the SEALs had been told to nab and grab her without any advanced warning. For reasons unknown to them, she had refused to leave Matamoros and would likely resist an escort out.

Why? Did the silver spoon in her mouth interfere with common sense?

As she vanished from her windows, Gabe tempered his impatience, and their forty-eight-hour reconnaissance continued. Waiting and watching was SOP—standard operating procedure—but to men who thrived on action, it felt like torture.

Throughout the morning, Rodeo regaled them with stories of the various Mustangs he had tamed and the time he had wrestled a mountain lion. He showed them the scars on his forearm to back up his claim, though Doc's eye roll suggested some embellishment.

Around midday, a looter intent on pillaging the abandoned office building tried to get into their command center. When he shot at their locked door and stumbled into their hideout, a brief firefight ensued, leaving the looter dead.

Gabe fumed as he dragged the man's body downstairs, depositing him on the street corner to be collected by anyone who recognized him. Poor guy. He probably had kids at home, waiting to be fed.

Let that be on Elizabeth's conscience, not mine.

Next, they watched Rodeo, who could fix anything, replace their doorknob, lock and all, with hardware appropriated from an office down the hall. Gabe called Home plate to apprise Lieutenant Commander Strong of the scuffle. Strong suggested they relocate, but a move at this juncture would delay the recovery of the target, and their view of El Instituto was so good that they voted to stay.

Their wait ensued. Gabe regarded Doc who had a surprising skill set. The medic could recite verse verbatim, allowing him to spout off lines of literature or poetry that fit just about every occasion. "Noah, give us some Shakespeare to ennoble this tedious situation."

Doc thought for a split second. "'Beware the leader who bangs the drums of war in order to whip the citizenry into a patriotic fervor.'"

As though in response to Doc's words, a spate of gunfire rang out. The weather had cleared, and the drug cartels were creeping back into the puddle-filled streets to kill each other. All the SEALs could do was watch and wait.

Home plate sent an update that the Mexican National Guard was planning to besiege the city in two days and wrest it from the cartels. The Miami Marlins needed to win the World Series and leave Matamoros with a trophy before then.

Gotcha.

An endless and boring evening crawled by, enlivened only by the reappearance of Elizabeth Clark at dusk when she pulled the shutters closed on what had to be the room where she slept.

Watching her, Gabe's pulse quickened with a visceral feeling he reluctantly acknowledged was attraction. She was gorgeous. But her worried expression made his eyebrows pull together. If she was so concerned by her circumstances, why hadn't she left the institute *days* ago when it was still safe to flee?

At long last, darkness descended over the city, and the streets fell quiet. It was finally time to reconnoiter. The night belonged to the operators.

Gabe guided his squad down the stairs of their building and cut the side door. Seeing the body of the looter still there, guilt assailed him. *Not my fault,* he reminded himself.

Their best point of entry into El Instituto was near the rear gate, which emptied onto an alley unseen from their hideout. Zen Suzuki, who had the moves of a ninja, leaped off Doc's back and hurdled the wall, glass shards and all, before opening the gate to them. As the metal bolt grated open, a dog in the neighborhood behind them started barking.

Doc and Zen went one way; Gabe and Rodeo went the other, mapping the area and testing all the doors and windows. They finally rallied up at the steps of the sandstone chapel and compared notes.

Someone had secured all points of entry. If the princess had done that, she got points for being thorough. Unfortunately, the only way for the SEALs to get to her was to scale the three-story building where she slept. Its colonial architecture made that feasible since every window above the ground floor was fronted by a narrow wrought-iron balcony. Gabe, who weighed the most, climbed atop Rodeo's and Zen's shoulders to assess the viability of the wrought-iron structures. If they could hold *his* weight, they could hold Rodeo's.

The exercise confirmed something Gabe was already well aware of—he hated heights. *Thank you, Princess, for raising my blood pressure.* Nor did he relish the prospect of the ornate little balconies tearing away from the sandstone wall while he scaled them.

The worst part was stepping atop the slender railing of the *second*-story balcony to grasp the bottom rung of the *third*-story balcony so he could pull himself up and *onto* it, dreading all the while that it would give way, plunging him to his death.

Three stories in the air, with a tremor in his fingers, Gabe wedged the point of his Gerber blade in the crack between the two halves of the shutters, gauging his ability to flip the latch on the inside. A debit card would have done a better job, but he managed to wedge the blade where it needed to go. Sending a thumbs-up to his teammates and blowing out a shaky breath, he started the long trek down.

Their plan, to be executed the following night, had come together neatly. So why did it feel as if everything was about to go wrong? If only Miss Clark were a cooperative target—or, better yet, if they'd been given her cell phone number so they could have arranged for her to meet them at the gate. Unlike Zen, who was obsessed with superheroes, Gabe had no desire to play Spider Man.

With the dog starting to bark again, the SEALs withdrew from El Instituto, exiting the same gate into the alley. Zen slid the bolt shut behind them, then scaled a tree growing near the wall. Swinging from a branch, he put one booted foot onto the glass shards before jumping into the alley to join them. Back to their command center they scurried, to wait for the following night.

Their second morning was much like the first. Gabe glared at Elizabeth Clark as she opened her shutters shortly after dawn.

Good morning, Princess.

Given her tousled hair, she hadn't slept very peacefully. Perhaps she'd sensed him just outside her window, plotting how to break in?

With the rain gone and the sun shining, Matamoros came alive like it hadn't the day before. Henchmen of the drug lords, displaying their loyalty to either the Zeta or the Gulf cartels by the colors they wore, barreled down the streets in the back of pickups, shooting arbitrarily at buildings or anyone unfortunate enough to cross their path. Doc flung himself away from the window just before it exploded inward.

Resentment followed Gabe's rush of adrenaline. If not for his psychic gift, Doc would have been maimed, maybe killed, all because Elizabeth Clark hadn't left town when she was supposed to.

The morning dragged on, marked by one aggressive foray after another. From their vantage, it appeared the Zetas had gained the upper hand. Then, just as suddenly as it had started, the craziness subsided as the cartel members withdrew from the heat. Into this lull, the sound of a motorcycle jerked Gabe out of a somnolent state. He peered outside just as the motorcycle slowed, then stopped by the school's closed gate.

Gabe snatched up his mini assault rifle and watched, gobsmacked to see the princess herself poke her head out the front pedestrian gate. *Lady, what the heck?*

"Guys, look at this!"

As his teammates shot to the windows, Gabe kept the driver in his rifle's crosshairs while Elizabeth negotiated some kind of deal with the man. She showed him the money in her pocket, but with a nervous glance around, the rider shook his head and shot away, his motor roaring.

Looking crestfallen, the princess slipped back inside the gate, appearing a short while later as she ran back toward her dorm.

Rodeo shot Gabe a mystified look. "What was that about?"

Doc had the answer. "She offered him money to do something dangerous."

"Like take her away from here?" Gabe clapped a hand to his forehead. They had just missed the perfect opportunity to snatch her off the street.

"Hey, so she must have a phone," Zen pointed out, "assuming she called that guy to come to the gate. Why don't we have her number?"

"We're supposed to catch her off guard, that's why." Gabe stewed at the woman's imposition on their time and safety. She had to be a nut. Why else couldn't they advise her of their proximity?

The hours crept by. With anticipation Gabe didn't care to

analyze, he waited for Miss Clark to shutter her windows for the night. Under a lilac-colored sky, her slim, bare arms looked flawless.

Just you wait, Princess. Tonight's the night.

At zero-one-hundred hours, Gabe's squad packed up their possessions and slipped their packs on their backs. With their mini-SIG Sauers cradled in the crooks of their arms, they left their hiding place for good. Cruz had parked his taxi right outside the building. They dropped their packs in his trunk before crossing the street and making their way to the alley at the back of the school while Cruz took off to wait for them elsewhere.

Breaching the wall as they'd done the night before, the SEALs slipped inside the compound without causing the dog to bark—a good omen. Zen and Doc would guard their perimeter while Gabe and Rodeo scaled the building, broke into the princess's bower, and nabbed her, tranquilizing her if they had to. They would sweep her away from El Instituto and into Cruz's taxi.

Easy day, Gabe kept telling himself.

The climb to her window was only slightly less terrifying since he knew the balconies would hold. Reaching the second story, he waited for Doc to boost Rodeo up behind him before stepping atop the first flimsy railing and pulling himself onto the balcony jutting over him.

The feasibility of breaking in this way angered him. If *he* could climb up Rapunzel's tower, then so could any thug intent on harming her. Did Miss Clark not realize how quickly she could vanish—very much alive but dead to herself and dead to the world? The more he thought about the trouble and effort required to rescue her—not to mention the looter's pointless death—the angrier he got.

By the time he inserted the tip of his Gerber blade into the space between the two shutters, he didn't care if he was particularly loud.

Ping!

As the shutters drifted soundlessly outward, Gabe sidestepped them only to face a screen. In the dark void of the room beyond, a white veil shimmered around a four-poster bed—mosquito netting, he realized. As its occupant rolled over, Gabe signaled over the railing for Rodeo to wait.

The SEALs didn't move again until Gabe was sure Miss Clark was sleeping. Waving up Rodeo, he pushed on the frame of the screen, and it swung silently inward, at which point he stepped gingerly over the low windowsill, one foot at a time until he was standing on the chamber's tiled floor.

There, he drew his monocular from the wide pocket on his shorts and IDed the woman in the bed. Yep, both the mane of golden-blonde hair and the piquant tilt of her nose matched the photo he'd seen when his squad had been briefed.

As Rodeo joined him, slipping through the window with stealth Gabe envied, the monocular went back into Gabe's pocket, and the two of them drifted apart, keeping to the shadows, as planned, to approach her bed from opposite directions.

Once they boxed her in, Gabe would quietly announce them. Depending on her response, he might have to tranquilize her using the loaded syringe in his other pocket. Obviously, they couldn't make a furtive exit with a shrieking woman.

But, just then, someone outside of the school's campus loosed a bloodcurdling scream, and the sleeping princess lurched straight up in bed, hair swirling around her shoulders, eyes wide and fearful.

Gabe flattened himself against the armoire at his back. Rodeo, on the opposite wall, blended into a bookcase.

Well, this was awkward. How was he supposed to cue the woman to their presence without scaring her to death?

CHAPTER 2

Alarm crackled up Libby's spine as she stared at the open window. How had the shutters farthest from her bed fallen open, and the screen frame, too? Either she had forgotten to secure that window or... someone had opened it. But that was impossible, right? She slept on the third floor!

Heart racing, Libby plumbed the shadows of the large chamber, seeing nothing amiss. The croaking of tree frogs outside suggested all was well.

Peeling back the sheet that stuck to her damp skin, she scooted toward the edge of the mattress, intent on crossing the room and closing the shutters—securely this time. As she ducked under the mosquito netting and reached for her wrapper, the sound of a man clearing his throat startled a shriek out of her.

A silhouette emerged from the shadow of her armoire, saying something. Libby jumped back onto her bed, unable to hear his words over the roaring in her ears. He swiped aside the mosquito netting, forcing her to jackknife off the far side of the bed, clutching her wrapper and managing to avoid his outstretched hand as she shook off the mosquito netting.

With a squeal of fear, she bolted toward the door that faced the bed, only to plow into a second man who halted her progress. The first man caught her up from behind, clamping a gloved hand over her mouth and stifling the scream that erupted from her throat. Reacting instinctively, Libby swung her elbow up and back straight into her captor's nose.

Crunch. The man blurted a Spanish expletive, but his grip only tightened. Libby fought desperately to free herself.

"Now calm down, ma'am. We're not here to hurt you."

The words issued by the man in front of her, spoken with a Western drawl, were slow to penetrate.

"We're U.S. Navy SEALs, ma'am. We're on your side. I'm Rodeo and that's Lobo." He nodded at the man subduing her. "We're here to take you home."

Relief liquefied Libby's bones turning her limp in her captor's clutches, though her heart still pounded. That must have been what they'd said to her earlier.

As the gloved hand came off her mouth, Libby sucked in a shaky breath. Her captor released her abruptly, and she staggered a couple of steps away while assessing the pair.

Thank God they weren't a threat, but— "You broke into my room to tell me this?" She gestured at the open window, then hastily donned her wrap. "You snuck in through my *window?*"

Lobo was clasping the nose she might have broken. "This is a clandestine operation." He spoke on a growl, clearly in pain and angry with her. "Did you want us to pull up in a Humvee and blow the horn?"

Libby narrowed her eyes at him. Given the swarthiness of her attacker, she could be excused for thinking him a local—not his partner, though, who looked and sounded like a North American gunslinger.

"Wait." She processed the rest of what the SEAL said. "So, you're here to take me home? As in back to the States?"

"Do you have more than one *home*land?"

Granted, she'd probably broken his nose, but Lobo's surliness was bordering on rude. "How did you know where to find me?" Surely these men had better things to do than to hunt her down.

Rodeo replied, "The State Department issued an evacuation *days* ago, Miss Clark. Your life is in danger, and your father wants you home."

Ah. And there it was. They even knew her name.

Libby heaved an inward sigh. "My father. Of course." She should have guessed her insistence on staying with the young women wouldn't deter her overprotective dad. Not being able to reach her by phone, he had to be frantic by now. "Well… as much as I appreciate your help, gentlemen, it's not that simple."

Lobo cut her off. "We were told you wouldn't want to leave. Rodeo, hold her still."

"What?" Libby took a wary backward step as Rodeo came her way. Before she could take two steps, the shorter man grabbed her, subduing her resistance with astonishing ease. Fright rose as she watched the dark SEAL produce something small and cylindrical from the pocket of his pants. As he pulled off a cap, a needle glinted in the dark.

They were going to *drug* her? "Stop! I'll go with you. You don't need to do that!"

Lobo drew up short, clearly weighing the truth of her statement. Whatever he might have said was interrupted by a knock.

Before Libby could blink, both SEALs were pointing semiautomatics at the door.

"No, don't shoot!" She pushed down Rodeo's weapon.

"*¿Profesora?*" a tentative voice called through the thick wood.

"Who is that?" Lobo hissed.

"That"—Libby managed to free herself from Rodeo's grasp— "is a *student*. There are two young women left at this school with no one to protect them. Don't you think I would have evacuated Matamoros *days* ago if there wasn't a reason why I *couldn't*?"

Without asking for their permission, she went to answer the door.

~

Gabe tensed as Miss Clark threw the door open, displaying two young women standing in the dark hallway. As Rodeo clicked on a penlight and shone it on their terrified faces, Miss Clark reached for them, assuring them in excellent Spanish that the intruders weren't a threat. Their big eyes and dark hair made Gabe think of his kid sister, Isiris. He and Rodeo lowered their mini assault rifles.

Crap. He knew something would go wrong with this rescue op.

The taller of the two murmured, "Are they here to take us home, *Profesora?*"

Elizabeth looked back at Gabe with a challenging expression. "Yes."

"No," he said at the same time.

She faced him. "Well, we can't just leave them here." One slim hand was propped at her waist while the other held her robe closed. "They live in Valle Hermoso. That's only an hour to the south. I assume you have transportation, so let's go."

"Slow down." Gabe's nose throbbed with every heartbeat. He jabbed a finger at his chest. "I am the one in charge here. You are the recovery target and the *only* one we are extracting from Matamoros."

Her jaw dropped with a look of utter disbelief. "Are you heartless? Don't you realize what could happen to these young women if they're left alone? We are not leaving them here!"

"Sir, a word?"

Gabe glanced over to see Rodeo gesturing for him to cross the room for a private conversation. Following his chief to the open window, Gabe checked his watch. The luminescent hands told him the sun would rise in just three hours. He wanted to be landing in Brownsville by then. Kyle Clark would be waiting there for his daughter's safe return.

"We don't have time for this." Rodeo's blue eyes shone like the tritium that made the hands on Gabe's watch glow. "Keep in mind the National Guard is going to take back the city tomorrow and drive the cartels out. Power will be restored, and everything will go back to normal. The young women are safe here."

Were they, though? Even if they weren't, Rodeo was right—they *didn't* have time for this. Gabe pitched his voice too low for the others to hear. "Okay. You tell the women what you just said to me. I'll grab Miss Clark and tranquilize her, and then we'll leave."

"If it makes you feel better, sir, we can send a message to the National Guard asking them to check on the girls once they take the city back."

"Yeah." Glancing back at the young women, Gabe could tell the princess was straining to overhear what they were saying. He looked back at Rodeo. "Ready for this?"

"Sure."

Good because he wasn't.

Together they recrossed the room.

"So, listen," Rodeo began, addressing the younger women, "do either of you speak English?"

Both girls nodded.

"Good. Here's the deal. We don't have the time or the means to get you two home. But"—he forestalled Miss Clark's protest by speaking over her—"the National Guard is taking back Matamoros tomorrow. By this time tomorrow, the cartels will be gone, and order will be established."

"You don't know that." Miss Clark sounded both incredulous and skeptical.

"We're optimistic." Gabe took over for Rodeo. "Our orders are to deliver you to Brownsville, Texas, by sunrise. These ladies need to return to their rooms, lock their doors, and not come out until the National Guard comes knocking. Got it?"

"You have *got* to be kidding me." The princess stamped a foot. In the glow of Rodeo's penlight, her eyes burned with indignation.

Rodeo said before Gabe could, "We're perfectly serious, ma'am. Now you can say good-bye and come with us, or we'll take you anyway."

"*Ven,* Sara." The taller girl was already tugging the smaller girl back up the hall.

Libby protested, switching to Spanish. "No, girls, wait. Don't make this easy for them. They have transportation. They can take you home."

Gabe's patience was wearing thin. "We're not taking them home, and that's our final decision. Let them go."

The princess balled her fists. "I am *not* leaving them here! Either they come with us, or I stay. You can't force me to leave."

Gabe's temper got the upper hand. "Actually, we can. Rodeo."

His chief moved so fast the princess never had a chance. As he grappled Miss Clark's arms behind her back, the other girls fled, disappearing into another room.

Gabe pulled the syringe out of his thigh pocket and popped off the lid a second time. Then he took out his penlight.

Elizabeth Clark was thrashing in Rodeo's unbreakable hold. The edges of her white robe had fallen open, revealing a thin, white nightgown underneath. Why couldn't she be wearing normal clothing?

"This is going to hurt more if you don't hold still."

His warning brought a growl out of her. "You are a *jerk*, you know that?"

The words hit him like a slap across the face. Was he turning into his father? "No," he refuted fiercely. "I am an operator with a job to do, and you're going to thank me later. Rodeo, hold her still."

The chief laughed at her feistiness. "I'm tryin'."

Without waiting, Gabe jabbed the needle into the muscle of Elizabeth's thigh.

"Ouch! Both of you are jerks!"

Rodeo held her fast in case she toppled over.

Watching her for signs of debilitation, Gabe capped the syringe and slid it back into his pocket. "Don't worry, Princess. We'll have you back home in no time. Then you can complain to your father and get us into big trouble. I bet you'd like that."

"Hah." She weaved on her feet. "That just proves how little you know me." Her words sounded slurred. "Make sure you grab my phone by the bed. Oh, gosh." Her eyes rolled back, and, in the next moment, she started to drop. Rodeo caught her on the way down.

For a second, neither of them moved. Gabe shone the penlight on her unconscious face, then tracked it down her scantily clad frame. "We can't take her home like this." He swiveled toward the armoire searching for suitable attire.

The princess had a lot fewer clothes in her closet than he was expecting. While sifting through them, he changed his mind. Changing her out of what she wore would give her something *legitimate* to gripe about. He pulled a long, white sash out of the drawer, deciding it went to the robe she was wearing. Beneath the sash lay a little bound diary that instinct urged him to grab. Jamming the diary into his pocket, he carried the sash back to Rodeo. "This will help." Holding the edges of her robe together with one hand, he looped the sash around her slim waist and knotted it securely.

"Better grab her phone," Rodeo reminded him.

Finding it right where she'd said it was, powered off, Gabe pushed it into his bulging pocket. As he helped Rodeo carry their target from the room, he tried not to notice how Miss Clark smelled like fresh herbs—rosemary, mint, and maybe lavender.

As they were headed down the stairs, Gabe tabbed his inter-team radio. "Doc, advise Cruz to pull up in two minutes."

"Hooyah, Lobo."

Rodeo shouldered open the door at the bottom of the stairs. On his way out, Gabe paused to ascertain that it would latch behind them. All things considering, their nab and grab could have gone down worse than it had. Only one thing concerned him besides his broken nose: The princess wasn't happy with them. Despite her comment about how little he knew her, Gabe wouldn't put it past her to press charges. And, as OIC, he would take the fall for any manhandling Rodeo might have done at Gabe's behest.

To be honest, the princess had done more damage to *them* than they had done to her. Even though she clearly had a screw loose, he had to admire her spirit. At least they'd get her to Brownsville right on time, provided they didn't run into any snags.

Libby awoke to the thunder of rotors chopping the air with a deafening *whuppa, whuppa, whuppa*. Opening her eyes, she found herself strapped to a gurney in the cabin of a helicopter that was surging through a brightening sky. Memories rushed back to her. Given the peachy sunlight, she must have been unconscious for a couple of hours.

Still woozy, she turned her head and encountered the brooding stare of the swarthy SEAL who'd drugged her. His eyes weren't brown as she might have guessed but, rather, jungle green. Rimmed by thick curly lashes, they were set in a ruthlessly handsome face— now disfigured by his badly swollen nose.

"Almost there." He spoke with the faintest accent that suggested he'd grown up speaking Spanish.

Craning her neck, Libby counted three more SEALs in the cabin. Their silence conveyed annoyance, for which she couldn't blame them, considering the trouble they'd gone to. Honestly, though, how hard would it have been to return Sara and Jessica to their families before flying her back to the States?

Libby's stomach lurched, a sure indication that the helicopter was descending. Lying flat on her back, she couldn't see more than a pinkish-gray cloud cover. Why was she strapped down anyway? Seeing how to free herself, she manipulated a buckle and released one of the spring-loaded straps. The SEAL sitting by her head reached over to help with the others.

"Sit up nice and easy, ma'am. You're going to feel lightheaded for a while."

A glance up and back revealed a lean face and gentle eyes. He wasn't anything like Lobo, who still watched her with a frown on his face. Maybe he was mad at her for ruining his perfect face. Sorry about that, but she'd thought him a thug from one of the cartels.

Chagrin pinched her as she put herself in his shoes. Poor guy, he'd only been following orders. She shook her head, incredulous that her father had managed to persuade the Navy SEALs to pluck her to safety. He'd probably even told these men that she'd resist leaving—hence the unnecessary tranquilizing. Her father's fears were understandable, truly they were. But, at some point, he needed to let her live her own life.

Concerned SEAL helped her to sit up slowly. Encircling her

wrist in a light grasp, he felt for her pulse, which led her to believe he was a medic.

"How do you feel?"

Sending him a smile, she blinked at the realization that one of his eyes was deep blue, the other golden brown. The word *hete-rochromia* popped into her head. "A little dizzy." As she adjusted her wrapper, which now hung askew, she spied her sash, tied and double-knotted at her waist. How'd that get there?

Glancing up into Lobo's watchful gaze, she guessed he'd tied it himself. And, given his wary expression, he was clearly expecting her to gripe to Daddy. Did all four of the SEALs hold her in such low esteem? The one immediately to his right was an Asian American, who appeared to be meditating. To the right of him was Rodeo, who sent her a wink. Clearly, he wasn't as worried as Lobo was.

"Did you grab my cell phone?" She found it easier to talk to him, even though he'd manhandled her the worst.

Rodeo tipped his head toward his leader. "He's got it."

Lobo reached into the pocket on his thigh, having overheard them. Her cell phone and then her mother's diary came into view, the latter eliciting a grateful gasp from her.

"Oh, my gosh. Thank you," she added when he passed them across the cabin. The fact that he'd salvaged her most-prized possession forced her to reevaluate him. A true jerk wouldn't have gone to the trouble.

Concerned SEAL handed her a bottle of water next. "I bet you're thirsty."

She was parched, in fact. "Oh yes." Setting her personal effects on her lap, she twisted off the top and slaked her thirst while watching the helicopter descend. Rooftops and treetops came into view before it touched down with a lurch.

"Welcome to Brownsville." Rodeo was the first man on his feet. Pulling open the chopper door, he admitted a blast of moist spring air.

Libby's gaze went straight to the trio of men standing a hundred yards away. Her father's silver hair made him easy to spot in the presence of his two bodyguards and backdropped by his private plane.

Libby drew a breath of resolve while screwing the lid back on the bottle. "Thank you. I hope you recycle." She passed the bottle back to Concerned SEAL.

He smiled and dropped it into a bin beneath his seat.

Looking back outside, Libby girded herself for the talk she was going to have with her father on the way home. There'd be plenty of time to convince him to stop being so protective. Instead of flying to Austin where home used to be, they were going all the way to Northern Virginia, where her father had moved while running for the U.S. Senate.

Seconds later, Concerned SEAL cupped her elbow and escorted her off the chopper. Self-conscious of her bare feet and sleeping attire, Libby slipped her cell phone into the pocket of her robe but held fast to her mother's diary. The three other SEALs trailed her and Concerned SEAL across the tarmac. Given the hair whipping into her eyes, they wouldn't be sticking around once they delivered her.

"Libby!" Her father, a tall brawny Texan, abandoned his bodyguards to rush at her with his arms outstretched.

She eyed him with exasperation. But then guilt pinched her as she spotted the tears welling in his brown eyes. "Hey, Daddy."

As he engulfed her in a bear hug, lifting her off her feet, she forgot her frustration with him. She'd put him through an emotional wringer.

"I thought I might have lost you."

"I was fine." *You didn't need to call up the troops to fetch me.* She swallowed the admonition for now. There'd be time for that on the way home.

"Well, you're here now and that's all that matters." After putting her down, he focused on her rescuers.

"Gentlemen, I can't thank you all enough. Kyle Clark. I'm in your debt." Her father jutted out a hand. "Thank you so much. What is your name?"

In typical Kyle fashion, her father made a point of meeting each man at a personal level. That was how she overheard Lobo's real name.

"Lieutenant Gabe Villalobos."

"Gabe." Her father pumped Lobo's hand for an extra-long time. "Something tells me you're the leader—am I right?"

"Of this squad, yes, sir, but we couldn't have done it without our higher-ups."

"Of course, of course. But you all did the hard work. Looks like you got a little banged up in the process. Nothing serious, I hope."

Gabe's gaze jumped to hers like he expected her to interject right then that she'd broken his nose because the SEALs had mauled and drugged her. But Libby kept her mouth shut. Why was he so certain she would throw him under the bus like that? He had seriously misjudged her, and that rankled. If only he knew what she was really like.

Sensing the SEALs were eager to leave, Libby caught her father by the arm and tugged him away. "Come on, Daddy. We've wasted enough of their time."

Her father frowned at her. "Well, I think you should thank them yourself first."

Libby raised her eyebrows, then looked back at Lobo. "Hmm." She could tell he was holding his breath. "Of course." She started with Concerned SEAL first, managing a sincere smile for him as she thanked him, then the Asian-American SEAL, then Rodeo who grinned, clearly not holding a grudge that she'd cuffed him across the face.

As she jutted her hand toward Lobo, an idea took hold: A chance to show him who she really was. "Lieutenant." The instant their palms met, a surge of awareness traveled up her arm, jolting her pulse. His mistrustful gaze held her steady one. "I'll see you around."

His quick frown assured her that he'd heard her words. If she had her way, then they would meet again under different circumstances. And then he'd change his opinion about her.

Swinging around, she started for her father's plane, relying on him to catch up to her.

He did so quickly, shooting her sidelong glances. "Are you upset with me, sugar?"

She cast him a wry smile. "We'll talk about it on the way home, Daddy."

He threw his hands up. "I know. I know, I went a little far, but I was so worried about you, Libby."

She huffed out a breath. "My work is going to put me into danger every now and then. You need to accept that." She cut herself off, knowing the reason for his overprotective behavior.

Sorrow wreathed her father's face. "You sound just like your mother, and look what happened to her."

"I know." Her gaze returned to the plane they were approaching—not much bigger than the plane her mother had been taking on her way to Brazil when it crashed. "And that could happen to me, too, but—"

"Please don't say that." Horror laced his voice.

"We can't afford to sit on our hands doing nothing, Daddy. The world is falling apart. Someone has to do something."

He threw an arm around her, pulling again. "I can't talk about that now. I'm just glad to have you back."

His words summoned the idea that had rooted earlier. As she prepared to board his plane, she glanced back at the helicopter starting to rise. Her gaze went straight to Lobo, who seemed to be watching her through the window. "What do you say we thank the SEALs in a grander manner, Daddy?"

Her father followed her gaze, then looked back at her with interest. "Oh? What do you have in mind?"

Libby smiled as she stepped up into the aircraft. "I'll tell you on our way home."

CHAPTER 3

Gabe straightened out of his Dodge Charger and stretched his six-foot-two-inch frame with a groan. The three-and-a-half-hour drive from Virginia Beach to Northern Virginia had taken a torturous six hours, no thanks to the midsummer thunderstorms that had broken over the I-95 corridor, triggering several fender benders.

By the time he'd finally arrived at Kyle Clark's address in McLean, the sun was setting. The man's brick mansion with its thick white columns and Georgian architecture called to mind Thomas Jefferson's Monticello. Gabe's upper lip curled with scorn.

Why had he come here exactly? An invitation to attend an evening soiree at the oil tycoon's home could mean only one thing: Gabe was about to get the dressing down he'd been expecting all along. While the other three members of his squad had also been invited, why put Rodeo, Doc, and Zen in the hot seat when they'd merely been following orders?

Gabe would have declined the invitation outright if that didn't smack of cowardice. What better way to banish Elizabeth Clark from his dreams—which she haunted with annoying frequency—than to be publicly berated by her father?

As he strode from his parked car up the curved driveway, Gabe sneered at the sheer number of luxury vehicles parked outside. Rich people loved to flaunt their wealth, like Wendie Pheifer's parents, who'd gifted her a brand-new Jeep Grand Cherokee for her sixteenth birthday.

Tugging the wrinkles from his dress white uniform, he approached the steps to the wide portico supported by the thick columns. While it wasn't yet dark outside, flames danced in the twin gas-powered lanterns that flanked the double door, giving the house a warm and welcoming appearance.

His pulse quickened with both anticipation and dread. Was it Elizabeth's idea to invite the SEALs to his house, or was that entirely her father's doing? Would she even be here?

The strains of a Frank Sinatra song reached Gabe's ears as he climbed the steps to the porch and greeted the tuxedoed doorman, recognizing him as one of Kyle Clark's two bodyguards.

"Evening, Lieutenant." With an inscrutable once-over, he pulled open the door.

Nodding his thanks, Gabe stepped into a vaulted foyer, his gaze sliding up the double-wide staircase to the crystal chandelier and the thirty-foot ceiling. It was hard not to gape as he took it all in—gleaming hardwood floors, Persian carpets, elegant wallpaper. *Wow.* So this was how billionaires lived.

Leaving his white-billed cap hanging with a few men's hats on the elaborate coatrack, Gabe passed a dining room filled with glittering guests and a table groaning under trays of delicacies. Sounds of lively conversation beckoned him toward the open-concept room at the back of the house where fifty or more impeccably dressed guests milled about holding cocktails.

I'd rather free fall into enemy territory than join this party.

With a reminder of all that he'd overcome in his thirty-two years—personal hardship and prejudice, followed by the most rigorous military training program in the world—Gabe summoned his courage and stepped into the big room with his head held high.

"You're late." The dulcet voice at his shoulder caught him off guard.

He swung around as Elizabeth Clark pushed off the wall, a half-empty tumbler in hand. She wore a silk crimson cocktail dress that hugged her perfect figure and imbued her honey-blonde hair with tawny highlights. Every thought went out of Gabe's head as his neurons backfired. She was even prettier than he remembered.

Back in Mexico, she'd resembled those sweet-smelling flowers blooming despite the lawlessness on the streets. Tonight, she called to mind a red hibiscus, right up to the decorative comb that kept her long hair coiled in a knot at the back of her head. Her equally thorough appraisal of him kept him tongue-tied for an embarrassing amount of time.

"Miss Clark." He managed to find his voice.

"Libby." She thrust out a hand. Taking it automatically, Gabe experienced the same visceral awareness that had hit him the first time he'd held her slim hand. She hadn't seemed so delicate when she'd slammed her elbow into his nose. "Gabe Villalobos," he reminded her.

Her lips quirked in that insubordinate smile he'd carried in his head for weeks now. "Yes, I remember." Pulling her hand back, she eyed him over the rim of her glass while taking a leisurely sip.

Was that a martini she was drinking or club soda? "Sorry for my late arrival." It wasn't like him to be anything but exactly on time. "Traffic was bad. Lots of thunderstorms."

"I figured you'd just chickened out." Her gray-blue eyes seemed to laugh at him as she lowered the glass, then gestured with it. "Can I get you a drink? There's an open bar at the end of the room."

"No, I'm fine. I have to drive back tonight."

She shrugged, drained her glass, and set it down on the nearest tabletop. "Let's tell Daddy that you're here, then." With a familiarity that made him gulp, Libby looped her arm through his and drew him into the crowd.

Oh yes, let's tell Daddy, who might have invited him here to publicly denounce him for mauling his daughter. The cotton T-shirt under Gabe's uniform stuck to his suddenly sweaty back. Conversations dimmed as heads turned in their direction. He should have thrown the invitation in the trash and just gone on with his life.

Kyle Clark, who stood two inches taller than Gabe, looked larger than life in a tuxedo that emphasized his broad shoulders and barrel chest. Keeping a small crowd of people enthralled with whatever story he was spinning, he brightened at Gabe's approach, cutting himself off and lighting up the room with a smile that eased a portion of Gabe's apprehension.

"Lieutenant Villalobos!" His greeting silenced the chatter in the room. Stepping toward Gabe, he thrust a bear-sized hand at him. "Welcome, welcome. So glad you could make it."

"Thanks for inviting me."

The tycoon pumped Gabe's hand with seeming pleasure and not a trace of a grudge. Maybe he wasn't going to give him a public dressing-down.

"Well, of course. I could hardly overlook the man who saved my daughter's life. May I have your attention, everybody?"

He already had the room's attention. Gabe held his breath, uncertain of what the man might say.

"I'd like to introduce tonight's guest of honor. Everyone, this is Lieutenant Gabriel Villalobos, a U.S. Navy SEAL."

Guest of honor? Gabe shot Libby a startled glance. Her exaggerated shrug suggested this was her idea, which her father had seized on and run with. What the heck kind of game was she playing with him?

"A toast," Kyle Clark continued, holding his scotch tumbler aloft, "to America's finest."

The crowd echoed his words with, "Hear, hear!"

Finding a champagne glass thrust into his hand, Gabe tossed back a bracing sip. *I never should have come.*

Guests swarmed him, offering words of gratitude. He managed to keep one eye on Libby as she retreated to the open bar and ordered a drink—of Sprite, apparently. While acknowledging his admirers, Gabe simmered inwardly. This party had to be her way of avenging him for being a jerk in Matamoros. He got his back pounded and his hand wrung countless times.

An effusive, perfumed woman in her fifties kissed him lingeringly on the cheek. "We are *so* very grateful to you, Lieutenant." Her clinginess made him want to tear himself away, but he gritted his teeth and suffered through it.

Men asked him questions that he wasn't supposed to answer. He fell back on the standard glib reply, "I could tell you, sir, but then I'd have to kill you."

Gabe glanced at his watch. How soon could he get away with bowing out?

"Would you like to see the gardens?"

Suddenly, Libby was at his elbow, intervening before the next guest could assault him. She threaded her arm through his again and drew him toward a French door that opened onto a broad stone porch—even the balusters and railings were made of stone. As a breeze greeted him, Gabe caught whiff of Libby's herbal scent, transporting his memories back to Matamoros.

With the storms safely gone, an orchestra was setting up their stands and chairs outside. Libby drew Gabe past the orchestra, down a set of stone steps into the damp backyard. The sun had finally set, leaving the backyard dark, except where gas lamps beamed, throwing puddles of light onto the lush, wet lawn and the elaborate flower beds.

"Sorry about that." Removing her hand from the crux of his arm, Libby started down the winding path, taking them through the flower beds. The amusement in her voice suggested she wasn't sorry at all.

Gabe stopped in his tracks, refusing to go farther. When she turned around inquiringly, the light from the house shone in her blue-gray eyes.

"That was your idea, wasn't it, making me the guest of honor?"

Her mouth wobbled as she fought to keep a grin in check. "Of course. You saved my life, Lieutenant; you deserved every ounce of recognition." Her smile grew sassy. "I have to confess it was fun watching you squirm. I bet there aren't many situations that make you uncomfortable, are there?"

He didn't know whether to be offended by her manipulations or impressed that she'd gotten one over on him.

"You seemed to take it all in stride," she added, easing his annoyance. "Well done."

"So, what comes next? Do you disgrace me with allegations of manhandling?"

Her smile abruptly faded. "No, I think the broken nose is sufficient payback for that." She frowned as she focused on it. "Was it crooked like that before I broke it?"

Her needling amused him. "People like it better, actually, as I was too good looking with a straight nose."

"Hah." The arrogant comment brought her smile back. "Well, you were right about one thing." Turning away as she talked, she headed for the far end of the yard, clearly assuming Gabe would follow, which, of course, he did, lured by her scent and the graceful way she moved.

"About what?"

"The National Guard returned order to Matamoros. It took them three days, but they finally chased out the cartels."

His conscience pricked him. "Any word on the young women?"

She stopped and looked back at him. "Do you care?"

Gabe frowned. What kind of man did she think he was? "Yes, actually."

A slight smile touched her face. "They're fine, back with their families for the summer and planning to return to the *Instituto* this fall."

Gabe tensed. "What about you. Are you returning?"

Instead of answering, she started forward on her strappy sandals, headed straight for the dark trees in front of them. "Come on. I want to show you something."

With reservation, Gabe stepped off the winding path into the grass, then under thickly leafed tree branches. With the lamplight failing to extend this far, it felt like he was wading into an ambush, except these woods had clearly been thinned, with fallen branches removed and hardly any brush for cover.

Libby, who'd stopped to wait for him, grabbed his hand, setting his pulse to race. Over the strains of a violin warming up on the patio, Gabe detected the sound of trickling water as Libby towed him deeper into the darkness.

What the heck was she up to, luring him out here? He hadn't pegged her for the type to throw herself at a man, even if he was a Navy SEAL.

"I come out here all the time." Her conversational tone held no trace of a premeditated intent. "See the bridge?"

Through the tree trunks ahead, he made out a Japanese-style garden bridge arching over a shallow ravine. The water he could hear had to be a brook wending its way through the expansive property.

"Nice." Still wary of a trap, he let her lead him to the bridge's height.

At the top, she released his hand, clasped the railing instead, and drew a deep, cleansing breath. Gabe cautiously mirrored her motions, inhaling the fragrance of pine needles and freshly cut grass, but most especially Libby's herbal scent.

Her reflective words filled his ears.

"Whenever I stand here, I like to close my eyes and imagine I'm the water, racing to the Potomac and then out to the Chesapeake Bay, flowing all the way to the ocean. We're all a part of this amazing planet. We forget that sometimes."

The solemn statement drew a puzzled glance from him. He found her eyes closed.

"Try it," she invited in a coaxing voice.

Gabe shut his eyes, but all he could focus on was the heat of Libby's arm where it brushed his.

"Put yourself in the water. Let it carry you away. What do you picture?"

With a frown of concentration, he envisioned himself rushing out to the Potomac River, then to the Chesapeake Bay, then to the Atlantic Ocean. "I see dolphins and fishermen trolling for fish."

"Yes, because water is life."

As she turned toward him, Gabe's eyes sprang open.

"Our planet is at a tipping point." Her voice took on a note of urgency. "Almost two-thirds of the world's population experiences water scarcity for at least one month of the year. Severe water shortages will affect the entire planet by 2040. If we don't come together as a people—governments, scientists, indigenous communities, everyone—to protect and preserve this indispensable resource, then we're done for. It's over."

Gabe hadn't envisioned their conversation taking this turn. But her passionate stance made one thing terribly clear to him. "Tell me you are not going overseas again."

She pulled away from him as if shocked by his statement. "Of course I am. There's work to be done, Gabe."

His name on her lips sent an odd thrill through him. "But you could do that work from here. The places where water is scarcest are inherently dangerous."

She *tsked* her tongue. "Well, isn't this the pot calling the kettle black?"

"Excuse me?"

She propped a slim hand on one hip. "I would have expected a Navy SEAL, of all people, to understand. You can't make the world safer from terrorists without venturing into their lands. It's the same story for an environmentalist like me. I'm not going to make a difference in the world's drinking water by hiding in my house. We're the same, Lobo. We're both warriors on a mission."

Gabe gripped the wooden railing until his knuckles ached. *We are nothing alike.* He bit back the words, wanting to add that he had fought for everything he had. But the thought of her leaving this oasis to put herself in harm's way claimed his full attention. Who would rescue her the next time she got herself into trouble? The same frustration he'd had with her in Matamoros reared its ugly head. "Do you think your privilege is going to protect you?"

Even in the dark, he saw her eyebrows rise. "My privilege? I'm no more privileged than you are."

"Hah. You were born with a silver spoon in your mouth. You have no idea how small and defenseless you are."

She made a scoffing sound. "Says the man whose nose I broke."

One minute Gabe was gripping the railing; the next, he was gripping her upper arms, letting her feel the force in his hands.

He'd never in his life wanted to intimidate a woman. But the thought of Libby Clark waltzing right back into danger after he'd just saved her from a terrible fate made him want to shake her until her teeth rattled. "You think being an American is going to protect you?"

She swallowed visibly. "I've traveled extensively. Of course, I know that's not the case."

"What happens when your luck runs out, Libby, and there's no one around to protect you? Do you really want to end up on the black market, or worse, murdered and left to rot in some landfill somewhere?"

A quivering indignation strummed her tightly held frame. "That's not going to happen to me. I have God and my mother protecting me."

"Your mother?" Surprised by her reply, Gabe loosened his grip but, for the life of him, couldn't seem to release her. "Your mother is dead. How can she look out for you?"

Libby's eyes narrowed. "How do you know my mother's dead?"

Gabe shrugged, not revealing that he'd looked her up online when he couldn't shake her from his thoughts. "We were told that in a briefing before recovering you."

"Hmm. Well, that was her diary you grabbed out of my wardrobe. She's an angel in Heaven now, and she looks out for me. In fact, she came to me in a dream recently, telling me where to go next."

The words made him release her abruptly. "That's crazy talk."

Suddenly unsupported, Libby staggered backward before catching herself. Disillusionment vied with hurt. *Crazy talk?* Maybe she'd misjudged Gabe Villalobos. She had thought for certain if she illustrated the importance of her work, he would understand how much alike they were. Not only did he not get that, but he mocked her faith and her vision. She watched him rake his hands through his hair.

"Look, I'm sorry for manhandling you—again. Something about you brings out the worst in me, but that's no excuse."

Her disappointment dimmed. At least he had a conscience.

"And, honestly, if you're compelled to fly around the globe fighting for clean water, there's nothing I can do."

"Compelled." Libby seized on the word. "That's a good way to describe it." She contemplated the word for a moment. "No, actually, it's bigger than a compulsion. It's a calling, Gabe. Just as you were called to protect our nation, I was called to protect the world's drinking water."

He turned his head and frowned at her, making her think he finally got it.

"We should go back."

Desperation got the upper hand. "Wait." Operating entirely on instinct, Libby threw her arms around his shoulders and embraced him firmly.

After a split-second's hesitation, he gathered her closer, burying his nose into her hair with a long, indrawn breath that told her he liked the way she smelled.

"What's this for?"

The confusion in his deep voice had her looking up with a smile. "I have no idea. Maybe it's an apology for breaking your nose or for having to rescue me in the first place."

For a long moment, he merely regarded her. When his hand rose toward her face, Libby's breath caught. Caressing her cheek with his thumb, he slowly lowered his lips to hers, bestowing a lingering but chaste kiss on her lips. Even so, the bridge beneath her went into a slow whirl.

When he raised his head, his eyes glittered in the darkness. "You're a nut," he said without disparagement. "A dangerous nut."

"Me, dangerous?" Her gaze fell to his mouth. *Please kiss me again.*

But then, not far away, a twig snapped, shattering the romantic mood. As Gabe stiffened, she released him, watching him home in on the sound.

"Someone's out here," he determined.

"It's probably just another guest."

"Shh. Let me listen."

Libby hung her head. It didn't matter if the interloper turned out to be a raccoon. Their unexpectedly magical interlude was over. She would take off for Paraguay a week from today and probably never see Gabe Villalobos again. Strange that she could be so drawn to a man who thought so poorly of her, who couldn't see how they both strived to make the world a better place.

It took Gabe's addled senses a moment to sharpen. They were definitely *not* alone. Someone was prowling through the woods at the edge of Kyle Clark's lawn. Probably one of the security guards.

"Don't move." He murmured the words while resenting the bodyguard's competence. If they hadn't been interrupted, he might have stolen several more kisses which, gauging by the first one, would have made his discomfiture at being the guest of honor all worthwhile.

Scanning the dark tree trunks, he tried to spot the interloper. All at once, a lamp in the yard backdropped the man's silhouette, letting Gabe know he *wasn't* approaching their hiding spot. Instead, he was creeping toward the patio at the back of the house. Why would a security guard move that furtively?

"Who is he?" Libby had caught sight of him, too.

"Good question." Now that Gabe could see him better, the man wasn't either of Kyle Clark's bodyguards. Tall and broad, he put a shoulder against the trunk of a tree and raised his arm. As the outline of an MK11 sniper rifle came into view, an alarm went off in Gabe's head. The suppressor bulging out on the end of the barrel could only mean one thing.

"Shooter," Gabe whispered. The man was about to assassinate somebody.

CHAPTER 4

Given the sultry strains of a viola floating over laughter and conversation, the party had moved outside. If Gabe didn't take immediate action, somebody was going to die.

Clapping a hand over Libby's mouth, he dragged her down to crouch with him.

"Do you have your phone with you?"

Her wide eyes caught the faint glow of the oil lamps as she shook her head no.

Putting a knee on the bridge, Gabe teased his own phone from his front pocket and thrust it into her hands. "Someone's aiming a rifle at the house, and he's not your father's man. Go that way off the bridge and block the light of the phone. Passcode is 757345. Call the police if you hear a pop and a hiss. Go."

She went without hesitation, melting quickly and quietly off the far side of the bridge while Gabe went the other way. He moved as swiftly and stealthily through the unfamiliar forest as he could while lamenting the absence of the Desert Eagle semiautomatic locked securely in his car. Without night-vision goggles, all Gabe could do was feel his way toward the target. Pine needles crackled under his soles. Branches raked his uniform. A backward glance satisfied him that Libby was keeping out of sight.

Gabe was still fifty yards from the sniper when the man adjusted his aim. There wasn't any way to follow the man's line of sight, but the target became clear when Gabe glimpsed the silver head of Kyle Clark amidst his guests.

Barbra Streisand's *The Way We Were* created a poignant soundtrack to the impending drama. Seeing the assassin's shoulders rise and fall as he settled into his kill, Gabe charged him with a "Hey!"

But he was still too late. With a pop and a hiss from the suppressor, the hypersonic bullet zinged through the air. Glass shattered and people screamed as Gabe tackled the shooter, bearing them both to the ground. The rifle bucked a second time just before falling from the shooter's grasp. Bits of wood and leaves rained down as Gabe plowed his fist into the man's face, grunting in surprise when his knuckles slammed into a granite jaw.

The man jackknifed, utilizing a wrestling move Gabe had only experienced once during close-quarter combat skills training. Finding himself flat on his back, he jerked up a knee to deflect an elbow to the gut. Then he seized the man's head and tried to gouge out his eyes, but the shooter had a hold of his throat.

The sniper's savage grin flashed in the darkness as he squeezed Gabe's windpipe. Dismayed by the power in the fingers restricting his airways, Gabe executed a desperate countermove that, fortunately, freed him. Lunging upward, he hooked the giant's neck while springing onto his back. But his opponent immediately flipped him off, heightening Gabe's concern. Not only was he half again Gabe's size, but he was a trained fighter.

A glint of light was Gabe's only warning before a gaudy gemstone, a thick gold band, and four knuckles plowed into Gabe's cheek. He turned his head to diminish the blow. Even so, pain radiated through his skull.

Over the ringing in his ears came, "Freeze where you are!"

The beam of a flashlight strafed the tree trunks, catching the assailant in its glare. As the man threw an arm up to block the glare, Gabe used his distraction to send him sprawling onto his side. But the shooter kept rolling. In one athletic motion, he snatched up his fallen rifle and came to his feet before crashing into the dark forest.

The guard with the bright flashlight took off after him.

Gabe pushed to his knees, his cheek throbbing. Before he could climb to his feet, a twig snapped, and the snout of a pistol gouged his spine.

"Don't move."

Was this the second bodyguard? Pain encapsulated Gabe's whole head. He wasn't certain he could move in any case.

"Who are you?" A penlight shot through the dark, stabbing the backs of Gabe's eyes as the man pointed it at his face.

"He's the guest of honor, Ken." Libby saved him, wading out of the darkness with Gabe's illuminated phone lighting her way. "Was anybody shot?"

The guard promptly removed his pistol. "No, thanks to you two, I'm thinking."

Gabe gingerly felt his face. "Better go help your partner. The shooter's a pro."

"Right." As Ken hurried away from them, Libby helped Gabe to his feet. "Are you okay? Oh, your face," she added when he turned toward the light in her hand.

Having felt the welt on his cheekbone, her exclamation came as no surprise. Gabe picked the leaves from his hair and brushed the dirt off his dress white uniform. The stains would be worth it if he'd saved Clark's life. "Who would want to kill your father?"

"My father?"

Until that moment, it was clear she hadn't realized who the target was.

"Daddy!"

Gabe caught Libby's arm as she started for the house. "Not so fast. There could be a second shooter. Follow me." Tugging her behind him, he ignored the throbbing in his cheek and headed for the seemingly quiet lawn, using his body to shield her as much as possible.

The scene awaiting them made Libby fight his hold. He roped her against him as he climbed the steps to the deserted veranda.

The guests had fled indoors. The glass in one of the large French doors had been shattered. As they passed the toppled orchestra stands and scattered musical scores, glass crackled under their shoes. At least there wasn't any blood that Gabe could see.

After entering the mansion, they located all the guests huddling pale-faced and subdued on the grand staircase, the only place in the house without windows.

"Daddy!" Libby broke away to run at her father, who stood among his guests.

Clark visibly melted as he caught sight of her. "Libby." Rushing down the steps, he embraced her fiercely, tears brimming his eyes. "When I couldn't find you, I feared the worst."

Watching them, a pang pierced Gabe's chest. If only his own father had loved him like that.

Libby turned and caught his eye. "I was showing Gabe the bridge in the backyard when we saw the shooter. He saved your life, Daddy. Gabe went after the man and fought with him. Your body-guards are chasing him right now."

The guests reacted with chorused dismay, then with gratitude.

Clark's eyes had rounded with astonishment. "You fought with him?"

That had to be obvious given that Gabe's cheek was still swelling. "Yes, sir."

The oil tycoon's horror morphed into wonder. "So now you've saved my life as well as my daughter's." Pulling Libby along with him, he approached Gabe to lay a heavy hand on his shoulder and stare deeply into his eyes. "Thank God you were here with us tonight, Lieutenant Villalobos. Thank God. I don't know how I'll ever repay you."

Uncomfortable with so much attention, Gabe kept quiet as the guests reiterated their host's words.

A fighting light had entered Kyle Clark's brown eyes. "Did you see what he looked like?"

Gabe nodded. "I did."

"Good. Good."

The wail of several sirens penetrated the home's thick walls, relieving Gabe that the police were here so quickly. Libby had done well. If only shootings in Miami garnered such a quick response.

Libby was tugging on her father's sleeve. "Who would want to kill you, Daddy?" Her eyes flashed with outrage. "What's this about?"

Clark patted her hand. "No idea, honey, but I guess it goes with the territory. Not everyone's keen on having an oilman as their next Texas senator."

"Senator." Gabe had thought the gossip about Kyle Clark running for Senate was just a rumor, but didn't it figure since only the wealthy could afford to run for public office?

"That's right, son. I'm tossing my hat into the ring. 'Bout time I gave back to the country that's given me so much."

The humble remark didn't jibe with the cynical thoughts in Gabe's head. A pounding at the door kept him from suggesting that the man hire more bodyguards.

"Police!"

"I'll get that." Libby responded first, thrusting Gabe's phone at him on her way to the door. For a split second, their eyes locked, filling him with a burst of satisfaction. Working together, they'd thwarted an assassination attempt. He watched her peer through the peephole first before she swung the door open.

The princess was good in a crisis; he'd give her that much.

Two hours later, the search for Kyle Clark's shooter had earned national media attention. A pair of German shepherds had been loosed to track the suspect, but they hadn't found him yet. Media choppers and law enforcement helicopters vied for airspace and shattered the suburban quiet, thundering late into the night.

Still, no arrest was made. The shooter seemed to have evaporated into thin air, leaving the security guards, then the local police, and then the FBI, who were last to arrive on the scene, all scratching their heads after canvassing the guests. As Gabe and the first bodyguard were the only two who'd glimpsed the shooter's face, the FBI kept Gabe from leaving and requested that he walk them into the backyard and show them where the confrontation took place.

Libby trailed him and the special agents into the tree line, now bright with their flashlights. As Gabe detailed his struggles with the suspect in the exact spot where he'd taken the man down, she listened to every word, determined to discover who would want to harm her father.

"He was trained in hand-to-hand combat, possibly Special Forces," Gabe said, "but I'm thinking more like mixed martial arts since he had some moves I'm not familiar with. On top of that, he was taller than me and maybe fifty pounds heavier. When he punched my face, the ring on his right hand clocked me pretty hard."

"Are you sure you didn't let him get away?" asked the older special agent.

Silence. The affront on Gabe's shadowed face only heightened Libby's attraction to him.

"Why would I do that?" The cold note in his voice eliminated the possibility of a conspiracy.

The agent waved dismissively. "Just a question."

After wringing every last detail out of Gabe, the FBI returned to the house to corner Daddy in his living room. Libby kept a worried eye on her father as he paced the Persian carpet and murmured replies with a pained expression. No one, to Libby's memory, had ever disliked her warmhearted father. It had to disturb him deeply to discover someone hated him enough to want him dead.

Would this attempt on Daddy's life deter him from running for the Senate? She hoped not. This country needed more leaders like her father—good men who had the interests of their country at heart. Surely, he would just hire more bodyguards and stay in the race; after all, he was running in honor of Libby's mother, who had always encouraged his political aspirations.

Gabe touched her shoulder, reclaiming her attention. "Hey, the FBI says I can leave now. You going to be all right?"

Disappointment shackled her. Since receiving his RSVP to the party last month, she'd been anticipating this evening. But now that it was over, she might never see him again.

"Please don't leave." She wasn't too proud to play on his protective instincts. "I'd feel safer tonight if you stayed. Besides, you look tired. Why don't you sleep here and drive back in the morning after a good night's rest?"

His long stare conveyed a mix of suspicion and temptation.

Hearing a lull in the conversation behind her, Libby turned and enlisted her father's aid in persuading Gabe. "You don't mind if Lieutenant Villalobos stays the night, do you, Daddy?"

He brightened at the suggestion. "Of course not. He must stay. Consider yourself family, Gabe."

An odd-sounding laugh rasped in Gabe's throat.

"It's settled then." Slipping her arm through his, Libby guided him toward the kitchen, half-expecting him to balk, but he didn't. "Let's get you something to eat first."

Once in the massive kitchen, located in its own wing off the dining room, she sat him on a stool, bringing him a plate full of delicacies left over from the party. He pounced on them, clearly famished. "Water?" She slid a cold bottle of Perrier in front of him.

He spoke around the little sandwich he had popped into his mouth. "Thank you."

Helping herself to a cheese square, Libby set about storing leftovers in glass containers and sticking them in the fridge.

"Don't you have staff to clean up?"

She slanted Gabe an admonishing look. "Of course, but Daddy sent them home after the incident, and they won't be back until tomorrow. This will all go bad if it's not put away tonight."

"Waste not want not."

"That's right."

"Even if you have the money to buy more."

She swung around, leveling a frown at him. "My father has money, yes. But that doesn't make him careless. He also sponsors more charities than anyone I know."

Gabe had nothing to say to that, draining half of the bubbly water before putting down the bottle.

"All done?" He had eaten everything she'd put before him.

"Yes, thank you. I'm stuffed." He patted his flat abdomen.

Libby cleared his plate, slid it into the dishwasher, then drained the rest of his bottle before she lobbed it into a recycling bin. "Let's find you a bedroom, then."

As she gestured toward the upper level, Libby noted the watchful look in Gabe's eyes with amusement. Did he think she had less-than-honorable intentions? Most men would welcome that, so why was he so wary? "Follow me." She led him out of the kitchen and up the back staircase toward the guest bedrooms, all located in the west wing where her own room was.

Casting open the door of a room not too far from hers, Libby snapped on the light. "Think you'll be okay in here?"

The queen canopy bed and marble-topped armoire sent Gabe's black eyebrows winging. "This is a guest room?"

"It's one of them." If her father had purchased a more modest second home, Gabe wouldn't feel so out of his element. She sighed inwardly. "Help yourself to the shower across the hall here. There are clean towels under the sink." She angled her face up at him. "Can I get you anything else?"

Gabe, who'd stepped into the room, glanced back, his gaze sliding to her mouth before jumping back to her eyes. "No, I think I'm good. Thank you."

Pondering the mixed messages she was receiving, Libby sent him a quizzical smile. "Well, sweet dreams, then." Turning away, she marched the short distance to her own room and shut herself inside.

An hour later, she lay in her bed, still wide awake. She had over-heard Gabe showering before retiring for the night. Since then, he hadn't made so much as a peep. She, on the other hand, still tossed and turned while wondering who would want to kill her sweet and selfless father. Someone who didn't know him well, obviously.

Her thoughts returned to the magical moments before Gabe had spotted the would-be assassin, and she sighed, reliving the sweetness of their chaste yet alluring kiss.

Back when she'd suggested her father throw a party and invite Gabe's squad to be the guests of honor, all she'd wanted was a chance to rectify his misconceptions about her—although watching him squirm with discomfort had certainly been enjoyable. It wasn't until he'd kissed her that romantic thoughts had entered her mind, even though she knew they were foolish. Libby didn't have time for a relationship, nor did Gabe, she suspected. They both had important work to do. If only he had acknowledged they were more alike than different.

Maybe in the morning they would get another chance to talk. If he left McLean with the realization that she was way more than just the precious daughter of a wealthy would-be politician, then she would be satisfied... at least until the memory of his kiss taunted her with possibilities that could never be realized.

Waking up in a strange bed in a dark room, Gabe peered around the shadowed enclosure, disoriented. *Where am I?* Memories of the night before came rushing back to him. Ah yes. He was sleeping in a guest room in Kyle Clark's house, and Libby's bedroom was just down the hall.

Coming wide awake, he checked his watch. This was when he always woke up, at zero-five thirty—so half an hour before sunrise in August. If he got up now, he'd be sitting here alone for at least another hour, probably more, as they'd all retired late last night.

Gabe envisioned sitting around waiting for them to wake up. What would he even say to Libby when he saw her again? And why were both she and her father so adamant that Gabe should stay overnight? *"Consider yourself family, Gabe."*

He analyzed the words for a hidden agenda. Was the man angling to have a SEAL for a son-in-law? Did he think he could get insider information on Special Operations that way, or was he just looking for a man who could tame his stubborn daughter?

Hah, good luck there. In all honesty, Gabe sympathized with Clark's quandary. Having a daughter who felt called to defend the world's clean water supply would make any man crazy—especially if that man had already lost a wife who died defending the rights of the indigenous population in Brazil. Something bad was bound to happen to Libby—how could it not?

Gabe shook his head at her naïve faith in God and in her dead mother. If only it worked that way.

I never should have kissed her.

The kiss he'd pressed onto her supple lips had been impulsive— thoughtless. Yet, closing his eyes, he relived its unexpected delight. And it wasn't just the sweet texture of her mouth and the herbal scent of her skin that made it memorable. Something beyond desire had risen to life inside of him, stirring up possessive feelings he had no business entertaining.

With a self-deprecating mutter, Gabe flung off the luxurious sheets and fluffy duvet as he rolled out of bed. Those feelings would only magnify if he saw Libby again this morning. He had to leave now, while the leaving was good. Yes, she was going to think poorly of him for vanishing without a word of thanks. Maybe he could scrounge up a pen and leave a quick thank-you note to mitigate his rude behavior.

Eighteen minutes later, dressed in his stained uniform and with the words *Thank You!* written on a scrap of paper and left on his bed, Gabe recovered his combination hat from the hat rack in the foyer and jammed it on his head. As he let himself out the front door, he ran directly into a bodyguard who jerked upright, having nodded off to sleep in a chair. They exchanged a terse "Good morning" before Gabe locked the door behind him and pulled it shut.

Coming down off the wide portico, he strode beneath a mauve-colored sky along the curved driveway toward the only car still parked outside. If he drove home fast enough, maybe he could outrun the regret chasing after him.

Good-bye, Princess. I can't afford to have feelings for a girl like you.

CHAPTER 5

The C-17 Globemaster III descended onto the empty runway in Mariscal Estigarribia, Paraguay like a fat mallard hitting the tarmac smoothly before braking with unnecessary urgency. The Air Force captain piloting the plane clearly wished to convey that he could land a Tomcat on an aircraft carrier in a hurricane if need be. Good for him.

As the transport aircraft screeched to a halt, flinging all thirty-four SEALs sideways on benches that lined either side of the plane, Gabe saw Master Chief Bukowski roll his eyes at the pilot's antics.

"All right, everybody, listen up." The task unit commander, Maximus McDuff, shook off his harness and stood. Built like a double-wide refrigerator with a bristling brown mustache and small slate-colored eyes, the CO reminded Gabe of a bull walrus in a perpetually bad mood.

"The less attention we draw to ourselves, the better. So grab your gear, head to the bus that's taking us to camp, and board it quickly."

The locals weren't supposed to know that the men in desert-patterned fatigues were U.S. Navy SEALs on a mission dubbed

Operation Anaconda. Under the guise of training the Paraguayan Special Forces stationed at the old military base in town, they had come to defend the American-owned oil wells from Hezbollah extremists believed to be training in the region. Gabe hadn't asked which oil company *owned* the oil wells. He was afraid he'd find out that Clark Petroleum had Special Operations at its beck and call.

Not that Kyle Clark was CEO of Clark Petroleum anymore. While running for the Senate, the Texan tycoon had relinquished control of the company to avoid any conflict of interest. As a senator, he would probably have more influence than ever, but it wasn't Gabe's job to question the ways of politics. His job was to stop Hezbollah from using South America as a staging platform for jihad—period, the end.

For the umpteenth time that day, he thrust thoughts of Libby and her father out of his head.

Mad Max, as the CO was called by the SEALs, but never to his face, swiveled toward his second-in-command. "Anything to add, Master Chief?"

Michael Bukowski's auburn head barely cleared the CO's chin, but his reputation as the SEAL who'd seen more combat than any active-duty SEAL made Master Chief a giant in the Teams. Bukowski's black-brown eyes swept over the men's eager faces.

"We'll be staying in an old Army installation where you'll be surrounded by civilians, not one of whom needs to know of our agenda. So watch what you say and who's around you when you say it. Clear?"

"Hooyah, Master Chief!" Two platoons, each comprised sixteen men, made the hull of the plane reverberate with their chorused reply.

Mad Max pointed toward the rear hatch. "Move out."

As the leader of Echo Platoon, Gabe got to head off the plane right after Bukowski and Mad Max. His two experienced chiefs, Rodeo and Doc, followed closely behind him, accompanied by Charlie Platoon's leaders.

As they streamed out of the plane onto a hot tarmac, a desert-like breeze wafted through the light canvas of Gabe's desert BDUs. The air, smelling of untouched wilderness, reminded him of Libby's herbal scent. She would be fiercely protective of this place, part of the Gran Chaco, a hundred thousand square miles comprised jungle to the north and arid lowlands to the south, where they were now. The dry savannah stretched as far as the eye could see, sprinkled with patches of wild grass and gnarly old trees. Libby would be jealous that he got to see this place.

Stop thinking of her already!

Every time he opened a bottle of Perrier or bent over a water fountain, thoughts of her would geyser up in his mind, whether he wanted them there or not.

Shouldering his backpack, which was stuffed with everything he needed for a month-long stay, Gabe waited for his platoon to line up behind him before leading them to the waiting bus.

It wasn't until all thirty-four SEALs were jammed inside and the bus was lumbering away from the airfield that his antenna for danger went up. Whose idea was it to pack them all into one large vehicle? If Hezbollah had any advanced knowledge of their arrival, a single rocket-propelled grenade could take all of them out in one fell swoop. Obviously, the Paraguayan attaché who'd organized their transport hadn't counted on word of their arrival to reach Paraguay before the SEALs did.

Crowded with bodies, the temperature in the bus rose quickly.

"Open the windows!" Mad Max barked as they swung onto a highway being used by several cars.

Through the window he'd just lowered, Gabe spotted the modest city of Mariscal Estigarribia in the distance. Home to a mere 2,500 people, the little town with a big name was nothing more than a hodgepodge of adobe and cinder-block structures clustered around the walls of an old military facility. One ugly stucco mansion lorded over the town atop the only hill.

As they drew closer, the color scheme of the simple buildings brought Matamoros to mind. Pink, yellow, and blue walls clashed with the red-tiled roofs. A layer of sand covered every surface, including the street, making it hard to tell whether it was even paved.

Glimpsing an olive-green Jeep barreling toward them in the oncoming lane, Gabe assessed it as a potential threat. His gaze snared on the honey-blonde hair streaming from the driver's side window. Wait, that wasn't... As it barreled past the bus, he ducked his head hoping to see inside. A glimpse of a piquant profile made his stomach cartwheel.

Libby?

It couldn't be. His eyes had to be playing tricks on him because why would she be here, of all places, in the wilds of Paraguay?

But the thunderstruck expression on Rodeo's face as he tore his gaze from the window suggested there was nothing wrong with Gabe's vision.

"Was that who I thought it was?" Rodeo sounded incredulous.

Gabe flicked a wary glance at Bukowski, whose right ear seemed to turn in their direction. "No." Master Chief wouldn't appreciate them knowing anybody in the area who might blow their anonymity.

Rodeo lapsed into silence, but the growing smirk on his face suggested the impossible: that Libby Clark was really here. No way was that a coincidence. Someone had to have made that happen— which meant Gabe was right to be suspicious of her in the first place. Was Kyle Clark throwing his daughter at Gabe? What would be the point?

He ground his teeth together. If Kyle Clark thought Gabe would drop everything to be with Libby, then the man had another thing coming. The last thing he wanted was to become a pawn in a game played by the powerful and wealthy.

I'm not going anywhere near her.

Libby averted her eyes from the bus crammed with men in uniform. They didn't look like locals. Were they U.S. servicemen? Her thoughts went immediately to Gabe, whom she'd been trying to forget since he'd vanished from her father's house with just two inadequate words scribbled on a piece of paper. *Thank you* hardly expressed what she hoped to hear him say—that he respected and supported the work she did. Libby nodded. Yes, that was all she wanted.

Sure.

To be honest, it was probably best that he'd left without them conversing. She couldn't stop thinking of him, as it was. Given the important work she was here to accomplish—protecting El Chaco Boreal's two rivers from contamination—the last thing she needed was a distraction in the form of a flowering romance.

Maybe one day she could afford to fall in love, but not anytime soon.

Recalling the challenge lying ahead of her, Libby swallowed hard. In the scant days she'd been here, she had yet to perform her duties for International Water Institute on her own. Her colleague Jaime had been the one to drive their Jeep on the treacherous tracks to the remote locations where they collected soil and water samples. Jaime also carried a pistol on his hip, and he knew how to use it, as evidenced by the day he'd shot and killed a poisonous snake about to spring at Libby's calf. With Jaime at her side, Libby felt no qualms about striking out into the semiarid wilderness.

Without him? Not so much.

But today Jaime's wife was having a baby. Libby had insisted he remain at the hospital for the baby's birth. Since a report was due to IWI by Friday and it wouldn't get done without more tests completed, Jaime had reluctantly turned over the keys to the Jeep, as well as the company satellite phone, so Libby could finish the last few tests by herself.

It wasn't until she started driving to their remote laboratory that doubts began to percolate. At times, the dirt tracks appeared impassable. And even with GPS on the sat phone to guide her, the unmarked roads made them difficult to find. More than that, El Chaco Boreal was the dead last place that a woman ought to venture out alone, which was why Libby donned a grass cowboy hat whenever she worked in the field—it helped to conceal her gender.

The porous border area between Paraguay, Bolivia, and Argentina offered a haven to drug traffickers, smugglers, and counterfeiters. There were even rumors of extremists training in the area.

"You were born with a silver spoon in your mouth. You have no idea how small and defenseless you are."

Gabe's cynical words made Libby grip the steering wheel more tightly. Roaring up the Ruta Transchaco, one of the only paved roads in the area, she raised the volume on her radio and let her long hair whip in the wind.

God had given her a mission, delivered to her in a dream by her very own guardian angel. So long as Libby was doing God's will, harm would not befall her. She latched on to that reassurance, ignoring the memory of Gabe's response when she shared her mission with him.

"That's crazy talk."

Maybe she was crazy—especially to do this on her own.

The 1930s-era military installation turned out to be an impressive enclave of red brick buildings circumscribed by a high wall and boasting spacious rooms with flaking paint and paddle fans that barely stirred the hot air. The unreliable plumbing might not have been updated since the Chaco War almost a hundred years earlier.

Freed to settle into their barracks, Gabe divided his platoon into four groups of four, selecting the same firing squad he'd taken to Matamoros to be his roommates. Leading them down a corridor to the biggest room at the end of the hall, Gabe claimed the bottom bunk on the right for himself. To test the mattress, he stretched out on it, ignoring Rodeo's pointed stare.

"I know that was her, sir." Rodeo tossed his rucksack on the bunk over Gabe's head. "I'd recognize her anywhere."

The statement wrested Zen and Doc from a game of rock/paper/scissors as they contended over the bunks on the other bed.

Doc met Gabe's eyes. "Are you talking about Elizabeth Clark?"

"Shh." Gabe hushed him.

"You saw her, too?" Rodeo asked.

"No, but she jumped into my thoughts when we landed. She's here, in Paraguay, isn't she? Why?"

Rodeo turned back to Gabe. "That's what I want to know. She was driving a Jeep out of town as we drove in."

Gabe drew a measured breath. "Shut the door."

Zen kicked it shut with his heel, muffling the sound of the task unit settling into their new digs.

"Listen." Still lying flat on his back, Gabe leveled a stern look at his companions. "You heard Master Chief telling us not to rub elbows with the locals. So, even if that *was* Elizabeth Clark—and I'm not saying it was—we are *not* to reach out to her or even acknowledge her existence. She knows what we do, and rumors would start to circulate."

His colleagues didn't need to know his personal reasons for avoiding her—mistrust.

Suspicion flattened the customary quirk on Rodeo's lips. "What's she even doing here?"

"Something to do with water maybe," Gabe suggested the most innocuous possibility. "She's obsessed with safeguarding the world's drinking water."

Doc hummed approvingly. "That is *so* cool."

Gabe frowned at him. "No, it's dangerous."

Rodeo was still ruminating. "I'm surprised her father let her leave the country again."

So was Gabe, who couldn't stop brooding over Kyle Clark's agenda.

Rodeo crossed his arms over his chest. "I wonder if the oil wells we're protecting from Hezbollah belong to Clark Petroleum."

Zen whistled. "If that's true, Kyle Clark sure has friends in high places."

Gabe scrubbed a hand over his face. "Of course he does. First we get sent to Mexico to save his daughter, and now she just happens to be where we're operating? I don't like it. My suggestion is we ignore her, forget we even saw her." He rolled abruptly out of the bunk to unpack his rucksack. "We're not here to socialize anyway."

Rodeo's crooked smile made a sudden reappearance. "You tryin' to convince yourself or us, Lobo?"

Gabe's dark scowl sent most men scuttling away from him. Rodeo chuckled as he turned away. Glowering at the chief's sun-streaked hair, Gabe had to admit Rodeo was right. He was trying very hard to convince himself.

International Water Institute's laboratory was situated in a cinder-block building topped by a tin roof and surrounded by a chain-link fence. Erected in a desolate area between Mariscal Estigarribia and the wilds of El Chaco, it took Libby forty minutes to arrive at the guardhouse.

She leaned out of the driver's-side window with a smile. "Hey, Enrique."

Setting aside the comic book he was reading, the full-time security guard frowned to see her all alone. "Where is Señor Jaime?"

In fluent Spanish, Libby explained Jaime's happy circumstances, adding that she would be testing samples on her own today and not to worry. Frowning, nonetheless, Enrique unlocked the gate and swung it open, then locked it again as Libby parked the Jeep inside.

A minute later, she was pressing the four-digit code into the combination lock on the lab's only door and letting herself inside. The generator running nonstop out back kept the lab at a chilly sixty-six degrees Fahrenheit. In contrast to the dry heat outside, the interior felt like a refrigerator.

Libby flipped on the lights and dropped into the chair at the computer—also run by the generator—where she logged in and opened the document requiring her to input data on the titrimetric, electrometric, and colorimetric tests she intended to run on their latest samples.

She was just getting up to start her work when a loud *pop!* sounded over the grinding generator. Libby froze, then crossed to the door to peer through the only window—set into the door itself. A vision of four bearded men dressed in military-style uniforms, brandishing pistols and standing over Enrique's prone body, made her blood run cold. "No!"

Heart pounding, she whirled toward the landline phone and snatched up the receiver. Dead silence greeted her. After pushing useless buttons, she hung up, picturing with regret the state-of-the-art satellite phone Jaime had put into her hands, clipped uselessly to the Jeep's front dash. She'd forgotten to bring it inside with her.

Now what? The only thing left for her to do was to hide and hope the soldiers couldn't break in.

With her heart racing, Libby sought a place to conceal herself. She scurried behind a tall shelving unit, flattening herself against the wall to squeeze in deep behind it. Her mouth turned desert dry as she waited. *Lord, please let the locked lab door keep them out. Please don't let them find me.*

As the seconds ticked by, curiosity got the better of her. She edged toward the opening to peek out of her hiding place. In that same instant, the man looking through the inset window spotted her, and she jerked her head back—too late, for their eyes had already met. He pounded at the door, demanding entrance.

What do I do? Racking her brain for a way out of her predicament, Libby could think of nothing.

She startled and cringed as the intruders fired shots at the lock. A cold sweat bathed her entire body as the door yawned open, admitting a wedge of sunlight. Libby squeezed farther into the narrow space but could go no farther when she ran into a wall. The soles of boots scuffed the floor, approaching the shelves behind which she stood. Libby braced herself, stifling a whimper.

Her heart seemed to jump up her throat as a handsome bearded face peered behind the shelf at her while pointing his pistol at her. She guessed him to be Middle Eastern, possibly Lebanese, since many from that country had immigrated to Paraguay as early as the nineteenth century.

Please don't let these be the extremists I heard about in town.

As the man continued to stare at her, Libby found her voice. In breathless Arabic she greeted him. *"As-salam alaykum."* Treating everyone with dignity and respect was a tenet of her faith and a key to peace.

"Step out," came the firm reply, spoken in perfect British English.

With no other choice, Libby edged obediently toward him. Her skin seemed to shrink as the man's turquoise gaze ran over her conservative yellow blouse and lightweight capris. He stepped back as she sidled into the open with her knees knocking. Three more men, two of whom struck her as dangerous, gathered around and stared at her.

I should never have come to work without Jaime.

If these men had killed Enrique, then they *had* to be the extremists she'd been warned about. Surely they would shoot her, too—or worse.

"You're with International Water Institute?" The handsome one in front of her reached for a tendril of her blonde hair and slid his fingers down its length.

Libby cleared her throat of the fear clogging it. "Yes."

"You're American."

It wasn't a question, so she didn't answer. Being American was more likely to get her killed.

"We are looking for nitric acid. You must have some here."

The unexpected information made her blink. Her brain churned back into gear. If she gave them what they wanted, maybe they would let her live. "We have several liters."

"Excellent. Show them to me." With an eloquent wave of his hand, he freed her to walk away from him.

On spongy knees, Libby led the foursome toward the shelf by her desk while reeling at her predicament. Nitric acid, stored in brown bottles, was used to detect trace metals in fresh water. She pointed to where they lined the bottom shelf. "Those six bottles there are nitric acid. Help yourself." God forgive her if they had nefarious plans for the stuff.

As the leader holstered his weapon, issuing a soft order that set two men to work placing the brown bottles into an empty box, the fourth soldier, the one with a scar across his cheek, kept his pistol trained on her. His dark stare prevented Libby from drawing a deep breath.

She cringed as the youngest man plucked up a bottle carelessly. "Oh, be careful! It's dangerous to inhale and corrosive."

Once all six bottles were placed in the box, the leader spoke with quiet authority, exhorting the others to take the box outside. Two of the three soldiers exchanged suspicious glances, but the youngest, who bore a resemblance to the leader, turned unquestioningly to the door and his companions followed reluctantly. Only the scar-faced man protested, uttering the word "Amricki" as he gestured angrily at Libby.

But the leader remained resolute, waving him away with quiet authority.

The door slammed in the scarred man's wake, signaling his protest.

As the leader pulled his pistol from its holder, the blood in Libby's veins rushed to her pistoning heart. *Father, I don't want to die yet!*

Keeping his gun trained on her, the interloper sifted through the paperwork she had printed out and left on her desk. He picked up a sheet and scanned it.

"Elizabeth Clark?" He turned his head to look at her.

Realizing he'd read her name on the printout, she stared back at him, too terrified to speak.

The color of his eyes brought to mind amazonite, a semi-precious stone named after the Amazon River near which it had been found.

"Is that your name?"

His reasonable tone encouraged her to nod. No one knew she was the daughter of the former CEO of Clark Petroleum, so what difference did it make?

"Hmm." He folded the printout and slid it into his breast pocket. Then, to her horror, he flicked off the safety on his pistol.

"Please don't." Libby's voice cracked with fear. How could he be so handsome and so ruthless at the same time? Her thoughts went immediately to Gabe, and regret rolled through her. *God will protect me,* she'd told him. He would never believe her work was a calling if God let her die.

"Turn around." The terrorist gestured with the point of his pistol.

Tears rushed into Libby's eyes as she struggled to accept what was happening. It made no sense. Her father would never recover. How could God allow this? Dread-filled, she slowly turned her back on her killer. She choked out a protest. "I must protect the water here. God gave me a job to do."

Bang! A bullet cracked through the air, and Libby's legs buckled, her knees striking the cement floor.

I've been shot. The unthinkable filled Libby's consciousness, keeping her frozen. *Ka-thump. Ka-thump.* But her heart was still pounding, and she felt no pain other than her knees smarting.

Looking down at herself, no stain of blood caught her eye. The cool cement floor grounded her to reality. *I haven't been shot.*

With a gasp, she craned her neck to regard her assailant. Had he missed? Evidently not, for he stood with his pistol aimed straight up at the ceiling, and sunlight beamed through a hole in the tin roof above them. He'd fired straight up, sparing her life.

Seeming almost angry with himself, he holstered his gun before stepping toward her and crouching until his face came within inches of hers. "Say nothing of this to anyone." His soft voice raised goose bumps on her skin. "You came here, and you found the guard dead, the place broken into. Do not mention me or my friends, and I will let you live. If not"—he nudged her chin up with the tip of his finger, his warm breath fanning her cheek—"I will find you, and I will kill you. Am I clear?"

His perfect English screamed of an Oxford education. Libby sought her voice. "Yes."

"Good."

When his gaze dropped to her lips, the fear that he would kiss her made her hold her breath. But then he straightened and air whooshed from her lungs.

Without a backward glance, he stalked on booted feet to the

exit. The door opened and closed firmly behind him. She heard him bark instructions to his companions. Their footsteps tramped across the yard until they were drowned out by the generator. In the distance, an engine rumbled to life before it became inaudible as it carried them away.

Libby didn't move. Her breath flowed in and out as she waited to see if the terrorists would return. But then she remembered Enrique, and she clambered shakily to her feet.

Sunlight blinded her as she staggered outside and across the yard to the guard lying face down in the dust. Getting a closer look, she clapped a hand to her mouth in horror. There was nothing she could do for a man whose brain was partly gone.

The last ten minutes replayed themselves in her mind, drawing her gaze upward. Enrique had gone to the next life. And God, in His mercy, had kept her alive—further evidence that she had a critical task to fulfill. If only He had spared Enrique, also, who'd done nothing to deserve his fate.

"Say nothing of this to anyone." The leader's warning tolled in her head. By firing that one shot he'd led his companions to believe she was dead. If she didn't heed his words, she could end up dying as Enrique had.

Weaving with shock, Libby hovered over the guard's body a moment longer, whispering, "I'm so sorry. I'm so sorry."

Then she tottered to the Jeep, where she retrieved her sat phone, relieved to find it hadn't melted for standing in the shade. With a tremor in her hands, she dialed International Water Institute's headquarters, and when the operator answered, she heard herself tell him exactly what the soldier had told her to say.

Being the only blonde American within a hundred-mile radius, it wouldn't be hard for the extremist to hunt her down. Leaving Paraguay was not an option—not when her quest to protect the area from her family's oil wells compelled her to get busy. So she stuck to the story that she'd arrived at the lab to find Enrique dead, the lab broken into.

After hanging up, her eyes went back to the dead guard. She said a prayer for his soul and for his family, then went to sit inside, where she waited until the distant wail of a siren penetrated her shock. International Water Institute had called the authorities for her. She wouldn't tell them a word about what had really happened.

Only the top brass within the task unit were invited to the meeting with their CIA contact, so, of course Mad Max and Bukowski were in the room, while Lieutenant Commander Strong looked on via WebConnect—Joint Special Operations' version of Zoom. As one of the two platoon leaders, Gabe got to sit in on the meeting, along with his chief, Rodeo, plus their Charlie Platoon counterparts.

If the slim, dark-haired CIA case officer, Jaime Ramirez, felt intimidated in the presence of such highly trained operators, he didn't show it. To Gabe, he looked perfectly at ease, even a little tired as he plopped into a chair near the head of the table.

"You'll have to forgive me if I make little sense tonight."

Their makeshift Operations Center must have been the dining hall for officers during the Chaco War ninety years before. Two ornate chandeliers hung over the long wooden table, casting the shadows of Jaime's eyelashes onto his cheekbones.

"My wife just gave birth to our first child three hours ago. It was a long labor, but they're both doing well."

McDuff raised his bushy eyebrows. "Good for you. Boy or girl?"

"Baby girl." Jaime followed up with a heavy sigh.

Given the man's line of work, Gabe marveled that his family traveled with him.

"My wife is Paraguayan," the operative added, answering Gabe's unspoken question. "I met her here just a year ago."

"Didn't waste any time starting a family," Mad Max needled with a leer.

"I don't believe in wasting time." Jaime segued right into the task at hand. "So, let's get this started." In English touched by the faintest Mexican accent, the case officer explained that he'd first spotted Lebanese males wearing military-style uniforms while shopping at Mariscal Estigarribia's Saturday market. He had followed them to a camp miles away from town, where they trained with artillery and explosives. Further inquiries led him to discover that they called themselves the National Liberation Brigade. Their numbers had swelled in the past few weeks to seventy-two soldiers. They owned three armored trucks, along with an arsenal of military supplies flown into Mariscal Estigarribia from the Middle East.

"There are plenty of Lebanese in Paraguay, so most of the soldiers are Paraguayan by birth. However, the weapons they carry and the uniforms they wear come straight from Hezbollah. Here's where their camp is located."

Leaning over the table, Jaime helped himself to the laptop and brought up a map of the region that replaced Lieutenant Strong's face on the large screen for everyone to see. First Jaime zoomed in on Mariscal Estigarribia, then he toggled south and west toward Paraguay's border with Argentina. "It's ninety-three kilometers from town and only eight kilometers from the nearest oil well."

"Owned by Clark Petroleum," Mad Max finished.

"Yes."

Exchanging a cynical glance with Rodeo, Gabe fought to keep contempt from corroding his faith in the Joint Special Operations Task Force as an independent entity incapable of bribery or favoritism. He had thought it was the threat of terrorism that brought the SEALs here, not because some oil tycoon wanted his wells protected.

Lifting a small pile of papers, Jaime divided it in half and sent paperwork down both sides of the table. "Once you get your packet, turn to page 3, where you'll find a copy of my surveillance notes."

Gabe flipped to a crude drawing of the National Liberation Brigade's base camp and tried picturing it in his mind's eye while Jaime described it in more detail.

McDuff and Bukowski had a dozen questions for the operative, some of which Jaime couldn't answer.

"I'm sorry, I haven't learned that yet. My cover job takes up more of my time than I'd like. I'm working for International Water Institute as an environmentalist, if you can imagine that."

Gabe's blood flowed faster. Jaime Ramirez probably knew Libby, maybe even worked with her. How many environmentalists could there be in this tiny town?

"What do you do for them?" The question came from Lieutenant Strong, listening in from Virginia Beach.

"Lab tests, mostly. IWI is measuring the impact of the oil wells on the River Lindo. Normally my cover job and my intelligence work don't overlap, but there was an incident today at the lab that makes me suspect the NLB was behind it."

Gabe's skin seemed to shrink with foreboding. "What happened?"

"My colleague found our security guard shot in the head. The lock on the warehouse door was destroyed, and six bottles of nitric acid were stolen. As I'm sure you know, that's a base ingredient in most high-velocity explosives. I have a hunch the NLB is planning to blow up a target, possibly an oil well."

"Why would they do that?" Strong asked from the overhead. "All that does is draw attention to the group."

Jaime shrugged his bony shoulders. "That's a good point, sir, and to be honest, I have no idea. Maybe Hezbollah is goading the NLB to attack American interests abroad. Maybe they're hoping to increase U.S. reliance on oil from the Middle East. Who knows? At least Clark Petroleum is aware of the threat and upping their security."

McDuff tugged on one end of his thick mustache. "What makes you so sure it was the NLB who broke into the lab?"

That was Gabe's question, too.

"Because the gun used to kill the guard was Russian, a Makarov, and, of course, the Russians have supplied Hezbollah for years."

Max gave a low whistle. "Good thing you weren't there when that happened."

Jaime nodded his agreement. "Agreed. Even better that my colleague wasn't there as she's a woman. Who knows what the intruders might have done to her?"

Gabe must have made some kind of choking sound because every set of eyes swung in his direction. He cleared his throat and stared at his hands to mask his consternation. Only Rodeo could guess the reason for it. Jaime's colleague *had* to be Libby Clark. What other American female would be skirting disaster to protect river water?

The rest of the meeting passed in a blur. After taking a few more questions, Jaime glanced at his watch and said he had to be going.

Mad Max appeared nonplussed that the case officer was wrapping up the meeting so soon, but in deference to the man's status as a new father, he agreed that they could meet again later in the week. The CO stood, and the others followed suit, their height and breadth making the CIA contact look slight by comparison.

Driven to speak with Jaime in private, Gabe arrived first at the door, but then protocol dictated that he hold it open while everyone else filed out ahead of him—all except for Rodeo, who flanked him as they coursed the hallway.

He spoke to Gabe out of the side of his mouth. "I can't believe she works with our CIA contact."

Keeping his gaze fixed on Jaime's dark head, Gabe ignored the remark. When Jaime broke left to slip out a side door, Gabe gestured for Rodeo to proceed with the others. He waited for all of them to turn the corner before ducking out the same door Jaime had exited, hoping to overtake him.

Finding himself in a grassy area between the admin building and the outer wall, he glimpsed the last of Jaime as an unmanned gate clanked shut between them. Pursuing him, Gabe slipped through the same gate and found himself on the town's main road. The headlights of an approaching car lit up a lone figure crossing the street right in front of him.

Gabe checked the urge to call Jaime's name. Dodging the oncoming car, he chased the case officer, but the man had vanished by the time he reached the curb. Gabe searched the stoops of the squat buildings in front of him, a row of what were probably officer's quarters back in the day. Jaime might have slipped up the alley cutting between the two of them.

He waded into it, calling softly, "Mr. Ramirez?"

A scuffling sound was his only warning before he found himself flung face-first against a dried-clay wall. Its rough surface scraped his cheek.

"Why are you following me?"

While impressed by Jaime's stealth, the man was no match for Gabe. He submitted to having his arm twisted behind his back, nonetheless. "I just have a question for you."

The case officer released him, and Gabe shook his arm out as he swung around.

"You couldn't ask me this question earlier?" Light in the window next to them blinked on, forcing them to move farther into the alley. "So what is it?"

"Your colleague, the woman you work with. It's Elizabeth Clark, isn't it?" Even in the dark, Gabe could see Jaime's eyes widen.

"How do you know Libby?"

The sound of her nickname on another man's lips sparked a feeling akin to jealousy. "I'm a friend of her father's." Technically that wasn't a lie since he'd saved Kyle Clark's life. "Gabe Villalobos." He stuck out a hand and Jaime shook it, his grip confident and friendly.

"Oh yes, she mentioned you once." Jaime's gaze trekked over him, appraising him. "You're the Navy SEAL who got her out of Matamoros, leaving two defenseless students behind."

"I hear they're fine now."

"They're lucky."

"And so is Libby for not being in the lab today. Is she okay? You said she found the guard's body."

Jaime's gaze flickered toward the lit window where a silhouette moved behind the closed curtain. "Why don't you ask her yourself?" He gestured with his head. "This is her house. Mine's the one next door."

Gabe glanced toward the lit window. "No, I can't talk to her." But when he looked back at Jaime, the man had vaporized.

Gabe reconsidered the window. *Libby*. His pulse had quickened the instant he'd realized how near she was. He'd told his men they weren't to have any contact with her, and yet here he was, practically on her doorstep and, for the life of him, he couldn't find the willpower to simply walk away.

As he headed for her front door, casting guilty glances at the buildings across the street, he told himself he would only check to see how she fared, having come upon a murdered guard that day. Not that he owed Clark any sort of allegiance, but her father would appreciate him checking on his daughter's emotional state. Having justified his actions, Gabe mounted the stoop while considering what to say.

CHAPTER 6

The hair on Libby's nape prickled. She hadn't just imagined the voices outside her window. Having crossed the room to draw the curtain, she had glimpsed two silhouettes conversing in the alley not far from the Jeep, which she'd parked as deep into the alley as possible to make it less visible from the main road.

God help her if the men who'd killed Enrique were here. But why kill her now when she'd told no one about the threat to her life, not even Jaime? Hope beat back the cold shock slipping over her. Maybe the two men she'd seen outside weren't the extremists.

She peeked behind the curtain for a closer look, but they were gone. Fear spiked her bloodstream. She darted across the room to her kitchen to close the blinds there. As they snapped shut, the memory of Enrique's battered skull shot acid up her throat. Her gaze dropped to the bottle of *caña*, gifted to her by an elder of the Guaraní tribe on her first visit to the indigenous village. Made from fermented sugarcane, *caña* was a native remedy for stomach pains and parasites. Maybe it would settle her stomach. She unscrewed the cap, lifted the bottle, and tipped it to her lips.

The sweet, scalding liquid made her eyes water. She went to take another sip only to freeze when a knock at her door reverberated through her half-furnished rental.

Oh, help! Libby set down the bottle before she dropped it. Her heart hammered anew as she envisioned the man with the blue-green eyes on her doorstep. He might shoot her on the spot if she opened the door. But what if it wasn't him? What if it was Jaime looking to borrow an egg or something?

Libby edged toward the entrance, fighting the cowardly urge to run and hide under her bed. "Who is it?" Her voice quavered with fear. If only her door had a peephole.

"It's me, Libby."

The deep, familiar voice summoned an image of Gabe Villalobos. Impossible. The *caña* was making her hallucinate.

"It's Gabe Villalobos."

So she wasn't hallucinating. But how could Gabe be *here?*

"Open up. I want to know if you're okay."

He was still so infernally bossy. Relief had her snatching the door open. The light inside her home spotlighted every solid inch of him, from his long legs encased in desert-patterned cammies to his dark, wavy hair. Without thinking, Libby crossed the threshold and threw her arms around his shoulders, hugging his reassuring solidness. *I'm safe. I'm safe.*

"Whoa, hey, hello to you, too."

It was obvious he hadn't expected such a warm welcome. With a glance back at the street, he maneuvered them through her door, shut and locked it behind them, all without releasing her.

Libby told herself to let go, but her fingers were curled into the surprisingly soft canvas of his jacket. It took a great deal of willpower to unfurl them and step back, recovering her composure with a deep breath. "What are you doing here?"

He didn't answer. Jungle-green eyes raked her pale face, slicing down her rigid torso to the hands now fisted by her sides. "What's going on?" His tone was suspicious.

She shook her head. "No, I asked first. Why are you here?" A sudden notion had her clapping a hand to her forehead. "Did my father send you here *again?*" Outrage supplanted her fear.

"What? No."

His immediate denial had her narrowing her eyes at him. "Then he sent you here to spy on me." She bristled at her father's high-handedness.

"Wrong again. I just met your colleague, Jaime."

"Jaime?" What did he have to do with any of this?

"He mentioned what happened at the lab today."

An image of Enrique flashed before her eyes.

"Are you okay? You seem—" Gabe angled his head as his gaze slid over her again—"frazzled."

That was how she felt, like a jigsaw puzzle shaken into disjointed pieces, but she couldn't tell him that, or he'd guess what had really happened at the lab—and then she'd be killed for saying anything. Horror stiffened her joints. She needed a quick excuse for her behavior. "I think I'm drunk." She gestured to the bottle of *caña* sitting open on the counter.

Gabe frowned at it. "That bottle's still full." He focused back on her. "You sure you're not just scared out of your mind?"

Libby lifted her chin a notch. "Of course not." She ruined that assertion by jumping as Gabe laid a hand squarely over her thumping heart.

"Tell me what happened today."

Maybe she was dreaming him. She'd certainly done her share of that since he'd vanished out of her house with his two-word note. The fantastic odds of them both ending up in Paraguay made her want to confide in him right away, but then Gabe would move Heaven and earth to have her on a plane bound for North America before the sun rose.

"Nothing." She managed a convincing shrug.

"Nothing? I heard that the guard at your lab was killed today, and you found the body. That sounds like something to me."

News certainly traveled fast in a small community. The haunting vision flashed into her thoughts causing her to shudder. "Yes, it was awful."

"Did you see anything else?"

"What do you mean?"

"Did you see the people who murdered the guard?"

The word *murdered* inspired a wave of nausea. "No."

But she'd answered too quickly, making her denial sound like the lie it was.

Suspicion brightened Gabe's dark-green eyes. "You did see them. Who were they?" His tone sharpened with urgency.

Libby shook her head emphatically and backed away. "No. No, I didn't see anyone."

He pursued her, using his height and breadth to impose his will on her. "Were they foreign soldiers? Lebanese, maybe?"

Surely, he could see the pulse galloping at the base of her throat. "I don't know. I never saw them."

"Then why are you so terrified right now?"

"I'm fine." She cast a longing glance at the *caña*. A shot or two or three might just convince her of that.

"Libby." Gabe's large hands rose to capture her face.

The feel of his warm palms against her cold cheeks sent a frisson of awareness clear to her toes.

"Those men have links to Hezbollah. If you know anything about them, anything at all, we could use that information."

Oh. So *that* was why Gabe was here. He hadn't chased her to the Southern Hemisphere just to be close to her again. Of course not. Why would she even think that after he'd scoffed at her convictions? "You're hunting terrorists?" She gulped. The extremists to whom she'd given the nitric acid were *Hezbollah*? Oh, God forgive her!

Gabe abruptly released her, his expression inscrutable. "I can't answer that. As far as you are concerned, we're here to train the Paraguayan Special Forces."

"Right." But that wasn't the real story. Doubt undermined Libby's resolve. If the Hezbollah extremists were now armed with nitric acid, shouldn't she tell Gabe everything she knew? Might that not save lives later, even if it put her own life at risk? On the other hand, Gabe would certainly insist she leave the country, possibly even enlist her father's aid to force her to go home.

He flipped his wrist over to glance at his watch. "I have to be going."

Relieved not to have to say anything, Libby nodded and kept her thoughts to herself.

Gabe's gaze dropped from her eyes to her mouth. With a jolt of anticipation, she could tell he was tempted to kiss her again as he had on the bridge. *Yes, please.* She couldn't resist flirting with him. "Maybe I'll see you around?" Those were the words she'd tossed at him at the airstrip in Brownsville.

His dark eyebrows pulled together in a frown. "We're not supposed to rub elbows with the locals."

"Right. I'm not really a local, though, am I?"

Evidently those words were just the excuse that he was looking for. With a long step, Gabe closed the distance between them, hooked her waist, and pulled her close before lowering his lips intently to hers.

Pleasure cascaded over Libby as he kissed her more thoroughly than the last time—like it had been the only thing he'd thought about since their last kiss.

A growl of frustration rumbled in his throat before he abruptly released her. Frustration simmered in his eyes. "*Please*, stay out of trouble."

Pivoting on his boots, he stalked to the door, where he flicked off the interior light before he let himself outside. She didn't realize until the door clicked shut that he'd turned off her light to keep people across the street from seeing him leave. Like he'd said, hobnobbing with the locals wasn't allowed.

Hurrying to the kitchen window, Libby peeked under the blind, hoping to catch another glimpse of him. SEAL that he was, Gabe had blended into the night already. There was nothing to look at but her sandy front yard, a scraggly cactus plant, and an empty street. Across the road, lights shone in the ugly brick buildings that loomed behind a high brick wall.

Gabe Villalobos was here in Paraguay at the same time she was. What were the odds?

Touching fingers to her lips, Libby relived his perfect and possessive kiss while marveling that it was way more intoxicating than *caña.* What was God thinking throwing them together on a whole new continent? She couldn't afford to be distracted from the urgency of her work here.

Maybe Gabe's role was just to chase off the terrorists, and her attraction for him was something Heaven hadn't factored in— except God was all-knowing, so that couldn't be right. She couldn't help but wallow in gratitude for Gabe's presence. If the SEALs rounded up the extremists, then she didn't have to fear for her life quite so much. "Thank You, Lord," she whispered on a long exhale.

After stowing the *caña* in the cupboard, Libby headed for her bedroom, keeping the lights off. With any luck, she would dream of Gabe tonight and not the extremist with the blue-green eyes.

Libby cast Jaime a puzzled glance as he drove their Jeep down a dirt road that took them from the Guaraní village back toward the lab. "How do you even know Gabe?" The question had occurred to her in the middle of the night when she'd tossed and turned, reliving the nightmare of Enrique's untimely death and the astounding reality of Gabe's proximity.

Dark eyes flicked in her direction. "Who?"

"Lieutenant Villalobos. He's a friend of mine. How do you know him?"

"Oh, him." Jaime shrugged and sped up on a straightaway. "He's the SEAL who saved your father's life, isn't he? You've mentioned him before."

The hot wind whistling through the Jeep's lowered window sent Libby's hair into her eyes. "Yeah, but he's here in Paraguay now, and he said you told him about the incident at the lab."

"Oh, yes, we ran into each other at *La Cantina*. I stopped by for a drink after leaving the hospital."

"Huh." The *Cantina* was the only place for drinks in Mariscal Estigarribia, and while Gabe might have run into Jaime there, his kiss hadn't tasted of beer or liquor. Rather than press Jaime, Libby noted his reluctance to be candid and changed the subject. "Do you think that cow died from toxins in the Río Lindo?"

The dead cow had been the topic of conversation among the indigenous villagers who relied on the Río Lindo for their drinking water as well as to water their livestock. As Jaime shrugged again, Libby turned her attention to the view out of her passenger window.

An ugly wellhead swung up and down, looking like a monstrous steel creature feeding in the arid wilderness. A collection of tanks stood beyond it, containing what the wellhead brought up from deep beneath the ground. "That well there can't be more than two miles from the river. It has to be contaminating the river water."

Jaime searched a moment before spotting it. "Yet the water's alkalinity and the pH are both within normal ranges, and we haven't come across any significant hydrocarbons."

Libby frowned at the grotesque machine. There were two dozen more just like it in El Chaco Boreal, all owned by Clark Petroleum and powered by electricity garnered from solar panels, which she couldn't see. "So you don't think the wells contaminate the environment?"

Jaime sent her an ambivalent shrug.

"You don't think there's a link between the dead cow and the locals complaining of gastrointestinal trouble and dizziness?" Half the older population at the Guaraní village had mentioned similar symptoms in the last month.

"From the tests we've performed, that doesn't appear to be the case, Libby. The river water is clean."

So the tests suggested, but Libby, still skeptical, hummed in her throat. The dead cow and the sick elders indicated to her that the wells were leaking contaminants, just like her mother told her in her dream. In time, she would discover which wells were responsible and how costly the impact was.

Her thoughts went back to that morning. "Did the river look low to you?"

Jaime shrugged again. "I imagine it's always low this time of year. The rainy season doesn't start for another month."

"You don't think Clark Petroleum's using river water for their Poseidon Ponds?" Those were enormous reservoirs dug to hold water. Once siphoned from the ponds, the water was mixed with sand and chemicals and then injected under pressure into the shale, deep beneath the ground to break it apart, releasing the oil and gas trapped in the earth. If Clark Petroleum was sucking water out of the river, that would also degrade the lifestyle of El Chaco's natives.

Jaime pointed out a huge white truck kicking up dust on the horizon as it traveled the Transchaco highway ahead of them. "They haul it in. See?"

"From where?"

He shot her a puzzled glance. "Don't you know?"

She knew what she'd been told. "Supposedly it comes all the way from the Gran Chaco Forest, where there's plenty of water. But it takes four hundred tanker trucks to supply just one Poseidon Pond, and you saw how low the river is running."

Jaime flicked her wry glance. "What are you saying?"

She pursed her lips, not wanting to make accusations she couldn't prove.

"Clark Petroleum upholds the highest standards, Libby. I thought that was the reason you worked for IWI—to prove to the world that your father's corporation is harmless."

Libby snatched the hair out of her eyes, astonished. "You know who my father is?"

He chuckled. "Well, it's hardly a secret. You share the same last name. Plus, I saw your father's photo online, and you have the same stubborn chin."

Dismay clouded Libby's contentment. Would she ever get out from under her father's shadow? "He's not in charge anymore." She crossed her arms over her chest. "He stepped down as CEO so he can run for Senate."

"Ah." Jaime gave a dubious nod.

Libby frowned at him. "And I am *not* here to make Clark Petroleum look good. When my father started drilling in this area, my mother protested. She tried to talk him out of it. The thought of contaminants leaking from the waste barrels or the containment walls and finding their way into the river water troubled her a great deal. I know it's happening, and I intend to prove it."

Jaime shot her a pained look. "I'm sorry you lost your mother prematurely."

Grief rose, closing off Libby's throat and keeping her quiet.

"But the way I see it," he added, "Clark Petroleum improves the local economy more than it harms the environment. Have we seen any methane in Río Lindo? No, but the economy is thriving, people needing jobs are finding them, and industries are burning cleaner energy. It's all good."

Libby regarded him more closely. "You don't talk like an environmentalist."

He chuckled. "That's because I'm a realist first." His smile of amusement abruptly faded. "What's this?"

As he stepped on the brakes, Libby braced herself against the dash. By a hair's breadth, Jaime prevented their Jeep from T-boning a cargo truck, which pulled out of a trail onto the dirt road they were traveling without giving them the right of way.

Her eyes widened at the vision of olive-colored uniforms worn by the men riding exposed in the back. Their full, dark beards identified them as members of the same crew who'd broken into the lab. Unfriendly gazes glared at Jaime as he laid on the horn. The cargo truck swung around them, moving briskly in the opposite direction, headed into the wilds of El Chaco.

Libby struggled to breathe. Had any of those bearded men spotted her? One or two might have looked familiar. And if they'd seen her in the Jeep, then they had to know she wasn't dead!

Dragging in a tight breath, she realized Jaime had yet to get them moving. Instead, he was frowning down the narrow track, lined by quebracho trees, from which the truck had emerged.

Without a word of explanation, he turned their Jeep down the rutted track.

"Where are we going?" The possibility of encountering more terrorists sharpened Libby's tone.

He flicked her a distracted glance. "I want to see what they were doing."

As the trees thinned, the wellhead she'd been regarding earlier stood directly before them, swinging back and forth as it pumped crude oil from deep underground. As Jaime slid the gearshift into Park and killed the engine, Libby swallowed nervously.

"Stay here." Shaking off his seat belt, he leaned across her knees to pull his pistol out of the glove compartment.

"What do you need that for?" Her voice sounded like somebody else's.

He shot her a reassuring glance. "Don't worry. You saw them leave. I just want to know what they were up to."

That's not your job, she wanted to point out, only her throat was too dry to speak. Jaime's footsteps faded as he left her alone to wend his way cautiously through the spiny shrubs that carpeted the sandy soil. Apart from the humming of the wellhead, a hush seemed to have fallen over the area. Not a single bird soared across the sky.

Libby fanned herself, losing sight of Jaime's dark head as the land dipped, then spotting him again as he neared the wellhead. He peered up at it, shielding his eyes from the sun with a raised hand, before stepping toward the tank at the base that separated the gas from the sediment.

A ring of light flashed brilliantly, accompanied by a loud *BOOM* that blasted Jaime off his feet and sent him flying.

Libby shrieked in disbelief. Flames shot into the air. With a hand clapped to her mouth, she watched in horror as the wellhead stopped swinging. But then it emitted a terrible groan before falling in slow motion toward the very spot Jaime had landed.

CRASH! It hit the ground with enough force to shake the Jeep while sending dust billowing into the air.

CHAPTER 7

"No!" Libby thrust her way out of the Jeep. On legs unwieldy with fear, she sprinted toward the place where Jaime had been flung. Grains of sand floated in the air, obscuring her vision. The acrid smell of burning gas had her holding her breath as she dodged brush and cactuses to get to him.

"Jaime!" Coughing against the fumes and dust, she searched the ground around the fallen tower. Beyond the twisted remains of the wellhead, she spotted Jaime at last—not under the steel structure as she dreaded but on the far side of it.

As she rounded the defunct machinery, keeping a wary eye on the fire now raging out of the well, an image of Enrique's shattered skull flashed before her eyes. She braced herself for what she might see as she hit her knees beside her colleague. "Jaime, are you hurt?"

His long eyelashes fluttered but his eyes didn't open. Blood specked one side of his face, coming from a laceration on his chin. She ran shaky hands over his sand-covered frame seeking further injuries and finding none. "Jaime, wake up. Please!" She gave him a gentle shake.

To her great relief, his lashes lifted. "Libby." He glanced around, his eyes widening at the sight of flames shooting skyward. "What happened?"

"It exploded. The wellhead blew up, and then it fell over." She shot a wary look at the fire, grateful, at least, that it was burning off any escaping methane, but the heat of it was nearly unbearable. "We need to get out of here. Can you move? Are you hurt?"

He raised a hand to his cut chin and hissed. "I think I'm okay. What about you?"

"Not hurt at all. Let me help you back to the Jeep."

He held up a hand. "I just need a moment." With a grimace, he adjusted his bent leg.

She ran another worried gaze over him. "What's wrong?"

He didn't immediately answer. "I think I broke something. My back or my pelvis."

She eyed him helplessly. Looking over at the raging fire, she measured the distance to the Jeep. Jaime would never make it that far. "Stay right here. I'm going to bring the Jeep over."

Jaime mumbled a feeble protest, but Libby was already sprinting back to their vehicle. Adrenaline lent her speed. She scarcely noticed the thorny shrubbery that scratched her bare calves. With four-wheel drive, the Jeep could drive right over them.

Less than two minutes later, Libby parked the Jeep alongside Jaime's prone figure. To her relief, the fire had subsided slightly.

At Jaime's instruction, she grabbed him beneath his armpits, lifted him slowly off the ground and dragged him toward the passenger door, grateful for his slight build. Jaime couldn't use his legs for anything more than holding up his weight once they reached the vehicle. He, himself, opened the passenger door.

But by the time Libby had stowed Jaime inside, with his seat tipped way back to make sitting tolerable, Jaime had turned a sickly shade of gray. Sweat glistened on his brow and his upper lip. Libby closed his door and rounded the vehicle to jump behind the steering wheel.

"I'll get you to the hospital quickly," she promised him.

"I'd rather you went slowly and avoided bumps."

The agony in his voice plucked at her heartstrings.

After shifting the Jeep into Drive, she drove as gingerly as possible back to the more traveled road, turning in the direction of town. Focusing all her attention on getting them to the highway, she did her best to avoid potholes.

Jaime handed her his pistol at one point. "Here, put this back in the glove compartment and hand me the satellite phone."

She did as he asked, amazed when he placed a call with a pained but determined expression. Who was he calling?

"Yes, I'd like to report an explosion at one of Clark Petroleum's wells. Number 36 has been targeted and is currently on fire. Please advise the company."

He must have called the police. He gave them his name and a halting but thorough description of the truck full of bearded men. "I'm happy to give a statement. You'll find me at the hospital in Mariscal Estigarribia, where I'm headed now. Yes," he added after a moment. "Thank you." Ending the call, he gave the phone back to Libby. "Keep this on you and answer for me if anyone calls back."

Admiration for Jaime's bravery kept her quiet as she placed the cell phone back in the holder clipped to the dash. Her thoughts returned to the men she'd seen in the back of the cargo truck. The same men who'd shot Enrique had now injured Jaime. Guilt burned in her belly. God forgive her. The extremists had used the nitric acid *she* had given them to make a bomb. "Why would they want to blow up a well?"

Jaime had closed his eyes. "Why do you think?"

The answer was obvious: The men were extremists, terrorists, and probably even Hezbollah, according to Gabe. They hated Americans so, of course, it suited their agenda to destroy an American-owned oil well. Were the rest of Clark Petroleum's wells in danger of being targeted? Gabe and his SEALs wouldn't allow that to happen.

It came as a relief to finally reach Ruta Transchaco. Jaime gave a groan as the Jeep lurched off the dirt road and onto the pavement.

"Sorry." Libby accelerated until the land on either side turned into a streaming blur.

What felt like hours of driving was probably just thirty minutes before the red-tiled roofs of Mariscal Estigarribia came into view. Allowing the tension in her shoulders to ease, Libby relaxed her death grip on the steering wheel and headed for the hospital, located in the heart of town, just blocks from her rental.

At last, she pulled up before the doors of the modest facility where she laid a hand on the horn until the orderly taking a break outside tossed down his cigarette and called for a stretcher. Within minutes, Jaime was being wheeled into the building.

"Libby." He groped for her hand and caught it. "I need you to tell Gabe what happened."

The words made her blink. Clearly Jaime knew Gabe better than he'd let on. She nodded her agreement, secretly pleased for a reason to seek out Gabe. "Okay."

"Tell him to come and see me. Then you can tell Lucía."

"I will." She trailed the stretcher into the hospital, only to be banned from the examination room. Poor Jaime would have to be x-rayed, and the shrapnel removed from his chin. Shaken by the close call—he could so easily have ended up dead—Libby whirled and walked out.

When she got back in the Jeep, she took a moment to compose herself and to consider her next move. The military installation might be only four blocks away, but she had no idea how to find Gabe within it. Even though she had the sat phone, she didn't know his number. What's more, how would she tell Gabe about the explosion and Jaime's injuries without confessing her unintentional role?

"Be with me, Lord." Anger flickered in her. The terrorist who'd sworn her to secrecy had just made an unforgivable move.

"Come on, sir, just one more. Don't let him win."

Doc stood on one side of the chin-up bar cheering Gabe on, while Rodeo stood on the other, undermining his confidence.

"He ain't gonna win." Bright-blue eyes mocked Gabe's trembling arms as he continued his uncertain ascent. If he could just get his chin to clear the bar, Gabe would beat Rodeo's record of fifty-three pull-ups in one minute.

"You've got all the time in the world." Doc looked up from his wristwatch. "And plenty of power left."

Gabe wasn't so sure of that. His biceps, on fire for the last ten ascents, were about to explode. His knuckles ached from grasping the bar too hard, and a bead of sweat had dripped into his right eye, making it sting. Out of the corner of that eye, Gabe could see Rodeo smirking.

"You're all washed up, Lobo."

Gabe longed to point out that he had three inches and twenty more pounds of muscle to move, but he couldn't talk with his teeth clenched.

"You got this, sir."

Taller than either of them with those different-colored eyes, Doc had endured his share of harassment for being the kindest, most sympathetic SEAL Gabe had ever met. The man literally felt other people's pain. While the merciless instructors at BUDs/SEAL training had done their best to toughen his hide, Doc's empathy was what Gabe liked best about him, especially in times like this one.

"Argh!" The bar hovered six inches above his eyebrows, and it wasn't getting any closer.

The door to the workout facility burst open, admitting the youngest SEAL in Gabe's platoon. "LT!"

Glad for the excuse to quit, Gabe let his arms go slack. He dropped to the floor, ignoring Rodeo's crow of victory.

The blond-haired newcomer spotted Gabe amidst the room full of bare-chested men and hurried over. "Sir!"

Dubbed Bam-Bam for his willingness to club anyone he thought deserved it, the nineteen-year-old had developed a case of hero worship for his platoon leader. As the lowest-ranking SEAL, his job in Paraguay was to develop rapport with the Paraguayan Special Forces, whom they were here to train—allegedly.

Gabe grabbed his towel and wiped the sweat from his brow. "What's up?"

Bam-Bam's gray eyes were as big as quarters. "Sir, there's a woman at the gate asking for you. She's covered in blood and talking about an explosion!"

The announcement hit Gabe in the solar plexus. The weight room went suddenly quiet. *Libby?* Oh, crap. He'd known something bad would happen to her.

Snatching his T-shirt off the weight rack, he tunneled into it. "Doc and Rodeo come with me. Everyone else stays here." His order prompted groans of disappointment as it prevented the rest of his platoon from pouring out of the door, eager to see the woman covered in blood.

As they chased Bam-Bam down a maze of hallways, Gabe's fears sank talons into his shoulder muscles. "You said she was covered in blood. Is she hurt?"

The young SEAL thought for a moment. "I don't think it's her blood, sir."

Thank God. They exited the building from a door that put them near the main gate. Spotting Libby on the far side of the manned barricade, Gabe hurried toward her. She wore practical cargo capris, a blood-stained green blouse, and sturdy boots. Her bare calves were scratched and bleeding; there was dust in her hair, and she still looked beautiful. Paraguayan soldiers had lined up on the other side of the gate, professing concern as they ogled her with fascination.

Relief registered on Libby's flushed face as she caught sight of him. "Gabe!"

"Let her in," he requested of the Paraguayan soldiers, speaking to them in Spanish.

They took one look at his intense expression and unlocked the gate.

As he drew Libby inside, Gabe squelched the urge to pull her into his embrace. Holding her lightly by the elbow, he could feel her trembling as he led her under the shade of a tree. "What happened?" He, Doc, Rodeo, and Bam-Bam gathered around her.

Libby hugged herself. "It's my colleague. He told me to tell you what happened."

With words flooding out of her mouth, she told them a story

involving Jaime Ramirez, the Lebanese extremists, an oil well, and an explosion.

"The wellhead collapsed practically on top of him, and the oil was still burning when we left. It's probably still on fire." Her voice quavered as she relayed how she managed to get Jaime into their Jeep and drive him to the hospital.

"Who are you talking about?" Doc was baffled.

"Someone she works with." Gabe exchanged glances with Rodeo, who'd attended the meeting with Jaime the evening prior. "How badly hurt is he?"

Libby tapped her chin. "He caught a piece of shrapnel here, but his back may be broken. He can't walk, but he can stand." She bit her lower lip as her chin began to quiver.

My brave girl. Gabe squeezed her forearm, frankly amazed that she was keeping it together, but then he'd seen her keep cool under pressure before. "You did the right thing coming to me." Even so, her story chilled him. This was twice now that she'd come close to rubbing elbows with the National Liberation Brigade.

He turned to Doc with instructions. "Noah, go tell Master Chief about the explosion. Rodeo, you fetch the CO. Ask them to meet me in the TOC, stat. Bam-Bam, give us some privacy."

As the three men scattered with a "Yes, sir," Gabe looked back at Libby, unable to mask his concern for her. "Are you sure you're okay?" Raising a hand to wipe a speck of blood off her cheek, he was glad to discover it wasn't hers. "Do I need to call your father?"

At the question, she knocked his hand away. "Don't you dare." Her eyes flashed with affront.

He had to respect her independence. "Look, I'm concerned is all. Did you see any of the terrorists up close? Could you identify them?"

She blinked as if caught off guard by the request. A warm breeze dried the sweat off Gabe's skin as he waited for her answer.

"Well, they wore olive uniforms with pistols on their belts and rifles strapped over their shoulders. They all had full beards. And their leader has blue-green eyes." She looked away, sucking in a breath as if regretting having added that detail.

The words set off alarm bells in Gabe's head. "You were close enough to see his eyes?"

She wouldn't look at him. "I have good vision."

Her response confused him, but he didn't have time to analyze it. Right now, there were bigger fish to fry. If Hezbollah had targeted one well already, chances were they were planning to target the others. They'd probably used some of the stolen nitric acid to make the accelerant that fueled the explosion.

"Who else have you told about this?"

"Jaime made a call to the police, I think, reporting that Well 36 had been blown up and was still on fire."

"What about the people at the hospital?"

"I don't know what Jaime's telling them. He just asked me to tell you and then I could tell his wife."

"The fewer people who know, the better." He gestured with his chin in the direction of her home. "Go ahead and tell Jaime's wife now. I've got to go alert my superiors, but I'll find you later." He drew her back toward the gate. "Are you going to be all right?" Of its own accord, his hand found its way to hers. The way her fingers twined through his pleased his senses to a ridiculous degree.

She nodded, avoiding eye contact. "Sure."

Awash in protective feelings, Gabe cradled her hand a moment longer, loath to let it go. "Okay. I'll see you soon. Thanks for coming to me."

Releasing her with reluctance, he watched Libby turn away, pass through the gate under many an appreciative eye, then climb into her Jeep. Gabe glowered at the Paraguayan soldiers, sending the message that Libby would be his before any of them had a chance with her. Looking back at the Jeep as she pointed it toward her rental, he caught the pensive expression on her face before she roared away.

Once she was out of sight, Gabe swung toward the building, where Bam-Bam stood waiting for him.

"I've got a special assignment for you, Caleb."

"Sir?"

Gabe nodded toward the terra-cotta roofs of the little homes across the street. "See those houses right across the street from the wall? Miss Clark lives in the one with the yellow door. She's the daughter of a future senator, and nothing bad can happen to her. I want you to keep an eye on her."

"Yes, sir!"

"Don't let anyone near her without me hearing about it right away."

"Yes, sir!" His face alight with interest, Bam-Bam started toward the gate only to be deterred by the guards there. He signaled to Gabe that he would walk down the wall and observe Libby's little house from there.

Gabe sent him a thumbs-up and hurried back into the building. If only he were in Bam-Bam's shoes and not about to face Mad Max and Master Chief, who wouldn't welcome what Gabe had to say to them. Like him, they would want to know why Elizabeth Clark, whom the SEALs had recovered out of Mexico a mere four months ago, was now in Paraguay.

Still dressed in his PT shorts and shirt, Gabe strode toward the TOC with his thoughts in a whirl.

Jaime, who was a true professional, would never have let Libby, an innocent civilian, get so close to the Lebanese that she could make out the color of their leader's eyes. For that matter, how would she have known which one was the leader? She'd have to be standing directly in front of the man to see... A horrifying thought broke his stride.

He stood in the hallway pursuing that thought. What if Libby *had* stood directly in front of the NLB leader? What if she'd lied about not seeing who broke into the lab because she'd *been* there when the thieves broke in? Yet, how could she have done that and still lived to tell about it? Perhaps she'd been hiding, and she watched them steal the nitric acid. Then why not say so to the authorities?

Only Libby knew the answer to that. And the first free minute he managed to finagle, Gabe would wring the truth out of her.

~

Libby paced the floor of Jaime's home with a tiny bundle in the crook of one arm. After an hour of fussing, baby Maya had finally lapsed into a peaceful sleep. If only Libby's churning thoughts would subside, as well.

Poor Jaime. She fretted over his prognosis. What if his injuries prevented him from returning to work? She needed him for guidance and security. And now she might have to get the water samples required for the lab on her own. Why, oh why, had he wanted to know what the soldiers were up to in the first place?

Perhaps Lucía, his wife, would have some answers when she returned, which ought to be any minute now. Libby had been watching their baby for hours.

Carrying baby Maya to the bassinet in her parents' bedroom, Libby lowered the newborn gingerly inside it, then paused to tuck a small, soft blanket around her. Tiny and vulnerable, Maya slept on.

Resting her hands on her thighs, Libby studied the infant's perfection with wonder. She'd inherited her father's dark curls. Her chin sported a tiny cleft, and her tiny hands were a masterpiece of craftsmanship, right down to the perfect little fingernails.

Maternal feelings rooted in Libby's heart, catching her by surprise. For the first time in her life, she wondered what her own child might look like and how she would raise it. *Not here. Her* daughter wouldn't grow up anywhere close to danger.

Her lips quirked with irony as she straightened. She was thinking like her father now.

The sound of a key jiggling in the lock brought her out of the bedroom in time to see Jaime's wife close the door behind her. Lucía appeared careworn and more than a little frazzled at having left her baby for so long.

"How was she?" Her thick, black braid slipped over her shoulder as she stowed her purse in the closet, then hurried toward Libby while peering past her into the bedroom.

In Spanish, Libby assured the new mother that the baby was an angel. "She fell asleep after I changed and fed her the formula you left me."

"Oh, good. Thank you so much."

"Any time. How is Jaime?"

The worry lines etched in Lucía's face were not encouraging. She grimaced. "His tailbone was shattered from being thrown by the blast. Waiting for it to heal would take too long, so Jaime convinced them to remove the chipped pieces. He will have to stay a few days for observation. His chin required fourteen stitches, but he'll be even more handsome with a scar, I think." She forced a smile.

Libby laid a hand on the shorter woman's shoulder. "I'm so sorry this happened to him, Lucía."

"It's not your fault. He's been through worse. It's a small thing."

"But one that shouldn't have happened in the first place. I don't understand why he got out of the Jeep at all. It's not his job to worry about the oil wells."

Lucía dismissed the subject with a shrug. "Jaime is too curious for his own good."

"I guess he is. Well, I'll leave you to rest now unless there's anything else I can do for you."

"No, no. I'm so grateful to you. Jaime told me what you did for him today."

She hadn't had much choice. After offering Lucía a smile and a swift hug, Libby headed to the door. "Try to sleep, and I'll check on you tomorrow." She would also be calling IWI's headquarters to see whether they expected her to carry on her work alone.

As she stepped into the chilly night air, Libby's gaze went straight to the lights of the military installation across the street. A yearning to see Gabe stitched through her. His tenderness and concern that afternoon had shown a side of him she'd only glimpsed. What had she been thinking, mentioning the color of the terrorist leader's eyes? The explosion must have addled her wits. Or was it guilt for inadvertently contributing to Jaime's injury?

Thank God for the SEALs, who would surely put a swift end to further explosions. As she crossed the alley toward her own home, uncertainty assailed Libby. She mounted the dark stoop, reaching for the doorknob. *I should have left a light on.*

What if one or more of the terrorists had glimpsed her in the

Jeep today and recognized her from the lab? Her light hair and fair skin would have betrayed her immediately, letting the soldiers know their leader hadn't really killed her. Then he would be forced to rectify his mistake. Even parked way up in the alley, the Jeep was still visible, advertising her location. What's more, it sat between her house and Jaime's, which meant Lucía and her baby were in danger, as well.

With a tremor in her fingers, Libby used the key in her pocket to unlock her door. With her senses heightened, she pushed the door inward and reached inside, flicking on the lights. The vision of a man sprawled across her couch had her rearing back with a gasp. He, in turn, had jerked awake at the light flooding him. In less than a second, he was on his feet, pointing a pistol at her.

CHAPTER 8

"Gabe!" Libby stepped hastily inside, then sagged against the door as she closed it, relieved beyond measure not to be facing a terrorist.

For his part, Gabe jammed his pistol back in its holster. His forehead furrowed as he studied her, no doubt seeing the residual horror still on her face.

His jaw muscles jumped. "You were expecting someone else?"

"Of course not." To avoid his probing gaze, she turned around and locked the door behind her before facing him with a more assured demeanor. "You caught me by surprise, is all. How'd you get in?"

He ignored the question completely. "Where have you been?"

What was this about? She gestured next door. "I was babysitting so Lucía could visit her husband."

"Ah." His suspicious expression vanished. "How's Jaime doing?"

"He's having surgery in the morning to remove pieces of his broken tailbone."

Gabe nodded. "Good."

"Why are you here?" She could feel the truth about the lab incident rising toward her tongue. If he stuck around for long, she feared the consequences.

"I want to ask you something." He walked straight toward her.

Libby had to lock her knees to keep from backing up. With his jaw darkened by stubble, Gabe was doubly appealing. His hair had grown out since he'd rescued her in Matamoros. The glossy waves curled around his ears and at the back of his neck, making her want to feel their texture. Recalling the kiss they'd shared the other night, her pulse ticked upward in hopes of getting another.

"Ask me what?" He stood within six inches of her now, so close that she could smell the gun oil on the pistol he'd just pointed at her.

His gaze bored into hers. "What really happened the other day at the lab?"

Her heart skipped a beat, even as her eyes widened. So, he'd realized the detail she'd given him was a bit too specific—of course he had. And now he wanted an honest answer. Unfortunately, she had no ready lie available. "I can't tell you." Her words came out in a whisper.

If she told Gabe, he would immediately tell her father, who would alert International Water Institute. Her employer would insist she leave the country, and she wasn't remotely ready to go yet, having found zero contamination to date and no correlation between the oil wells and the dead cow.

Gabe regarded her through his curly eyelashes. "You came face-to-face with the men who killed the security guard, didn't you?"

The awful memory transported her straight to that awful moment. The blood drained from her cheeks, leaving the top of her head cold.

"What happened?" His voice roughened.

Libby shook her head. "I can't tell you." With her distress rising, she spoke louder this time.

His expression turned incredulous. "Your colleague almost got killed today, and you can't tell me what you know about the men who did it?"

She hesitated. *Do I tell him or not?* A vision of the terrorists pulling into the alley and mistaking her home for Jaime's gripped her vocal cords. Lucía and Maya could wind up getting killed instead of her. "No."

With a mutter of frustration, Gabe whirled away and stalked to the nearest window, where he fingered the heavy curtain while peering outside. Libby held her breath, wondering at his next move.

All at once, he drew the curtain closed. Libby's pulse spiked. She backed away from him as he strode toward her, pulling something from his pocket. When she saw it was just a folded piece of paper, her wariness subsided.

"Look at this."

Taking it and unfolding it, she found herself regarding a dozen mugshots. Libby scanned the title—FBI's Most Wanted—before studying the photographs of eleven hard-faced men and just one woman.

"Don't tell me anything. Just point with your finger if you recognize any of these men."

With reluctance, Libby examined the bearded faces in the photographs, fully expecting to recognize her nemesis. When she came to the last picture, she started again at the top, assuming she had overlooked him. On her second pass, the scarred face of a heavily bearded soldier stopped her heart momentarily. The man in the next photo also looked familiar.

"Point." Gabe was watching her closely.

Her finger seemed to rise of its own accord as she pointed out the two men who'd wanted their leader to kill her. "Him. And him."

"Only two? According to the report, there were several intruders."

Libby skimmed the printout one more time. "The other two aren't here."

"What about the one with the blue-green eyes?"

She looked again. "Not here." She would have recognized his picture anywhere.

"But these two were?"

"Yes." What terrible event had she just set into motion by breaking her word? "Gabe, he said he would kill me if I told anyone." The rush of whispered words escaped her.

Anger flashed in Gabe's eyes, accompanied by a Spanish expletive. But then his visage softened. "No one's going to kill you." He lifted her chin with his fingertips, forcing her to meet his gaze. "Do you hear me? These terrorists won't get anywhere near you. I won't let that happen."

She nodded, wanting very badly to believe him.

Seizing her elbow with his other hand, he drew her toward the couch. "Have a seat. I need you to tell me everything."

By the time Libby had concluded her story, Gabe's temples throbbed with frustration. Hearing her describe how she'd stood toe-to-toe with terrorists and lived to tell about it made him want to throw her over his shoulder and run for the airfield, where he envisioned her father waiting with his private jet to take her home.

Libby's sharp fingernails dug into his forearm. "Don't you dare think you can drag me out of here the way you did in Matamoros." Her blue-gray eyes promised a battle if he tried.

He exhaled forcefully, a harsh punctuation of sound that betrayed his frustration. "I've got to keep you safe. If anything happened to you, your father would never forgive me."

She scoffed at his assertion with a *tsk* of her tongue. "He would never hold you responsible, Gabe. Besides, you're going after these guys, right? You're going to find these extremists and arrest them, and then I'll be safe."

At least he hadn't violated his oath not to disclose their top-secret mission to any outsider. Instead, she'd guessed the purpose of their mission. "You can't tell anyone else about that."

"Why would I?"

Overwrought, Gabe raked his fingers through his hair, thinking. He made his decision. "Okay, I'll let you stay in Paraguay for now." Meaning he wouldn't hesitate to remove her from the country if things got any more dangerous.

Libby's eyebrows shot up. "You'll *let* me stay?" She loosed an incredulous laugh. "That's not your choice to make, Gabe. I explained this to you the night of the party: My work *matters*. It matters just as much as your work matters. I will *not* be leaving Paraguay until I have evidence that the oil wells are contaminating the rivers."

This wasn't the first time she sounded like a nut. "Those are your family's oil wells, Libby. Why would you want to impugn them?"

Her long-suffering sigh let him know he was missing the mark. "The people of Paraguay are my family, Gabe. Everyone on Earth is my family, even you."

She sounded as crazy when she'd told him back on the little bridge that her mother had told her in a dream where to go next. He shook his head, amazed by her idealism.

Libby wasn't done. "I couldn't care less about Clark Petroleum. Yes, my father founded the company and, yes, he's a major shareholder, but what's happening in this pristine landscape requires vigilance. Clark Petroleum's wells are poisoning the rivers here. Not only will I prove that, but I'm going to force Clark Petroleum to fix the problem or stop drilling altogether. Who besides me could possibly accomplish that?"

Gabe fell silent. Libby's adamant stance reminded him of Don Quixote's battle with the windmills. Reluctant admiration chased away the worry that something bad was going to happen to her. *How do I protect her?* He racked his brain, pondering his options. At least Bam-Bam was watching her front door.

"For God's sake, be careful." His hand sought hers and squeezed it. The feel of their palms connecting sped up Gabe's pulse. Her skin felt like warm velvet, making him want to touch her elsewhere.

This woman was a threat to his equilibrium. If he didn't leave right now, he was going to kiss her again, and once he grew addicted to her kisses, he'd be even more obsessed with her than he already was.

"I should go." He said the words, hoping to motivate himself to stand up and walk out. In just three hours, his platoon would pile into a couple of Humvees and drive toward the Hezbollah training camp to relieve Charlie Platoon's reconnaissance. He could certainly use the sleep between now and then to keep his senses sharp.

Libby's gaze dropping to his mouth was his undoing. With an inward groan, Gabe caught the side of her face with his free hand, pulled her closer, and kissed her with all the unreasonable feelings she unleashed in him.

Gabe's kiss wielded a strange sorcery over Libby, banishing all thoughts of her singular purpose from her mind. She relished the magic, unwilling and unable to stop herself from enjoying every second.

If not for the quiet knock at her door, causing her to pull back with a gasp, she could have kissed him all night.

Gabe frowned and glanced at his watch before bounding to his feet. Strangely, with him present, Libby suffered no concerns that a terrorist stood outside her door. Just as he had the night before, Gabe turned out the light before unlocking and cracking the portal open. Rodeo's blue eyes cut through the gloom, identifying him as the interloper.

"Hey, sir, sorry 'bout the interruption but we're due at an impromptu meeting at the TOC in three minutes."

"At this time of night?"

"Yep, we've got visitors."

Gabe had to leave. Disappointment vied with relief, pulling a shaky sigh out of Libby.

He looked back at her. "Sorry, but I can't stay. Be safe. Bolt the door behind me and don't open it for anyone. And don't go outside at all while it's dark."

Man, he was bossy! "I wasn't planning to."

"Good. See you around?"

Those words had apparently become their secret passphrase. A smile tugged at Libby's lips. "Sure."

Gabe hovered for a second longer, clearly loath to leave her. Then he vanished like a ghost, shutting the door behind him.

The instant Libby's rental turned quiet, fear pounced on her, speeding her heart rate. She shot up from the couch to turn the deadbolt and flick the light back on. As the memory of Gabe's kiss cascaded through her, she leaned against the door, suddenly weak-kneed.

Why, why, why did she have to be so drawn to *Lobo* of all people? "Lord, You have a seriously strange sense of humor throwing us together."

Libby shook her head. They were two strong-willed people on utterly disparate missions. A relationship would never work. For one thing, her purpose here took precedence over everything—and that included her love life. For another, Gabe, who was busy with his own quest, wanted to undermine her efforts, not help her fulfill them. Since she wasn't about to surrender her God-given mission just to become his girlfriend—assuming his intentions were honorable—this crazy magnetic attraction between them was a fluke, or maybe even a roadblock thrown up by the Enemy.

Libby firmed her lips and gathered her resolve. Clearly, she needed to ignore Gabe as much as possible and double down on the quest God had given her—that she save El Chaco Boreal from the oil wells dug by her own family. If she accomplished that much, maybe *then* she might consider a relationship with Gabe.

Her heart pattered as if to say, *Hurry up and do it, then!*

As they crossed the street and headed toward the pedestrian gate, Rodeo's grin flashed in the darkness. "You sounded super protective back there."

Gabe grunted, ignoring what was obviously a request for more information.

"I think she's crawlin' under your skin, Lobo."

Shaking off the yearning that still clamored in him, Gabe changed the subject. "Who the heck is visiting tonight? I was hoping to catch some shut-eye."

"It's Clark Petroleum's CEO. He wants to talk about what happened today."

Gabe's head whipped toward his chief. "Libby's father's here?"

"No, the new CEO."

"Oh." For a hopeful second, he'd thought Kyle Clark had come to collect his daughter in the aftermath of the explosion. A fragrant breeze, sharply colder in the night, banished the lingering heat from his skin.

"And he brought a general from USSOUTHCOM with him."

"No kidding." So, Gabe had been right about Clark Petroleum having friends in high places.

Rodeo shot ahead of him to swing open the gate for him, proving himself a top-notch NCO despite his taunting.

Concerns caught up to Gabe as he reentered the compound. "Does Bukowski know where I went this evening?"

Rodeo fell into step on his left side. "Nah, I told him you couldn't sleep so you went out for a run."

"Thanks." Gabe shot him a grateful glance.

"Bam-Bam knows where you were, though. He's the one who told me. Say, hi, Bam-Bam." Rodeo raised his voice.

"Hey, LT. I'm up here."

Startled by the voice behind him and way up in a tree, Gabe spun around and spotted a dark silhouette waving at him.

"And don't worry," Caleb added before Gabe could caution him to keep secrets, "I won't say a word about your girlfriend."

"She's not—" But the thought of Libby as his girlfriend hijacked Gabe's brain, leaving him speechless. He swiveled and stalked away, relying on Rodeo to keep up.

Soon they were in the warm building, headed for the Tactical Operations Center, or the TOC. As they rounded a corner, the sight of an immense stranger dressed in civilian clothing and guarding the door of the TOC slowed Gabe's step. He'd seen that man before… somewhere.

He nudged Rodeo. "Who is that?" he asked out of the side of his mouth.

"The CEO's bodyguard."

As the giant opened the door for them, Gabe searched his face, but the low brim of the man's baseball cap kept his eyes concealed.

Stepping into the TOC, Gabe confronted four frowning faces and promptly forgot about the bodyguard. The general from SOUTHCOM, an imposing Black man, was easy to identify, given his Army-green service uniform. That meant the burly blond man in the pink polo shirt was Clark Petroleum's new CEO.

Master Chief Bukowski's scrutiny of Gabe's rumpled jacket and mussed hair had him mumbling apologies before dropping into one of the two empty chairs situated directly across from the newcomers.

As Rodeo took the seat next to Gabe, McDuff rattled off introductions. "Gentlemen, this is Lieutenant Villalobos and his Chief, Rodeo. Lobo, Rodeo, this is General DePuy from USSOUTHCOM and the CEO of Clark Petroleum, Paul Van Slyke."

Regarding Van Slyke more closely, Gabe could tell he'd been a handsome man at one time, tall and broad like his predecessor, Kyle Clark. But years of comfortable living had put bags under his eyes and left him with a paunch. Van Slyke's blond hair had gray roots, which meant he dyed it. Eyes similar in hue to Libby's swept over those assembled as he addressed them.

"I apologize for the lateness of the hour, gentlemen, but I think circumstances certainly call for it." He spoke with an air of natural command, no doubt believing his wealth entitled him to a rapt audience. "Not only has Well 36 been destroyed, but now I fear for the fate of the other wells, not to mention my employees."

General DePuy chimed in with his opinion of the bombing. "This is just the beginning." His resonant voice took on an urgent note. "The CIA has been cognizant of the threat for more than a year before sharing their intel. I just hope it's not a question of too little too late. I consider the attack today a blatant declaration of war."

Gabe regretted that Jaime wasn't here to defend the CIA's position.

"Blatant," Van Slyke repeated. His hands, with their neatly

manicured fingers, graced the tabletop as he eyed Commander McDuff and Master Chief Bukowski expectantly. "The threat has got to be annihilated before any lives are lost."

Gabe fully appreciated Bukowski's perplexed expression. Why was the CEO of a private corporation telling Navy SEALs what to do? Even General DePuy was overstepping his bounds. It was the Joint Special Operations Task Force—JSOTF—that made decisions for Special Operations, not USSOUTHCOM. And while JSOTF fell under USSOUTHCOM's umbrella, it didn't answer to the larger command. Who had invited these men down here in the first place?

General DePuy comforted his companion in the ensuing silence. "I'm sure the SEALs are planning to take immediate action."

The scornful lift of Commander McDuff's mustache negated DePuy's assertion. "It's not our job to protect Clark Petroleum's property or its employees. So, unless and until we're instructed by JSOTF to take preemptive measures, there's nothing we can do for you right now."

DePuy's dark eyes bulged as he leveled a stern stare at McDuff. "Well, that's only a matter of time, Commander. I can assure you that *all* of the Joint Chiefs of Staff are in full approval of taking preemptive action against the terrorists in this region."

The CO narrowed his gaze at the general. "Our reconnaissance of the terrorist camp began twelve short hours ago. Thanks to the CIA, we have a rough head count of the hostiles but no knowledge of the extent of their arsenal. Raw force begets more violence. If we attack Hezbollah here, you can bet your wallet they'll retaliate elsewhere. We have diplomats and contractors in Lebanon who will want advanced warning before they find themselves targeted. When I hear from JSOTF, that's when we'll take action."

Van Slyke objected with a tragic sigh. "And, in the meantime, my wells remain vulnerable."

"Sorry you came all the way down here for nothing." McDuff didn't sound terribly sorry.

The new CEO waved aside the inconvenience. "Actually, I own

a house nearby, the one on top of the hill, and General DePuy is staying with me."

Gabe pictured the monstrosity on the top of the hill and stifled a snort. Van Slyke looked like the kind to live in the old stucco mansion. Since arriving here, Gabe had learned it once belonged to a top general during the Chaco War.

Mad Max looked less than thrilled to learn of the CEO's proximity. "How long will you be staying, General?"

"Oh, just for the night. Tomorrow I'll be back in Tampa, reaching out to my colleagues. Don't be surprised to get an action statement from JSOTF shortly." Having cast that prediction, DePuy pushed back his chair and stood.

Clearly, the man's rank allowed him to end their talk whenever he wanted to. As Van Slyke likewise came to his feet, Gabe's close regard finally caught his attention. The man sent him a smile, displaying teeth bleached so white they almost blinded him.

"Have we met? You look familiar."

"I don't think so." Not unless Kyle Clark had shared photos from the night of his party with the new CEO. In his peripheral vision, Gabe noted both Bukowski and the CO watching their exchange as they stood.

"Hmm." Van Slyke considered Gabe a moment longer before he shrugged and followed DePuy to the door.

Without so much as a backward glance, DePuy pushed through it, leaving Van Slyke's bodyguard to hold the door open for his employer.

Gabe racked his memory. *How do I know that guy?*

Muttering as he went, Mad Max headed for the door. "That man has some nerve."

Whether Max meant the CEO or the general, Gabe didn't know, but he fully agreed. Van Slyke's assumption that the SEALs were here to guard his oil wells reminded him of what he loathed most about the wealthy: They thought everyone else should cater to their needs.

After glancing at his watch, Gabe shot an alarmed look at

Rodeo. "We're relieving Charlie Platoon in an hour." It would take nearly that long to get to the NLB's remote camp.

Rodeo's crooked smile appeared. "Vehicles are gassed up, and the men are waiting."

Gabe could have hugged his chief for doing all the work while he napped on Libby's couch. "I owe you." On their way to the door, Bukowski's voice stopped him from making a quick exit.

"A word first, Lieutenant."

Gabe's stomach tightened. He freed Rodeo with a "Meet you out back" and retraced his steps. Did Bukowski know of his contact with a civilian in town? To his relief, the room had emptied out.

Bukowski wasted no time on preambles. "I know you weren't out running earlier, so where were you really?" His black-brown eyes plumbed Gabe's, demanding a straight answer.

Being an officer, Gabe could have told the senior enlisted man to mind his own business, but considering Bukowski's twenty-five years of experience and the fact that he'd survived some of the worst firefights in SEAL history, Gabe refused to play that card.

Dipping two fingers into his breast pocket, he pulled out the folded printout of the known Hezbollah extremists and handed it to Bukowski, who glanced at it quizzically.

"I went across the street to ask the IWI employee if the men responsible for blowing up the oil well looked like any of these guys."

Bukowski raised a russet eyebrow. "Ramirez's colleague? What makes you think she got a look at them?"

"She didn't—not today, anyway. But she was in the lab when they broke into it."

Bukowski frowned. "That's not what Ramirez told us."

"That's because she kept the truth from him. Tonight, she admitted to me she was in the lab when the thieves shot the security guard and broke in. Their leader, a man with blue-green eyes, threatened to find her and kill her if she said a word about it."

Master Chief's eyes widened before he lowered them back to the printout. "One of these men?"

"No. The leader isn't here, but she IDed two others on this list."

Taking the paper back, Gabe found a pen on the table and circled their photos before handing the page back to his master chief.

"Ashraf Al-Sadr and Musa Hamade." Master Chief lifted a grave look at Gabe. "These are dangerous men, Gabe. She's lucky she's alive."

He swallowed hard. Hearing Bukowski articulate just how lucky Libby was made him suddenly queasy. By some miracle, the terrorists had let her live. Gabe should probably get on the phone tonight and convince Kyle Clark to wrest his daughter out of the country before she wound up dead. Only he didn't have time.

Bukowski's dark eyes pinned him. "You made the right decision to question her, but next time you run it by me first." He paused, then added, "I hope you're not getting friendly with this woman."

The memory of kissing Libby's sweet lips brought heat to Gabe's face. "No, Master Chief. But you should know who she is."

"What do you mean, who she is?"

"She's Elizabeth Clark, the same woman we were tasked to recover from Matamoros."

Bukowski gave a slow blink. "And now she's here?" He looked every bit as dumbfounded as Gabe had been.

Gabe shrugged. "Go figure." Inclining his mouth toward the shorter man's ears, he added, "Then along comes the new CEO of Clark Petroleum telling us to hurry up and eliminate these terrorists who are threatening his oil wells. Makes you wonder whose interests we're protecting—America's or the oil company's."

Bukowski's expression gave nothing away. "That's a pretty serious insinuation."

Gabe straightened to his full height. "Well, I'm a pretty serious guy, Master Chief."

"We'd better keep these thoughts to ourselves for a while." The shorter man sent him a pointed look. "And I advise you to steer clear of the honeypot."

Another wave of heat climbed Gabe's neck. "Roger that, Master Chief." The thought of never kissing Libby again left him feeling distinctly cheated. "I need to get going."

"Hooyah." Stepping back, Bukowski freed him to leave.

Charging from the room, Gabe headed straight for the motor pool and the caravan waiting for him. *I should probably avoid Libby from now on.* His spirits sank at the thought. If only he could be sure her father wasn't hoping to get a SEAL for a son-in-law. Kyle Clark was already friends with General DePuy. Maybe he wanted a finger on the pulse of Special Operations also.

Only, who would protect Libby if Gabe didn't? She was on a mission, and nothing could stop her—except, perhaps, the NLB, should their leader have a change of heart about not killing her.

Gabe's intestines knotted at the thought. *I can't let that happen.* Moreover, it was probably too late to ignore Libby now. Like Rodeo had noted earlier that evening—she was under his skin. In fact, from the moment Gabe had first laid eyes on her, she'd been worming an inexorable path straight to his heart.

He murmured to himself as he made a beeline toward the convoy of vehicles idling outside, "You'd think I would know better."

CHAPTER 9

With his face caked in camouflage paint, Gabe joined Charlie Platoon's leader, Lieutenant Corey Cooper, in peering over the top of a sandy berm and a thicket of thorny bushes at the NLB's training camp. "Sitrep."

As Gabe settled in next to his peer, Corey sent him a look that, even in the dark, conveyed frustration. "There is no situation." Cooper didn't even bother to whisper. "As far as we can tell, no one's even here."

Seriously? Gabe stole a peek over the top of the rise. The training camp was circumscribed by tall coils of concertina wire, then a chain-link fence topped by yet more barbed wire. Inside the compound, Gabe identified a shooting range and an obstacle course, along with several crude wooden buildings. Not a single light flickered in the structures' few windows. There were no voices to be heard, no signs of movement anywhere. A chilly desert breeze kicked up spumes of dust here and there, making the camp resemble a deserted mining town.

Gabe looked back at Cooper. "I thought we had a confirmed sighting of unfriendlies earlier this evening."

"We did." Cooper came up on his knees next to him. "Four men arrived in that vehicle right there." He pointed to an old Range Rover, its doors dented and pocked by bullet holes. "They all got out and went into that door there." He pointed again. "And we haven't seen or heard from them since."

Gabe searched for movement and saw nothing beyond what the wind was causing. "Maybe they're sleeping."

"Without posting anyone on watch?" Cooper's tone conveyed skepticism. "Honestly, it's been so quiet, I'm wondering if there isn't another way out besides the only gate. I don't feel like anybody's here."

"You mean like an underground tunnel?"

"Yeah, maybe."

Gabe considered the possibility. The Chaco War had been fought here nearly a century earlier. How likely was it that either side had dug tunnels into the hard-packed clay? Or maybe the terrorists themselves had shoveled out an escape route.

Only one way to find out. But the standard operating procedure entailed a forty-eight-hour reconnaissance before any kind of action could be taken, not to mention that Mad Max had to wait for JSOTF's orders. So just because the camp *appeared* deserted, that didn't mean they should search it. The whole place could be booby-trapped.

"Okay, thanks for the update. We'll take it from here." Clapping the younger man on the shoulder, Gabe bade him good night while wishing he could tuck into his own rack about now. The only sleep he'd had in the past twenty-four hours was the nap he'd caught on Libby's couch while waiting to grill her about the leader with the blue-green eyes.

In his mind, he replayed the kiss they'd shared, reliving the way she'd softened, then kissed him back, her responsiveness kicking his desire for her into the stratosphere. If only he could trust that her father wasn't trying to influence the SEALs' agenda here, as General DePuy's overreach suggested.

How could Gabe carry on a relationship with a woman whose father used his influence to play God?

If the past had taught him anything, it was that the rich could not be trusted.

Yet the need to protect Libby was too real for him to keep his distance. All he could do was protect his heart while keeping her safe.

Rodeo cut into his thoughts as he spoke through Gabe's headset. "We're all in position, sir." His calm drawl brought Gabe back to the present.

Seven pairs of men, as well as Gabe, were spread out along the perimeter of the NLB's camp, watching it from every angle. Normally Rodeo would have remained at Gabe's side, but with Bam-Bam watching Libby's door, Rodeo had taken his place. So long as Gabe's men didn't rat on him, Gabe counted on Mad Max and Bukowski never hearing about Bam-Bam's side job.

Doubt speared Gabe belatedly. What if one junior SEAL wasn't sufficient to protect Libby? With a low growl of frustration, he dug his elbows into the sandy earth, settling himself so he could watch the camp comfortably without straining his neck. The compound lay beneath a gossamer-thin blanket of moonlight. With a pulse tapping at his temples, Gabe studied the dark windows and plumbed the shadows for the barest suggestion of occupation.

Nothing.

Could the NLB have suspected they were being watched—by no less than U.S. Navy SEALs? It wasn't beyond the realm of possibility that some enterprising villager had identified the SEALs' uniforms and sent gossip spreading throughout the region, alerting the Hezbollah loyalists to their presence. But what if the men who'd stolen nitric acid blamed Libby for summoning the American forces? What if they regretted letting her live?

Demonios, he couldn't stop fretting about her! What's more, if the terrorists weren't here at their camp, then where were they? Was Libby in danger right now?

∾

Ashraf Al-Sadr's black eyes glinted with accusation. "I'm telling you, that woman from the lab was in the Jeep we passed on the road. She is alive! You let her live!" He thrust an accusing finger at Salim Ghazal's face. "And now the Americans hound us!"

Salim heaved an inward sigh. He'd suspected when he'd spared the lab technician's life that he was going to be confronted for his weakness eventually. Even so, he would not have been justified in killing her. Her cooperation in locating the nitric acid amidst hundreds of vials of mysterious reagents had earned her a reprieve. Nor was he a cold-blooded murderer like Ashraf Al-Sadr, who had shot the guard unnecessarily.

But reports of an American military presence had circulated almost immediately following their impromptu raid on the lab. The rumors let him know Elizabeth Clark, despite her promise to keep their encounter a secret, had betrayed him. He had not expected treachery from a woman who clearly wished to stay alive.

Meeting the furious gazes of the Hezbollah volunteers, Salim paused to formulate his rebuttal. Their situation was already tenuous. Claiming an unpaid army of just seventy, they couldn't hope to drive out the Americans. Though only half their number, the American force would have an arsenal superior to theirs—not to mention superior training.

Not even Ashraf and Musa's experience in warfare could tip the scales in NLB's favor. Their only recourse was to disband.

Salim had sent his recruits back to Asunción, from whence most of them hailed. He, his brother, and the two Hezbollah volunteers had then rigged their camp to explode when the Americans forced their way inside. They'd promptly fled the area via a crumbling underground escape route that spat them out half a mile away.

It was now dawn, and the first suggestion of sunlight framed the shuttered window of the private home they occupied, situated on the outskirts of town, surrounded by a high wall, with only a few neighbors visible. Paid for with Hezbollah funds, the safe house was small but tidy.

"Your suspicions are correct, Ashraf." Salim acknowledged the warrior's accusation with a calculated mix of authority and humility.

"I did not kill the woman as I led you to believe. Forgive my deception, but I conceived then, and still believe, that she is of more use to us alive. Hear me out." He held up a finger as the man started to cut him off.

The main room, with a kitchen off the back, was strewn with rugs. They sat cross-legged in a circle, a loaf of bread and an empty ewer between them. The chai that filled their mugs perfumed the small space with its pungent aroma, while a single light fixture, a lamp in the corner, shed enough light to display Ashraf and Musa's glowering regard.

"As we know, the lab is owned by International Water Institute, a group comprised of esteemed scientists from all over the world. Imagine the pressure those scientists would put on Clark Petroleum should one of their employees be held hostage. Ransom for the woman's safe return would entail money, of course, but also action. I would like to see half of Clark Petroleum's shares in the hands of Paraguayan investors by the end of the year. If they can't do that, the hostage dies. If they can, we free her."

Interest lit only the face of Salim's younger brother, Nasrallah. Ashraf and Musa thirsted for the destruction of the American-owned wells, not the redistribution of the company's shares.

Ashraf tugged on his wiry beard while shaking his head. "It would be simpler just to blow up the wells, as we had planned."

Salim acknowledged his words with a shrug. "The American force has eliminated that option. They have come here to annihilate us. We would not be able to escape their notice."

"So, that's it? We abandon our objective without a fight?" The scar on Ashraf's face stood out starkly as his anger mounted.

"Of course not." Salim kept his voice calm and soothing. "Clark Petroleum has robbed Paraguay of her natural resources and robbed her of profits that are rightly hers. We cannot stand for that."

Ashraf, a mercenary, snorted. He couldn't care less about Paraguay's citizens or even the National Liberation Brigade, which he'd joined so he could train them. His only goal and the goal of Hezbollah, which sponsored him, was to undermine U.S. interests and claim the area as a homebase in the Western Hemisphere. Salim wasn't fooled into thinking their objectives were any loftier than Clark Petroleum's, but for now, Hezbollah aided his agenda.

"We could seize the woman tomorrow." The eager voice belonged to Nasrallah. "We will stop her on her way to the lab."

Salim nodded at his brother. "Good thinking, Brother, but she hadn't been to the lab since we broke into it. I've had her under surveillance. I know where she lives."

Nasrallah eyed him curiously, perhaps guessing that Salim knew even more than that. Prompted by his persistent visions of the blonde beauty and intrigued that her last name was Clark, Salim had researched his prospective hostage thoroughly. What he'd discovered made her a very desirable target, indeed. Only, he dared not inform his colleagues, especially those affiliated with Hezbollah, that Elizabeth Clark was more than an employee of International Water Institute. She was the daughter of the founder of Clark Petroleum himself.

How better to force the oil corporation to accede to his demands than to use Elizabeth Clark to issue his ultimatum?

But the Hezbollah loyalists must never discover what Salim knew, for they would use the woman to further their own objectives, none of which resembled the objectives of the NLB. Moreover, they wouldn't hesitate to abuse her and defile her, regardless of her political value.

And Salim could not have that. Her beauty was not made to be destroyed but rather cherished. He would take her hostage—yes. But he would protect her as he leveraged her value for the sake of his adoptive country.

"It's settled then," he announced, appeasing Ashraf's rabid desire to attack the enemy the only way they could. "We will seize the employee tomorrow night."

By the time Libby awoke the next morning, sunlight shone boldly around the curtains at her bedroom window. As her thoughts went immediately to Gabe, she willed herself to think of something else. *My work is more important than my feelings for him.*

Hoping IWI had reached out to her, she checked the sat phone by her bed for messages. Oh, dear. Yes, her employer had called while her phone was on silent. Accessing the message, she listened to it and blew out a breath. They were still looking for a scientist to fill in for Jaime; she could take the day off.

Relief vied with frustration. How would she ever fulfill her God-given quest if she couldn't get water samples to continue her testing? Perhaps she ought to venture into the wilderness alone. But after the incident at the lab and the explosion of Well 36, that sounded foolish. This mission was getting dangerous.

Jumping out of bed, she promptly stripped the sheets. Keeping busy would hold thoughts of Gabe at bay. With her bedding in the combination washer/dryer, she commenced cleaning her small one-story rental from top to bottom.

At noon, she crossed the alley that divided her home from Jaime's. Lucía, looking like she hadn't slept much, answered Libby's knock with the baby in her arms.

"Any news on Jaime?" Libby asked her in Spanish.

"*Sí*, he's in surgery right now. Any chance you could take us to the hospital at three o'clock to visit him?"

"Of course. I'd love to. Come get me when you're ready."

With hours to waste between then and now, Libby returned to her home and called her father, whom she hadn't spoken to since he'd driven her to the airport, begging her the entire way not to fly to her new job in Paraguay.

"Sweetheart!" His robust answer told her how relieved he was to hear from her.

"Hi, Daddy."

"I thought you'd never call me." His tone chided her gently for ignoring him. "I left several messages with your employer."

"Yes, I got them, thank you. I've just been too busy to call you back."

"Is this a number where I can reach you?"

"For now. It's the company's sat phone."

"Good. Well, how's your work going? Is Clark Petroleum defiling El Chaco like you expected?"

"I don't know yet, but I will soon."

Her reply elicited a skeptical grunt. "Well, if you do, just take your concerns to your uncle Paul. There's nothing I can do anymore."

"Uncle Paul?" Libby pictured the man he was referring to, her mother's brother and her father's high school friend. Paul and her father had founded Clark Petroleum together, using her father's money. They'd run Clark Petroleum like a captain and his first mate for two decades, yet her hopes of eliciting a response to her demands dwindled. "Great."

"What do you mean 'great'?"

Libby blew out a breath. "Uncle Paul's not like you, Daddy. Remember, he used to give Mom a hard time for caring about the indigenous tribes in the rainforest? He won't be open to mitigating any contamination done by the corporation."

"Oh, but he's family, Libby. I'm sure he'll do what makes you happy. Besides, I want you to hold him to the highest standards."

Hearing her father give priority to the environment buoyed her spirits. Her mother had left her gentle mark on him; that was certain. "Then, I will."

"Well, tell me all about Paraguay. How do you like your colleagues?"

Her father must not have heard about Well 36 being targeted by terrorists. Far be it from Libby to share that information first and make her father worry. "Paraguay is awesome." She described the desolate but still beautiful landscape. Next, she told him about Jaime, without mentioning his accident, and how reassuring it was to work with a man unintimidated by the savage environment. Her thoughts skipped immediately to Gabe, accompanied by a clamoring to see him again. "You'll never guess who I ran into down here."

"Oh, who could that be?"

Her father's smug tone brought a frown to Libby's face. *Wait just a minute.* It sounded like Daddy already knew what she was going to say. Only, how would he have learned the SEALs were in El Chaco Boreal?

"Lieutenant Villalobos." She waited, ears pricked to the slightest nuance that her father already knew.

"No kidding." He sounded pleased and not a bit surprised, cementing Libby's suspicions.

"You knew I'd run into him again," she accused. "How?"

A nervous chuckle sounded in her ear. "Now, what makes you say that?"

"I can tell by your tone of voice."

"Oh, pooh. Okay, I heard a rumor is all, and I had my hopes you two might run into each other again."

Astonished, even a little outraged, Libby lost the capacity to speak for several seconds. "Why do you like him so much?" For that matter, why did *she* like him so much?

"Oh, I guess he reminds me of myself when I was younger. Plus I feel better knowing he's around to protect you."

"I can take care of myself, thank you. Listen, I have to go visit someone at the hospital."

"Gosh, I hope it's not Gabe."

"No." She deliberated whether to tell him or not. "Actually, it's my colleague, Jaime. He was injured in an explosion yesterday."

The quiet on the other end made her realize she had said too much.

"The explosion of Well 36?"

So, he'd heard about that, after all. "Yes, actually." Why hadn't he mentioned it earlier?

"What on earth was your colleague doing near the well?"

She'd asked herself that very question. "I have no idea."

"Honey, you be careful down there. I don't like the rumors of Hezbollah terrorists in the region."

They're not rumors.

"It's bad enough that they're targeting Clark Petroleum's wells. I don't want them going after you."

A vision of the man with the blue-green eyes assailed her. "I'll be fine, Daddy." Gabe had said he wouldn't let the terrorists get to her—though he was too busy pursuing the said terrorists to protect her personally. "I've got to go." Talking to her father only fanned her fears and frustrations. "I'll call you when I have more news to share."

"You do that, honey. Be careful down there."

"I am. Love you. Bye." Placing the phone on her nightstand, she picked up her mother's diary and sprawled across her bed, hoping to find comfort in its pages. "Talk to me, Mama." How she treasured this tangible piece of her mother's spirit! When she read the entries, it felt as if her mother were speaking to her directly.

Libby thumbed through the pages, looking for the entries dated over a decade ago in which her mother jotted down her objections to her husband and brother prospecting in El Chaco. Ah, here they were.

As she read them for the dozenth time, her mother's voice, still a crisp memory, sounded in Libby's head.

It is the height of injustice to corrupt one of the last pristine wildernesses on the planet. Drilling in El Chaco will ruin the delicate ecosystem. Toxic waste will spill into the waterways and leach into the flora. The livestock of the native Guaraní will die off first. Eventually, the people living off their meat will develop various cancers and perish painfully.

A vision of the dead cow flashed into Libby's thoughts. Was that a manifestation of the process her mother had predicted? Then why hadn't any of the tests she and Jaime had run so far indicated any adverse influences on the environment? What were they doing wrong?

"We'll find it, Mama. It's just a matter of time before we get the data I expect." And when she did, Libby would stop at nothing to ensure remediations were made to the wells' containment walls. It was either that or dismantle the wells completely, which Uncle Paul would never allow. But as Jaime had said, drilling for oil was good for the economy. That being the case, she and her uncle would strike a compromise. Uncle Paul would put a stop to any leaking chemicals. It was that or Libby would sic IWI on a corporation founded by her own family.

A knock at her front door inspired a rush of adrenaline, even though it was probably just Lucía on her doorstep. The terrorists weren't likely to knock first. With no peephole, Libby called, "Is that you, Lucía?" just in case. Getting a positive response, she found the woman carrying baby Maya in a sling strapped to the front of her body.

"The surgery is over, and all is well," Lucía announced with a smile. "We can go visit now."

"Oh, wonderful. Give me one minute. I'll meet you at the Jeep."

"Perfecto."

Less than a minute later, Libby locked up behind herself and joined Lucía in the alley. The sun beating down on the Jeep's roof told her the car would be too hot for the baby. "Don't get in just yet. Let me open the windows first and cool things off."

Slipping into the boiling interior, she turned the key in the ignition intent on lowering the electric windows. Instead of turning over, the engine gave a *click, click, click.* Libby tried again, to no avail. With a grimace and a shake of her head, she got back out of the car and met Lucía's worried gaze.

"I'm sorry. Either the starter's given out or the battery's dead. So we can't drive. Shall we call for a taxi?" She had snagged the sat phone on her way out of the house.

Lucía gazed off in the direction of the hospital. "No, I think we can walk. It's not too far."

Libby considered the distance and agreed with a nod. "I'll carry the baby if you want."

But Lucía waved off the offer, striking out toward the heart of town.

Hurrying after her, Libby had second thoughts. Walking entailed passing three blocks of storefronts and walled-in buildings. With no sidewalks on the narrow, dusty road, they were forced to walk single file. She kept a wary eye on the few cars that zipped past them.

With every passing minute, the sun burned brighter, heating the top of her head. *Darn, I should have brought the straw cowboy hat.* She pictured it lying in the Jeep and chastised herself for her forgetfulness. As it was, her blonde hair drew the eye of every male they encountered, and there was one sector of the population in particular whose attention she desperately wanted to avoid.

Hopefully, Gabe was off rounding up the extremists. God willing, he and his teammates would eliminate the threat entirely before anything more awful could happen on top of Enrique's death, the destruction of Well 36, and Jaime's injuries. *Dear Lord, watch over us.*

CHAPTER 10

A ray of sunlight shot through the slats of the blinds, stabbing Gabe's closed eyes and rousing him from a midday nap. He raised his arm to check the time. Five hours of sleep ought to be enough to keep his platoon alert during their imminent briefing with the CO. He swung his feet out of the bunk, making sufficient noise to rouse his suitemates.

"Rise and shine, brothers. We've got a meeting with the CO in twenty-two minutes."

Half an hour later, Gabe's fifteen men, including Bam-Bam, who'd come inside reporting that Libby had walked off with Lucía in the direction of the hospital, had seated themselves around the long table. Mad Max and Bukowski stood at the front of the room while Lieutenant Strong's benign gray gaze regarded them from the overhead projector, giving Gabe reason to believe the task unit was mobilizing for action. Finally.

"All right." Mad Max raised his voice, causing the room to fall silent. "Let's get this underway. Master Chief, bring these men up-to-date." Folding his thick arms over his broad chest, he let Bukowski take over.

"Good afternoon, frogmen."

The room echoed with the unanimous reply. Gabe's platoon sounded alert and eager for action.

"As you saw for yourself last night, the NLB's training camp appears deserted. Charlie Platoon reports nothing has moved since they relieved you this morning. One hour ago, we were cleared by JSOTF to sweep the targets' camp. Tonight we'll find out where they disappeared to."

A wave of excitement rippled over the captive audience.

Bukowski toggled the laptop in front of him, causing Lieutenant Strong's face to vanish and an aerial view of the camp to take its place.

"At 20:00 hours, you will join Charlie Platoon on-site. While you all spearhead the sweep, Charlie Platoon will widen their perimeter, looking for squirters and alternative exits." Bukowski nodded at a sunburned man on Gabe's platoon. "You've got the best breacher in this task unit."

With his shock of red hair, pale skin, and freckles Carl Haskins, aka Ice, couldn't hope to conceal his self-conscious blush as his teammates cheered him.

"And odds are high that this camp is laden with IEDs." Bukowski's grim tone subdued their exuberance.

Ice, an ordnance disposal expert, hadn't spoken more than a dozen sentences in Gabe's presence the entire time he'd been with Team Six. All Gabe knew about the redhead was that he loved cats and never got angry. Even so, he'd earned Gabe's respect for his cool head around explosives.

Using a laser pointer, Bukowski proceeded to illustrate their entry in timed segments. Like choreographed dancers, Echo Platoon would breach the outer perimeter while Charlie Platoon broke away from the camp in an ever-expanding circle, looking for enemy combatants fleeing the scene—aka, squirters—either aboveground or via unidentified tunnels. At the same time, Echo Platoon, with Ice in the lead, would search the building into which the NLB had disappeared, keeping vigilant for trip wires or pressure plates.

With a trickle of foreboding, Gabe acknowledged someone in his platoon—himself included—might be maimed or even killed tonight, depending on how effectively the tangos had booby-trapped their camp. Would Libby even look at him twice if he lost a limb? Reassuringly, the answer was *Yes*. Libby was a champion for the weak, as her determination to help the young women at El Instituto proved. Heck, she would probably like him *better* if he got injured.

Catching his thoughts off-task, Gabe focused on the details coming out of Bukowski and then Strong's mouth as the operations officer chimed in from Virginia Beach. While both these men would remain in contact via radio, the platoon leaders, Gabe and Cooper, would be the highest-ranking officers on-site. The responsibility of ensuring everything happened as planned rested solely on their shoulders, while their chiefs, Rodeo, Doc, and the two chiefs in Charlie Platoon, dealt with the execution and unforeseen contingencies. They'd done this kind of thing a zillion times in training and half a dozen times in real life. They could do it again.

Except that nothing ever went down the same way twice.

"We're looking for tunnels." Strong's voice explained the black-and-white photos of miners standing at the entrance to a mining shaft. "Old photos and letters indicate there were gold mines in the area, later used in the Chaco War to hide supplies and men. Our guess is the NLB noticed or suspected our surveillance and used an old tunnel like this one to escape the area unseen."

The photograph of a wild-eyed, scar-faced terrorist replaced that of the mine. "One of the guys we're looking to capture is this Hezbollah extremist: Ashraf Al-Sadr, who is believed to be training members of the NLB."

Gabe, recognizing the man as one of the two Libby had identified, glanced at Bukowski, whose expression gave nothing away.

"Al-Sadr," Strong continued, "is believed to be responsible for the rash of car bombings in Beirut earlier this year. He fled Lebanon sometime in March to avoid arrest and has been indoctrinating and training the local Lebanese, spreading his hatred of the U.S. If you come across him, debilitate him if you must, but we want him alive. Any questions? Yes?"

As Zen asked a question about radio frequencies, Gabe looked past him and caught Bam-Bam eyeing him hopefully. The kid so obviously wanted to be included in the action tonight. With a subtle shake of his head, Gabe let Caleb know that—no, he needed to go right back to watching Libby's house. The only reason he was at this meeting at all was because Libby and Lucía had just left for the hospital, and Bukowski expected all of Gabe's platoon to attend this meeting.

The kid had the audacity to roll his eyes, but Gabe didn't blame him. No SEAL worth his salt would want to be left out of the action. Besides, if all went well tonight, they might catch the terrorists who'd threatened Libby's life, and Caleb wouldn't have to protect her any longer.

Standing by the installation's outer wall with a cicada trilling in the tree next to him, Caleb smeared his face with dark-green camouflage paint. The stuff went on like mud. It was even harder to take off than it was to put on. And while he hadn't been told he *had* to use it, the fact that he'd been spotted the previous night by Rodeo, who'd been looking for Lieutenant Villalobos, meant Caleb needed to step up his game.

The feeling that he was being left out of the highlight event in Operation Anaconda nagged at him. But protecting the daughter of a future senator was important, too. And if the reason had anything to do with that scar-faced terrorist, Ashraf Al-Sadr—whose very name made him sound like a sadist—then Caleb's protection detail might actually result in contact of the nasty kind, which he secretly hoped for.

Pushing the tin of camo paint into his breast pocket, Caleb verified that the clip on his MP5 was fully loaded, pushed his helmet more securely onto his head, and swung his muscular, six-foot frame up into the quebracho tree where he'd hung out for the past three days. The tree, one of a dozen that shaded the installation's yard, grew up close to the wall and well above it, affording Caleb a bird's-eye view of Miss Clark's home while keeping him within the camp's perimeter.

Fifteen feet in the air, Caleb reclined on a thick forked limb, finding the most comfortable position on the knotty bark. From his perch, he eyed Miss Clark's home, disconcerted by her unlit windows. Even with the sky turning indigo blue in advance of nightfall, she still wasn't back yet. He heaved a sigh and noted the stars leaping into view as darkness fell.

As a bright kid growing up in the hills of Kentucky, Caleb had checked out a book on astronomy and taught himself the names of all the constellations. El Chaco was the perfect place to recall what he'd learned, but the leaves shrouding him in his hiding place impeded his view of the night sky. Besides, he was supposed to be watching for Miss Clark.

Scanning the street for potential threats, nothing out of the ordinary jumped out at him. His gaze returned to a nondescript van parked a block down the road from her home. Was there somebody sitting in the driver's seat?

Flipping down his night-vision goggles, Caleb decided with a spark of interest that, yes, there was. The driver was either wearing a beard that covered his upper chest or he had on a fuzzy sweater. True, it got chilly at this time of year in the Southern Hemisphere, but a sweater? And why was the man just sitting there, doing nothing?

Hearing footsteps coming from the direction of town, Caleb turned his head and spotted two people hustling along the side of the road. The long hair and lithe figure of Miss Clark made her immediately identifiable as she hurried ahead of her neighbor, who carried her baby in a sling across her chest. They walked with haste along the unlit and uneven shoulder, looking antsy about the lateness of the hour.

All at once, the lights on the van facing them blinked on, catching them in its high beams as it pulled from the curb and rumbled toward them. Caleb sat straight up while splitting his attention between the women and the approaching van.

Miss Clark took note of the van's approach, and her stride faltered.

"Drive on by," Caleb murmured, hefting his submachine gun just in case.

The angles were not at all in his favor. With a screeching of brakes, the van slowed as it neared the women. Alarm seized Caleb as it blocked his view. He raised his weapon, only to realize a misfired shot might go through a window and strike either one of the women.

"Come on!" Not daring to take his eyes off the scene to find a better vantage, he stayed put.

Except he couldn't even see Miss Clark. He heard what sounded like a door sliding open. A rough male voice barked an order. *Oh, crap. This is bad.*

A woman screamed, prompting Caleb to take action. Aiming at the tires, he fired off two successive shots, *rat-tat, rat-tat,* and deflated both driver's-side tires. The van listed. But then a door slid shut and the van pulled forward, tires slapping the ground as it squealed away.

Jiggling wildly, the van accelerated, leaving one woman cowering on the sidewalk where there had just been two.

The blood drained from Caleb's head to his heart.

Miss Clark had been taken.

In retaliation for her kidnapping, he shot at the retreating tail-lights. They exploded under the onslaught of his bullets, but the vehicle didn't stop.

With a wild leap out of the tree, Caleb managed to land on his feet. He sprinted to the gate, yanked it open, and stepped out into the street, swinging up his MP5 up to shoot again—only to see the van disappearing from view having turned at the intersection.

Stunned, Caleb swiveled his attention to the neighbor now crying out for help near her home. Dreading the fallout, he shouldered his weapon and crossed the street to see if the woman was injured. How was he going to tell Lobo that he'd failed his simple task?

∾

This isn't a dream.

The blue-green eyes that had haunted Libby's sleep since the incident at the warehouse glinted within the shadowy interior of the vehicle, making it painfully apparent her circumstances had changed. One minute she'd been anticipating the warm shower awaiting her inside her rental, the next she'd been staring down the barrel of a gun and realizing if she didn't cooperate, then baby Maya and Lucía might be gunned down. So, she'd climbed into the van, as her nightmare became reality.

To the accompaniment of gunfire—coming from where?—the besieged van had lurched forward, and her nemesis had pinned her with a uniformed arm to her seat. The sound of shattering plastic paired with the *thunk* of a bullet embedding itself in the van's rear bumper meant *someone* had endeavored to prevent her abduction—not Gabe, most likely, as he was busy with his SEALs. Whoever it was, they'd been unsuccessful. Though hampered with flat tires, the van fled the scene, and the gunfire ceased.

Her heart hammering, Libby swiveled her head, glimpsing four silent figures in the dark van with her. The one who'd grabbed Libby's arm and hauled her into the van was the cruel one with the scar. He'd tossed her down onto a bench next to the man who'd saved her life, then dropped into a seat behind her. The youngest of the group stared back at her from the passenger seat up front and the fourth man drove.

With what felt like flat tires, the van floundered on.

Steeped in shock, Libby failed to respond to the spate of Lebanese being muttered in her ear. A brisk slap from behind stung her cheek and brought her sharply to reality. Not a dream at all.

"Enough," said the leader, speaking in English for her sake, evidently.

To her relief, the scarred warrior subsided, stewing on the seat behind them.

Taking heart from the leader's mercy, Libby eyed his handsome profile in the dark. His fingers bit into her arm, keeping her next to him, not that she had anywhere to go. He had spared her the last time. She could only hope he would do the same again.

But his taut expression and his refusal to look at her suggested otherwise. Dread chilled Libby to the bone. Her thoughts flew to Gabe, who'd expressed the desire to keep her safe—or better yet, send her home where she would *be* safe. Would he even come searching for her? What if he was too busy with his work to notice she was gone?

She was doomed—unless she admitted to these terrorists whose daughter she was. Would that guarantee her safety? Her father would pay any sum required to secure her freedom, but what if money wasn't their goal?

It probably wasn't. She shouldn't tell them anything.

Gabe would hear about her kidnapping through Jaime once Lucía reported it. He and his SEALs were pursuing these extremists. They would rescue her in the process of rounding them up, only how would they know where to look?

The sat phone! She could feel it in her rear pocket, possibly broadcasting her location with its built-in GPS. Hope surged through her, driving away the paralyzing effect of shock. But if the terrorists found it, they would immediately seize it and destroy it. She had to keep it out of sight, but how? Perhaps she could hide it right now before they realized what she carried.

Trying not to draw attention to herself, Libby slid her free hand along her seat toward her rear pocket. When her fingers encountered a crevice between the seat cushion and the seat back, she resolved to hide her phone there.

With the wobbling van masking her movements, she managed to tease it from her rear pocket. Her heart pounded. Avoiding the button that would light up the screen, she slid it between the two cushions, wedging it as deep as it would go.

Find me, Gabe! Her heart pounded with fear. *Find me and save me!*

Man, I hate spiders.

"Sir, wait!"

Carl Haskins's last-second admonition froze Gabe in the act of reaching past the EOD expert to sweep aside the spiderweb draped like a curtain from the tunnel's low ceiling. Directing his gaze downward, Gabe saw what he'd completely overlooked in his quest to keep all spiders from dropping onto his helmet and scuttling down his back: the glint of a needle-thin filament bisecting the tunnel right in front of the foot he was about to lift.

The terrorists hadn't been content with wiring their building to blow sky high. They'd booby-trapped their escape route, too, a tunnel the SEALs had discovered in the building's cellar.

A cold sweat bathed Gabe's pores. Bending his right arm to a ninety-degree angle, hand fisted, he communicated to Rodeo, who followed some distance behind, to halt.

"You might want to step back, sir." Ice sounded as calm as if he were suggesting Gabe should exfoliate once a week.

Swallowing hard, Gabe eased his foot slowly away from the trip wire. With his shirt sticking to his back and his mouth desert-dry, he watched the EOD expert crouch over the menacing filament and follow the path it took to a tin bucket standing inconspicuously off to one side.

The tunnel had been built just wide enough to allow a wagon to be pulled through it. Littered with relics of two past eras, it was filled with rusted trowels, buckets, and bottles, all vestiges of mining and war. The bucket didn't look any more suspicious than the others Gabe had seen. But Carl's low whistle suggested it was packed with enough gunpowder and hardware to shred a man's flesh.

As Ice went to work disarming the device, Gabe sought to slow the tempo of his trotting heart. His gaze flickered to the lumber and metal plates buttressing the crumbling walls. Over a hundred years old, the tunnel had obviously been put back into service by the NLB, who had used it to sneak past the SEALs' reconnaissance because they sure as heck weren't hiding in the camp. Nor were they down in this tunnel, not with the place rigged to blow sky high.

Come on, Ice. Gabe shone his penlight on the breacher while Ice held his own penlight between his teeth and methodically disarmed the IED. Gabe tried *not* to envision them being buried alive. A rivulet of sweat trickled between his shoulder blades.

I should have agreed with Libby that we're alike.

Of all the regrets he might have entertained, that was the one that came to mind. Reflecting back, he'd belittled the work she did. He might have even called her crazy. But what she was doing— pitting herself against a corporate giant to protect the last pristine water on the planet—that took guts. And now she might never know how much he admired her because he could die today. *I am a jerk.*

To distract himself, he keyed his mike. "Coop, this is Lobo." He had to work to smooth the tremor of dread from his voice. "Any idea yet where this tunnel ends?" He and his men had been following it for half a mile or more. If he knew they were close to an exit, he could chase off the sense of doom squeezing his rib cage.

Lieutenant Cooper's chipper reply was a balm to his ears. "Roger that, Lobo. We've located your exit. Looks like it was tres- passed a while back by our targets. What are your coordinates, over?"

Gabe read the coordinates off his watch.

"Yeah, you're close. You've got maybe two hundred yards to go."

Gabe briefly closed his eyes. *Just two hundred yards. We got this.* His earpiece crackled as another voice broke into the conversation.

"Sir, this is Zen. HQ reports a secondary situation."

"Go ahead." Gabe could never tell by Zen's voice whether something was urgent.

"Bam-Bam just reported to Master Chief that Miss Clark was abducted. She was grabbed right off the street as she approached her house. The perpetrators were driving a white van. Bam-Bam shot out the tires, but it drove off anyway."

The tunnel seemed to shrink in on Gabe. He'd barely heard a word beyond *abducted* as shock turned his blood to ice water. In desperation, he stared at Ice, who was bent over the IED, wielding a pair of specialized clippers.

"You need me to repeat, sir?" Zen asked.

"No." The fear that he might perish in a dark tunnel seemed like child's play compared to Libby's circumstances. Feisty, idealistic Libby in the hands of Hezbollah! An echo of the terror she had to be feeling reverberated through his body. "We have to find her before they…"

He couldn't bear to articulate what the terrorists intended with her. Instead, he focused on what it would take to find her. "Wait, Zen, she carries a sat phone for work! With any luck, she's got it on her. Tell Master Chief to get a hold of Jaime Ramirez, who's at the hospital, and find out what her number is. Maybe we can track her phone's GPS."

"Yes, sir. Over."

God, please… "How much *longer*, Carl?"

A soft *snick* preceded Ice's answer. "All done, sir." He rose fluidly to his feet. "You'll want to stay behind me," he chided gently as he slipped his tools back into his pockets.

Gabe acknowledged the admonition with a nod. The spiders could have at him for all he cared. And as much as he chafed to sprint for the exit, who knew how many more filaments lay in his path? Licking the salty sweat off his upper lip, he followed Carl cautiously forward.

This is a nightmare.

The terrorists, if they could see him now, would gloat. Here Gabe was, trapped in a tunnel laden with IEDs, looking for *them* while they were long gone. What's more, they'd seized the prize that Gabe had failed to protect.

The walls of the snaking tunnel blurred as the memory of Libby's sweet kiss taunted him.

He should have done more to keep her safe. One junior SEAL pitted against a handful of experienced extremists wasn't enough. If the worst happened to her—and the odds of that were sickeningly high—Gabe wouldn't even care if her father ruined his career. He would quit of his own volition.

A SEAL who couldn't keep his woman safe wasn't worthy to wear the Trident.

CHAPTER 11

L ibby awoke with a crick in her neck that came from sleeping sitting up while propped against a wall. *Where am I?* For a panicked second, her dark, cramped surroundings looked utterly alien. But the scratchy blanket under her hip and the numb fire licking up her arms brought her circumstances back to her, prompting a sick lurching in her gut.

She was locked in a closet, a prisoner of the same men who'd killed Enrique.

Her thoughts went back to the moment when the terrorist had thrust her out of the van, cuffed her wrists behind her back with a zip tie, and hustled her into a dark house. The sound of the van pulling away, taking her sat phone with it, had brought a cry of denial to her lips—one that was cut short by another stinging slap delivered by the scar-faced warrior.

Overwrought that her only hope, her satellite phone, had gone on without her, Libby had scarcely registered that her captors had stowed her on the home's second level, securing the closet door from the outside. Grateful to be left alone, she'd bewailed her circumstances and prayed with all her might for deliverance. At some point, she must have fallen asleep.

Wincing in discomfort, Libby used her shoulders and her feet to brace herself as she pushed to a standing position. Faint light shone through the seam around the door, suggesting it was morning. She had managed to sleep quite a lot then, but now her bladder needed relieving. "Hello." While the last thing she wanted was to draw attention to herself, she refused to pee in a closet. "I have to use the restroom!"

Putting an ear to the door, she detected footsteps on the stairs and drew back. Her heart thumped warily as one of her captors answered her summons. The knob gave a click, and the door yawned open, revealing the youngest of the three, the youth who resembled the leader. This morning, he clutched a deadly-looking knife that earned her full attention. Through eyes that were wide and wary, he regarded her with mistrust.

Keeping his dagger trained on her heart, he crooked a finger at her, gesturing for her to emerge. When she stepped hesitantly from the small space, he seized her elbow and roughly turned her around. Libby gasped at the feel of the knife sliding between her wrists, but in the next instant, the plastic cuffs snapped apart, freeing her to shake out her tingling arms. "Thank you."

"No talking." He gave her a shove. "Walk."

On quaking knees, she preceded him into a sparse bedroom. Given the two beds, a uniform folded neatly on one of them, and the scent of something like sandalwood, she surmised the room belonged to the leader and this youth.

"Stop."

Libby froze, sending an inquiring glance over her shoulder. The youth's English wasn't anywhere as good as his brother's. Keeping a mistrustful eye on her, he took a heap of gray material from the top drawer of the dresser and thrust it at her. "You may wash and put this on."

Wordlessly Libby accepted what looked like a robe and a head-dress. With a sinking heart, she backed away with the items into the bathroom, where she quickly shut and locked the door. The flimsy lock wouldn't keep anyone out for long. Turning, she assessed the possibility of escape only to have her hopes snuffed as she took in the high narrow window, comprised of thick, cube-shaped glass. Nobody could break through that, let alone see through it.

Perhaps she might find a weapon that she could conceal and use later?

But after peering into the cabinet under the sink and sifting through modest supplies, she realized why her captors didn't own a single razor—because they didn't shave. There was only soap, toilet paper, and a few thin towels for drying off. She had better make use of those amenities while she could.

Minutes later, shivering in the wake of a cold cat bath, Libby tunneled into the coarse chapan she'd been given, then pulled the hijab over her head. She'd learned the names for both garments on a well-digging retreat to Egypt back in college. The hijab covered her head completely, with just her face showing. Libby studied herself in the mirror. *I won't be here long*, she assured the pale, frightened woman staring back at her. But now that her phone was gone, driven off to God-knew-where, how would anyone track her down?

A knock at the door startled her. "Elizabeth Clark." The familiar voice with the perfect British accent thinned her blood. "Step out."

With the bone-chilling fear that she was walking toward her death, Libby scooped up her balled clothing and reluctantly unlocked the door, pulling it open. The gravity in her captor's stare drove the air back into her lungs.

"I never told anyone." The lie spilled out of her, born of desperation.

A cynical smile made his soft-looking facial hair twitch. "Indeed. Well, it makes no difference now. The Americans are here, aren't they? My name is Salim." He rendered a slight bow.

Stunned, Libby wasn't sure how to respond. "Your English is excellent."

His smile became pleasant. "As it should be. I studied at Oxford for six years—politics and environmentalism." His close regard made her wonder if he had looked her up enough to know she'd studied the latter also.

"What do you intend with me, Salim?" Her temerity surprised her.

His thinning lips conveyed disapproval. "A typical American, so forthright." His tone chided her gently. "Please, have a seat. Let us get to know each other whilst you eat."

Eat? As he turned toward the dresser, she spotted a plate of bread and cheese, along with a glass of some kind of juice.

He wouldn't be feeding her if he meant to kill her. The realization cheered her until she envisioned a lengthy captivity. Sinking into the chair he'd indicated, she stowed her clothing underneath and took the plate and juice he held out to her. As she lowered the plate to her lap, Salim took a seat on the end of the bed across from her, causing the springs to creak. He gestured for her to begin.

Highly conscious of his watchful gaze, Libby consumed a piece of cheese, discovering it to be goat cheese. Tasty. When he kept silent, she tore off a bit of bread and chewed, searching for the right thing to say. If communication was the key to world peace, as she firmly believed, she needed to bring up a neutral topic to ease the tension between them.

"The younger man, is he your brother?"

A fond look overcame Salim's handsome face. "His name is Nasrallah. It means 'victory of God.'"

"That's lovely. I wish I'd had a brother, but I'm an only child."

"Sounds lonely."

"Not really. My mother kept me company. She was an environmentalist who spent much of her life in South America."

"Hmm. I'm not surprised to hear it."

An awkward silence fell between them when he had nothing more to say. Did he know who she was, or didn't he?

Libby tried again. "What about the others? Who are they?"

His expression immediately tightened. "Their names you need not know."

His flat and dismissive tone made her say, "You don't like them."

He hesitated, then shrugged, as if deciding why not be frank with her? "I do not. They are Lebanese and I am Paraguayan. My family left Beirut in 1982 before I was born. This is my native country."

"Why do they work for you, then?"

"They were sent to me by Hezbollah to help me address the exploitation of my country by the American oil company."

Alarm pierced Libby. The sun in the window rose higher, throwing a shadow over the upper half of Salim's face. Would he say that if he knew who she was? "In what way do they exploit you?" It took all her courage to ask.

"The United States has no business sucking wealth from Paraguay. Now, I might feel differently if half of Clark Petroleum's shares resided in the hands of Paraguayans."

Libby thought for a second. "At least forty percent of Clark Petroleum's proceeds remain here in Paraguay. That was stipulated in the trade agreement." She had just read about that in her mother's diary.

Salim *tsked* his tongue and shook his head. "If only your father and the new CEO—your uncle—abided by the trade agreement."

Her scalp tightened, then tingled. He knew exactly who she was.

"With every year since the first well was drilled, the shares have been re-appropriated, and today, not a single Paraguayan is a shareholder in the company. So, unless and until Clark Petroleum sells ten million dollars' worth of shares to Paraguayan investors, you will remain my unwilling guest."

She considered denying who she was, then thought better of it as he paused, waiting.

"I'm sure your family adores you. And I'm counting on them to choose your life over the profits they earn from pillaging my country's resources."

Her *life*. So, he would murder her if his demands were not met. She took a quick sip of her juice—was it guava?—to counter her dry mouth. In her desperation, she cited the good things Jaime had pointed out the other day. "At least the economy is thriving because of the wells, right? For the first time in history, Paraguay exports oil without having to rely on Argentina's imports."

"Perhaps. That doesn't alter the fact that Clark Petroleum is profiting from resources that should be ours alone."

Libby reconsidered her kidnapper. It wasn't at all difficult to empathize with his viewpoint. "Honestly, I have to agree with you.

The reason I am here is to prove that the wells are spoiling the river water and to force Clark Petroleum to redress the damage done. El Chaco is the last pristine wilderness in the world. Like you, I want it protected, not exploited."

A glint of approval had entered Salim's bright eyes. "I will send a ransom note to International Water Institute." He waited for her to slip another morsel of cheese into her mouth to chew and swallow. "They will inform your uncle and your father of our demands. If Clark Petroleum responds to my requests, then I will release you." He sent her an encouraging smile.

Searching his expression for any hint of deception, Libby saw no reason to doubt his assertion. "But that could take weeks." Despite her resolve to remain brave, tears of reluctance and fear pushed into her eyes.

Salim gestured to the glass in her hand. "Drink. You have nothing to fear, Elizabeth—not from me or my brother. And we will protect you from the others."

The memory of the stinging slap she'd received made her doubt Salim's words. Intuition assured her this man and his younger brother were the only entities standing between her and the radical terrorists whom the SEALs were hunting. Complying with Salim's suggestion, she drained the cup's contents, deciding that the mildly sweet beverage wasn't juice at all but yerba mate, a tea enjoyed by locals.

"I must film you in captivity." With an apologetic grimace, Salim produced a cell phone from his breast pocket and accessed its camera feature.

Hope revived Libby as she eyed the Motorola. If people viewing the video wanted to find her, couldn't they use technology to determine where she was? *God, please let that happen!*

"You will identify yourself when I tell you to," Salim instructed, "and answer my questions succinctly. Also, you need not be so brave, Elizabeth. Things will go better for the both of us if you shed some tears."

~

Gabe paced the perimeter of the long table in the TOC, unaware that he was orbiting his colleagues like a satellite until Commander McDuff flicked him a censorial look.

"Have a seat, Lieutenant. You're making me dizzy."

Gabe dropped into the nearest empty chair. Dragging fingers through his crisp hair, he glared at the monitor. "How much longer?"

"Almost there," Bukowski promised as he worked to open several image files.

It had been twelve hours since Libby's abduction—the longest twelve hours of Gabe's entire life, feeling even longer than the nine days he'd unjustly spent in jail when he was eighteen. At least then, he'd only had himself to worry about. As overwrought as he was, it had scarcely bothered him when Commander McDuff tore into him for ignoring direct orders and befriending a woman living in town. The unpleasantness of that experience was nothing compared to what Libby had to be facing.

If Hezbollah realized what a prize they held, there was a good chance they'd ship her out of Paraguay on the first plane to Beirut, where she'd be held as a bargaining chip for the release of high-profile terrorists currently in U.S. captivity. She would become a political pawn, defiled and debased, never to see the light of day again.

The thought of informing Kyle Clark about his daughter's disappearance sickened Gabe—and not just because the man had the power to deep-six his career. Remembering the look of relief on Clark's face when he'd come to collect her in Brownsville and again after the assassination attempt at his party, Gabe could easily imagine Clark's devastation.

To prevent that, Gabe had used Clark's love for his daughter to convince McDuff that Libby's fate wasn't something they could ignore. They might not have direct orders from JSOTF yet to launch a rescue effort, but she was a high-value American target, and the fact that they'd rescued her once before set a precedent for doing so again. Moreover, informing Clark of his daughter's kidnapping ought to wait until they knew whether her sat phone provided them with any added intel.

While getting the sat phone's number from Jaime, Master Chief had learned that it was registered with AccuTracking, which meant that anyone in law enforcement could find it by plugging in her number. That information got the FBI involved, mostly because Lieutenant Commander Strong's wife was an FBI special agent. Charlotte Strong used AccuTracking to provide the SEALs with the exact latitude and longitude of Libby's satellite phone. Bukowski was working to download a satellite image of the area so they could see exactly where the phone was—eight miles north of Mariscal Estigarribia.

"Got it." Master Chief clicked on a link, and a photo popped up on the overhead. Gabe sat straight up in his seat as the pixelated image focused, showing the top of a white van amidst sand and scrub brush.

Master Chief toggled in, and more details came into view, like two broken taillights. The van looked empty. Next, he toggled way out. There was nothing but a rolling savannah and a couple of palm groves for miles in any direction. If Libby was in the same place her phone was, then she was out in the middle of nowhere.

Subsequent photos taken five and ten minutes later showed no movement, no signs of life whatsoever. Moreover, there was no option of seeing what had happened earlier, as the satellite had just begun to sweep over the area.

Rodeo, who was sitting quietly at the end of the table pointed out, "Someone walked away from there, headed back to town. See the tracks?"

The comment reminded Gabe that Rodeo was a trained tracker.

Bukowski frowned. "That's a *long* walk. How many sets of tracks?"

"Just one. Everyone else was probably dropped off somewhere along the way. Her phone just got left in the van."

Given the alternative—that Libby was lying in the van with a bullet in her head—Gabe much preferred Rodeo's explanation. "Can AccuTracking tell us where the van was before this?"

"No," said a woman's voice over their sound system. It took Gabe a second to realize Charlotte Strong was attending this meeting along with her husband, via WebConnect. "Only if she'd made a call along the way."

Gabe's hopes for a quick recovery died a painful death. He looked back at the overhead, his eyes burning from lack of sleep. *Kyle Clark is going to blame me for this.* He turned a hopeful gaze on Commander McDuff. "Permission to search for her, sir. We can start with the van and follow those tracks back to town."

Mad Max's long stare made his hopes falter. "What do you think, Lucas?" Max deferred to Lieutenant Commander Strong.

A long pause followed as their operations officer weighed the need for a quick response against the lack of any formal authorization. "Okay. Recon the van tonight when there's less chance that you'll be seen. Follow the tracks if you can, and get back to me."

"That we will, Lucas." Mad Max's slate-gray eyes focused on Gabe as he added, "Operation Anaconda was supposed to be a purely military operation. Now that there's a civilian involved—a high-profile *American* civilian—our activity down here is going to fall under public scrutiny, especially if we fail to handle this situation effectively and quietly."

In other words, the whole world was going to hear about the SEALs in Paraguay if they failed to liberate Libby. Their agenda would be discussed over dinner tables all across America, which was not a good thing. Gabe's temples throbbed with self-recrimination.

McDuff thumped the table with both hands as he pushed to his feet. "Get some rest. You can leave at dusk. Charlie Platoon remains here unless you require them for backup."

The only reason they would need backup was if they found Libby too well-protected to be rescued by just one platoon.

Gabe pushed wearily to his feet. As tired as he was, he couldn't imagine falling asleep right now, not with his imagination spawning vignettes of Libby being defiled and tortured. Protective feelings bound up in admiration stormed his heart, making him want to rage at God for not protecting her the way she had confidently asserted that He would.

Rodeo lay a comforting hand on Gabe's back as he followed him out the door and up the hallway. "We'll find her, Lobo."

"Thanks." Seeing the exit ahead of him, Gabe muttered an excuse about needing fresh air and darted out of it. Rodeo would advise the lower enlisted of their plans that afternoon.

Pushing into the sunshine, Gabe was taken aback to find it just another ordinary day. On the other side of the military installation's wall, the townspeople of Mariscal Estigarribia went about their daily routine, unaware and apathetic to Libby's plight. Gabe put his back to the building's sunbaked brick, hoping its warmth would drive away the chill deep inside him.

He'd been a SEAL for seven years, and in that time, he'd seen some horrific things. But there'd never been a circumstance that shook him as badly as this did. Why? Guilt he could understand, having promised both himself and Libby that the terrorists wouldn't get near her. But this wasn't just guilt he was feeling. It was raw and helpless fear, like he'd been personally attacked, like Hezbollah had robbed him of something that meant everything to him.

Demonios, had he fallen in love with Libby and not realized it? The possibility stripped the air from his lungs. Oh yes, he had.

He clapped a hand to his eyes and rubbed them. What was he thinking giving his heart to a rich woman—a woman whose father had a member of the Joint Chiefs of Staff sitting squarely in his back pocket? What a fool Gabe was!

And yet, Libby wasn't like her father, was she? She'd turned her back on all the privileges she'd been born into and was forging her own path the same way Gabe was. In that way, they were more alike than different.

He cut his thoughts short. Pondering their suitability was pointless when her future wasn't even guaranteed. All he could do was stick to the facts. She'd been kidnapped. She mattered to him. He needed to find her and save her from the fate Hezbollah held in store for her.

Yet he couldn't help but shake his head when he considered her faith. It was just downright *wrong* for a person so fueled by faith to be assaulted by evil.

Of their own accord, his eyes rose to the tops of the trees before him where leaves swayed under a sultry breeze. "God." His voice cracked, and tears flooded his eyes. "Don't You care about her?" The words escaped his gritted teeth. "I care, so You must care." He found his hands clasped together.

Staring down at his long, tan fingers gripped in supplication, it occurred to him that he was praying. The last time he'd tried praying was when he'd been sitting in jail over a decade ago. This time, he wouldn't give up. "You have to protect her, *Señor*. Please, protect her. I'll take better care of her if I get her back, I promise."

Dashing a tear from his cheek, Gabe dropped his hand and swiveled on the balls of his feet to haul the door open.

CHAPTER 12

Libby struggled to make sense of the argument raging downstairs, immediately below the closet in which she'd been locked all day. Her captors volleyed words at each other in Lebanese, practically at the top of their lungs.

She'd been let out only once since Salim had videotaped his interview with her that morning. She scrambled to her feet, putting her ear to the crack hoping to make sense of the discussion, but their dialect, so distinct from any Arabic she had ever heard, was completely unintelligible to her.

She could only think of one reason why they would bicker so heatedly: The Hezbollah recruits were demanding access to the hostage.

Dread made Libby's heart race and her stomach churn. Pushing away from the crack, she pressed her back against the wall, consumed by doubts. While she'd been kept apart from the other two men, how long could Salim keep that up, and how long before her ransom video was delivered to International Water Institute? Would they contact her father right away?

Lord, let it happen quickly. She couldn't live like this, trapped in a closet for hours on end. *Save me, Father. Save me, Gabe.*

Considering her last thought, she chided herself. Gabe wasn't obligated to do anything. Even if he could, how would he find her, given that her phone had been driven off with the van? Instead of leading a rescue party straight to her, the sat phone might, in fact, be sending potential rescuers on a wild-goose chase.

A sudden shout and the crack of a bullet brought a shriek to her lips. Libby clapped a hand to her mouth to stifle sounds that might draw attention to herself. Over her pounding heart came the sound of Salim speaking in the same authoritative voice he had used at the lab. Thank God he hadn't been shot. Without his protection, she was doomed.

The sound of footsteps climbing the stairs had her holding her breath. What was happening? The knob jiggled and the lock released. She backed farther into the corner. Would she be dragged downstairs and forced to face the others?

The door swung open, and Salim's brilliant orbs rested on her frightened visage. "Come." His voice was still gruff with anger. He held out a hand for her to take.

Operating purely on instinct, Libby placed her hand in his. He drew her briskly out of the closet to where his brother stood, guarding the top of the stairs with a rifle now braced across his chest. Sweeping Libby into his dark room, Salim shut and locked the door, leaving his brother to guard them on the landing. Then he flicked on a light powered by the generator grinding away outside.

His stormy gaze went straight to her uncovered head. "Where is the hijab you are supposed to be wearing?"

His misdirected anger made her blanch. "I'm sorry. I took it off. It was so hot in the closet—"

"Nasrallah!" He barked an order in Arabic, presumably asking his brother to fetch the head covering.

A moment later, the door cracked open, and Nasrallah lobbed the hijab into the room. Salim caught it, adjusted it in his hands, and draped it over her head himself. As he did so, his gaze slid over the curves of her body, only partially concealed by the shapeless chapan. The awareness that kindled in his eyes kept Libby rigid with mistrust. Had he brought her into his bedroom to protect her, or were his intentions lascivious?

Stepping back abruptly, he gestured brusquely for her to lie across the nearest bed. With her blood running cold, Libby shook her head no.

"Go to sleep." His impatient tone suggested her fears were baseless.

Still mistrustful, she reclined upon the thin mattress. Her muscles tensed as Salim whisked off his T-shirt, trading it for a fresh one. His slim torso made her think of Gabe, whose broad shoulders and powerful upper body inspired a wave of longing for his protection. Did he even know she'd been taken yet? How would he even suspect it?

Her pulse became erratic as Salim unbuckled his gun belt and started to remove his pants. Terrified, Libby turned her head toward the wall and squeezed her eyes shut. It took every ounce of willpower not to curl into a protective ball. *This isn't happening.* The pillow under her head gave off an odor she had come to associate with him—a blend of gun oil and sandalwood.

A vision of Gabe holding her chin between his thumb and forefinger while gazing deep into her eyes drove a shaft of remorse through her. Would she ever behold his handsome face again?

At the feel of something sliding over her rigid body, Libby started violently. Whipping her head around, she brought up her hands to fend off Salim. Only then did she realize he had covered her with a blanket.

"Rest." His sardonic smile mocked her frightened response—or perhaps it was himself he mocked. Straightening away from her, he turned toward the other bed and snapped off the light.

As the springs on the second bed scrunched beneath his weight, tears of relief slid from the corners of Libby's eyes. Regarding him through the shadows, she watched Salim drape his gun belt across his stomach, then notch his hands behind his head to stare up at the ceiling.

"Thank you," she murmured, her words as much for God's mercy as for her captor's.

"Do not thank me yet." His grim voice prophesied trials to come. "From now on, you must wear the hijab and do exactly as I say."

"I will." She'd do whatever it took to save herself.

A taut silence fell between them, filled with the sound of Salim's deep sigh as he wrestled with weighty thoughts. Libby closed her eyes and willed herself to sleep.

If only a pair of SEALs would come sneaking through the window as they had in Matamoros to whisk her away.

Viewed through his NVGs, the beleaguered van resembled a white whale beached on a solitary shore. The instant Gabe saw it, sitting under a starry night sky in the middle of nowhere, he knew Libby wasn't here. Even so, he gave the breeze a wary sniff, dreading the scent of death but smelling only fresh savannah air. The good news was she wasn't lying dead inside the van. The bad news? They had no earthly idea where she might be.

Gabe signaled for Ice to approach the vehicle first, just in case it was booby-trapped. Looking through the windows, Ice inspected the dark interior using a penlight. Then he went down on the ground, rolled onto his back, and disappeared beneath the van. A minute later, he wriggled back out, declaring it clean. Gabe reached for the door handle, surprised to find it unlocked, and slid open the door to the cargo area.

Doc joined him in searching the rear while Rodeo searched the seats up front. With penlights strobing every inch of the interior, they inspected the van for clues while the remaining members of Gabe's platoon formed a perimeter around them, just in case the terrorists had lured them here.

"Found it." Doc, who may have used his psychic gift to locate the phone, held it up. "It was wedged into the crevice of the seat— pretty clever of her. It still has some battery left." He passed it to Gabe.

Resisting the urge to put the phone to his nose, perhaps to catch a trace of Libby's scent, Gabe powered it down and slid it into his thigh pocket. "Rodeo, you see any registration papers? Anything with an address on it?"

Rodeo had just torn through the glove box. "Negative, sir."

Gabe swallowed down his disappointment. But the van hadn't been their only lead. "Any chance you can follow the tracks we saw in the photos, Chief?"

They all climbed out of the van to look for them. Panning the sand with his pen light, the only footprints Gabe could see were their own. Still hopeful, he fastened his attention on Rodeo as the chief squatted and studied the sandy ground through his NVGs. He flipped them up and looked again, using just the ample moonlight to see. In his youth, Rodeo—aka Adam Donovan—had been trained by the Native Americans of his home state of Montana to track game. As he stood and met Gabe's anxious regard, his blue eyes shone like sapphires.

But the grimace on his face said it all. "I'm sorry, sir, but the wind's blown them away."

Mother Nature had conspired against them. With a bitter taste in his mouth and with growing despair, Gabe accepted defeat. "Zen," he called to his communications specialist, "tell the head shed to come and pick us up."

Their search for Libby had hit another wall.

"Why do you work for International Water Institute when your father owns Clark Petroleum Corporation?" Salim's question, coming on the heels of their luncheon the following day, made Libby set aside her pita and hummus, only too happy to talk about her work.

In the time she had remained in his room, guarded either by him or by Nasrallah, she had lost any lingering fear of defilement or torture—at least at their hands. Only the others, whose restlessness she sensed and could sometimes hear, remained a threat. But for the time being, the warm upstairs chamber felt as secure a place as any. If only she were free to leave it.

"Like you, I am passionate about protecting the planet, Salim."

Approval danced in his amazonite eyes.

"My mother taught me that our planet is both a gift and a responsibility. We don't just live here. We're the stewards. I was about ten when my father decided to drill for oil in this region. I remember my mother trying to dissuade him, telling him that fracking would contaminate the last untouched wilderness in the world. Drilling was the only thing I ever heard my parents disagree on. My mother wanted my father to focus on clean energies, while my father believed drilling for oil was harmless."

"What do you believe?"

It pleased her that he seemed to care. "Well, the science says my mother is right, and once I've gathered sufficient evidence of contaminants in the river water, I'll show it to my father, and he'll make the better choice."

"And what if you discover that the wells have corrupted El Chaco irrevocably and that the region will never be the same again?"

Libby grimaced. "I hope that's not the case. To date, the tests haven't shown any significant toxin levels."

"Really? None whatsoever?"

Libby blinked at his sarcastic tone. "Why would I lie?"

Salim startled her by whipping out his cell phone, the same Motorola he had used to make her ransom video. "I have pictures to show you." Scooting closer, he thumbed his screen, then held out his phone and scrolled through photos of dead cattle rotting under a hot sun and swarming with flies.

Libby's eyes widened and her heart sank. "Where did you take these?"

"Twenty kilometers south of the Guaraní village, alongside the Río Verde. The toxins have built up there. They've seeped into the surrounding soil, poisoning the flora that these cows have eaten. Now they are dying. The people eat the cows and drink their milk. What will happen to them?"

Dismay shot through Libby. She and Jaime had been looking in the wrong places, by Río Lindo not Río Verde. "I've only seen something like this once." She relayed the story about the hapless cow belonging to the native ranchers.

Salim sat back and put his phone away. "That's how it started farther north."

Disillusionment spread through Libby. For the first time ever, she asked herself if IWI hadn't directed her and Jaime to collect their samples in the wrong places? Might the international company have allowed itself to be bribed by Clark Petroleum to limit their testing area? Salim's accusing gaze seemed to suggest that was the case and that Libby was their pawn.

She surprised herself by reaching for his hand and squeezing it. "If I find out that Clark Petroleum has influenced IWI to turn a blind eye to what's happening to Río Verde, then I promise you, Salim: I will expose the corporation and force Clark Petroleum to make restitution."

The cynicism in his expression faded, softening toward a grudging smile. "I believe you. And I pity your uncle, who will have to face such determination."

The intimate and emotional energy arcing between them prompted Libby to release him. Feeling in some strange way she was betraying Gabe, she stood with her plate and, leaving it atop the nearby dresser, stepped toward one of the two windows covered with a wrought-iron grill.

She had peered out of this very window many times before, envisioning her father's response to the ransom video and praying for Gabe and his SEALs to materialize out of thin air and rescue her.

Her captors' home stood in a grassy area surrounded by a wall, a few trees, and a field. The closest building she could see was another like this one, perhaps a hundred yards away, with the roofs of the town visible beyond it. *If I ever get out of this room, I know which way to run.*

"Elizabeth."

Salim's voice sounding in her ear made her jump. She hadn't

heard him get up. His hands settled gently on either of her shoulders. The heat of his palms seemed to burn through the cloying fabric of the chapan.

If she had never met Gabe, hadn't experienced the deep connection between them, she might have thought herself drawn to Salim's gentle touch. It didn't frighten her the way it ought to. If anything, the warmth of his hands was a comfort as she allowed him to turn her around.

"I think we have more in common than you realize." His striking eyes roamed her face centering on her lips.

She stiffened as he started to incline his head. "Please don't."

His eyebrows quirked with puzzlement. "I won't hurt you. You and I were meant for each other. Don't you see? With your help, my protests have credibility. Together, we can keep El Chaco untainted. We can expose the corporation exploiting her purity."

His words mesmerized her, for she would like nothing better than to leave the children of Paraguay such a legacy, but his offer came with the implication that they would become a couple. "I can't." She shook her head while picturing Gabe's brooding gaze. How ironic that the man she'd recently pledged herself to resist had a claim on her already.

"Why not?" Salim's tone remained patient. "I'm well educated. I come from a good family. Is it my religion? I'm not a Muslim, though don't tell the men downstairs that. Most of the Lebanese in Paraguay are Christians."

If anything, this information made her decision harder. They even shared the same faith. Reaching up, she drew his hands off her shoulders and squeezed them tightly. "You're a good man, Salim, though I question your decision to kidnap me. And your words make sense, but... but my heart is already spoken for." The words emerging from her mouth both amazed and dismayed her. God might have been a bit too ambitious pairing her and Gabe together—assuming Gabe even returned her feelings.

Salim abruptly pulled his hands from hers.

Still reeling from her discovery, Libby kept a wary eye on Salim as he turned his head to avoid looking at her. In the beginning,

Gabe had been more of a hindrance to her work than an asset. Yet even when she'd balked at his heavy-handedness in Matamoros, he'd had her full attention. The night he'd chased off her father's would-be assassin, then here in Paraguay when he'd figured out what had really happened at the lab, he'd proven both brave and insightful.

He wasn't just a thorn in her side. He was her hero.

But seeing the disillusionment harden Salim's handsome profile, she both regretted the truth and resented it. Why Gabe? A relationship with him entailed all manner of complications, while she and Salim shared a common vision—though he *did* associate with some questionable characters. Plus, she objected to his radical tactics to eject Clark Petroleum from his country.

Stepping closer to him, she sought to lessen her rejection. "Salim, if you let me go, I swear I will help your cause." Getting no immediate objection, she added, "My father is a reasonable man. If he saw your pictures and received lab reports to corroborate them, he would address the situation immediately."

"But your uncle now runs the company, not your father." Salim's voice had turned flat. As he looked back at her, she could see the idealistic flame burning in his eyes earlier was gone, making him look suddenly older than she guessed him to be.

"Yes, but Uncle Paul will do whatever my father asks him." At least she hoped that to be the case. "Please." The distant way in which Salim was regarding her worried her. "Let me go, and I swear I will rectify these issues with the environment. Nothing would please me more."

A thin smile curled the edges of Salim's mouth. "It's too late for that."

Turning his back on her, he went to collect her plate. Fear ambushed Libby's hopes as he carried it to the door and let himself out. Muttering orders to Nasrallah, he locked her inside before the sound of his footsteps signaled his descent down the stairs.

By kidnapping the daughter of Clark Petroleum, Salim had set the ball rolling toward some unknown catastrophe. Libby closed her eyes and prayed. Her heart harbored little hope of this situation ending well—not for her, not for Salim, not even for the country he loved.

Gabe let himself into Libby's little house using his credit card. The scent of lemon cleaner blended pleasantly with her one-of-a-kind herbal fragrance, causing his heart to clutch with the fear that he might never see her again. The sun reflected brightly off her kitchen countertops and table. Everything looked so neat and tidy.

Drawn to her bedroom, he stood at the door, his gaze drawn to the imprint of her body on the comforter topping her bed. She'd lain there, perhaps reading the leather-bound book, still lying face down where she'd left it. Recognizing it as the same little diary he had grabbed that night in Matamoros, he picked it up and flipped through it, skimming several passages and absorbing the words of an intelligent woman on a passionate mission to improve the world. It sounded just like Libby talking, except Libby had been a teen at the time, according to the dates written above each entry.

Her poor mother. Gabe's research online had informed him that Melinda Clark had been headed to the Amazon jungle in Brazil to protest the deforestation of indigenous lands when her plane crashed. And now Libby was on an equally harrowing mission here in Paraguay when random violence interrupted her work. A shudder racked his spine. *Have mercy, Señor.*

A knock at the door had him setting down the diary with a leap of concern. He'd asked his chiefs to come fetch him the instant there was news.

Doc's half smile beat back Gabe's foreboding. "We've got a lead."

"What lead?" Joining Doc on the stoop, Gabe locked the handle from the inside before closing Libby's door behind him.

"The International Water Institute received a ransom letter in the form of an email that contained a link to a site like YouTube, except you can post videos there without them being vetted first." Doc started walking, forcing Gabe to match his long strides.

They waited for a car to pass, then crossed the street together. Hope vied with dread at the prospect of seeing Libby in the video—overwrought and at the mercy of her captors. A video posted to the Internet wouldn't stay secret for long.

"The CO's waiting so we can watch it together."

"Wait, does that mean JSOTF is aware of the abduction, and we have orders to respond?"

"I don't know, sir. I imagine the CO will tell you."

Arriving at the TOC, Gabe found every SEAL in the task unit already seated, over thirty men either sat or stood around the long table with their eyes glued to the Internet browser projected on the overhead screen.

The CO glowered at Gabe as he and Doc walked in. "There you are."

Gabe found his seat while muttering an apology. As Doc cut the lights, Mad Max clicked the link, and Gabe found himself staring at Libby, covered from the head down in Middle Eastern garb. A single lock of her honey-blonde hair escaped the headscarf. A lump of helplessness swelled in his throat as the camera focused on her luminous eyes, glistening with tears which she bravely held in check.

The window behind her was covered with a wrought-iron grill. A rooster crowed outside. Then a male voice declared in a cultured British accent that Elizabeth Clark, an employee of International Water Institute, would remain a hostage of the National Liberation Brigade of Paraguay unless Clark Petroleum met the Brigade's demands.

Gabe catalogued clues as he listened to the terrorist speak. The man had been educated in England, obviously. He sounded polished and intelligent and not at all unhinged—or was that just wishful thinking? Given the view through the window, Libby was being held on a second floor. The crowing rooster suggested the location was more rural than urban.

"Our demands are simple," the voice continued. "We require Clark Petroleum to cease operations entirely until ten million dollars' worth of corporate shares are sold to Paraguayan investors.

The sale of these shares must take place before closing hours Friday or the hostage will be put to death."

Was that the only ultimatum? Gabe glanced at the faces of his leaders to gauge their reactions. Aside from the threat of death, the demands sounded feasible, not like the radical ultimatums for which Hezbollah was famous. Surely Kyle Clark would do whatever it took to get shares of Clark Petroleum into the hands of Paraguayan investors. But wait. Libby's father wasn't the CEO anymore—Van Slyke was.

The screen flickered and the video ended at just over a minute in length.

"Has IWI responded publicly to the captor's demands?" Gabe blurted this question.

Bukowski looked over at him. "Not that I'm aware of, but I'm sure they've seen the video by now and reached out to the oil corporation. The victim's father most certainly knows because General DePuy was the one who advised SOUTHCOM, who advised JSOTF, who told us about the video. Our chain of command is worried. Once Hezbollah realizes this woman's political value, they'll leverage it for all she's worth. Given the reasonable demands of her captors, they can't possibly have realized who Elizabeth Clark is just yet."

Gabe swallowed hard. "Then Clark Petroleum should jump at the chance to meet the NLB's demands. Maybe they'll release her before that happens."

Mad Max raised his eyebrows. "Do you *hear* yourself, Lieutenant?"

Yeah, he sounded totally naïve and hopeful, but the alternative was too awful to contemplate.

Bukowski followed up on a kinder note. "The problem is this video was posted to the Internet, which means the media will jump all over this any minute now. As soon as the public sees it, somebody's going to comment on Elizabeth Clark's identity. At that point, the ransom demands are bound to change."

Worse and worse.

"The FBI is working with the website to get the video taken

down," Bukowski added, "but there is one plus to having it posted on the Web. You want to tell them, sir?"

Mad Max cleared his throat. "Yes, the FBI has narrowed down the location of the upload to a region on the northeast side of Mariscal Estigarribia. The target isn't far from here."

Hope stormed Gabe's heart as Mad Max gestured to the blank screen.

"Adding clues from the video, like the fact that she's being held on a second floor—there aren't very many two-storied structures on the northeast side—we can whittle down her location to maybe a dozen buildings within a five-square-mile area."

Bukowski tapped a few keys on the laptop, and a map of the area jumped onto the overhead projector. "Here's what we're going to do," he began.

～

A shout downstairs jarred Libby from a light slumber. She sat up slowly on the spare bed and held her breath, listening. It was the middle of the night. A hint of moonlight patterned the tiled floor, and Salim's bed stood empty, suggesting he couldn't bear to be with her after she'd rejected his offer to work together.

Earlier that night, the sound of a television show downstairs suggested Salim and the others had mended their differences. She'd been reassured enough to fall asleep as soon as the sun went down. Only in her dreams could she escape captivity.

But the angry accusations penetrating the tiled floor now suggested the fragile peace was over. Straining to hear the tenor of the argument, she panicked at the certainty that the disagreement directly impacted her safety. Over the faint hoot of an owl floating through the window, she detected Salim's voice, familiar to her now. He sounded angry, defensive.

Unable to fall back asleep, Libby swung her feet to the cool floor, crossed to a window, and peered longingly outside. The light shining in the neighboring house—so close yet impossible to reach—tormented her.

The sudden crescendo of footsteps, accompanied by a warning cry from Nasrallah, had her whirling toward the door in alarm. The door opened, and Salim pushed his brother inside the room before following on his heels and locking the door behind him. A puddle of moonlight betrayed his alarmed expression as he instructed his brother to help him shove the dresser in front of the door. It scraped noisily across the tiles as they moved it.

Breathing heavily, Salim turned to regard her standing by the window. "I'm so sorry."

His apology brought her closer. "What's wrong? What's happening?" Foreboding clamped down the muscles at the base of her neck. The whites of Nasrallah's wide eyes did nothing to reassure her.

"The others have discovered who you *really* are, not just an employee of IWI. It was on the news, word of your kidnapping. The media identified you as the daughter of the founder of Clark Petroleum. I should never have posted the video online. My mistake. Now Ashraf and Musa know, and they want to take you back to Beirut with them tonight. I forbade them," he added with a tremor in his voice. Apprehension seemed to ooze from his pores.

His fear spilled into her. "Will they listen to you?"

As he reached for her hands, the trembling of his fingers vaulted her alarm to unprecedented levels.

"I will protect you with my life."

Both his words and the whites of his eyes shining through the darkness sent shock ricocheting through Libby's body. *This is it.* Counting on Salim's protection, she had hoped that she would ultimately be spared, but his portentous words made it terrifyingly clear: His colleagues had turned on him, denied his status as their leader, and were making plans to wrest her from his control.

The sudden bark of gunfire from the bottom of the steps nearly stopped her heart, even as it confirmed her fears. Salim gave his brother grim orders in Lebanese. Then he drew Libby toward the bathroom. "Stay inside, lock the door, and stand inside the shower." He pressed an object into her hand.

Looking down, Libby recognized the dagger Nasrallah had used to slice off her cuffs. Salim started to close the bathroom door between them, and she glanced up, frozen in horror. Even knowing what he would do next, she made no move to stop him this time as he leaned forward, pressing a heartfelt kiss to her lips. His soft beard tickled her face. His gentle lips tasted of fear and farewell.

He pulled away. "I'm sorry."

The door closed behind him, and Libby quickly locked it, recalling with a sick lurch in her stomach that it wouldn't keep anyone out for long.

CHAPTER 13

G abe held up a hand, signaling for the men ghosting him to hold their position. Leaning into the shadows of a stuccoed wall, he thumbed his mike. "Did you hear that?"

"Gunfire." Rodeo, who brought up the rear of their scouting party a soccer-field length behind him confirmed his guess. "Couple of blocks west."

Relying on Rodeo's excellent judgment, Gabe glanced at the compass on his watch before leading his platoon in that direction while sending two scouts in the opposite direction. They shouldn't put all their eggs in one basket.

Every structure on the northeast side of town looked the same— a squat cinderblock or adobe dwelling surrounded by a yard and a sturdy wall five to six feet high. The objective of their reconnaissance was to locate and map every structure with two or more stories, leaving a pair of SEALs to observe each one. So far, they'd only encountered five buildings fitting that description. Gabe was left with just six men, including himself, though the other ten could be swiftly summoned, if needed.

Keeping his footfalls stealthy, he led them down a narrow road pitted with potholes. Sand crunched beneath the soles of his boots.

Where are you, Libby? An herbal scent had him sniffing the air, but what smelled like Libby was probably just the bougainvillea climbing the wall next to him.

Most of the homes stood in darkness, their occupants sleeping. His toe collided with an aluminum can, sending it rolling noisily into the dirt street, which prompted a dog to bark. Gabe froze. So much for being quiet.

That was when he heard it: another spate of semiautomatic gunfire.

He glanced back at Rodeo, who'd caught up to him. "Talk to me, Chief."

Rodeo pointed. "Dead ahead, sir. Coming from across that field, on the other side of those trees. See the light? Right there."

"Everyone, pick it up." With that order, Gabe broke into a run.

The *rat-tat-tat* of semiautomatic gunfire sounded like cannons going off.

Libby pressed herself into the corner of the tiled shower, one hand clamped over an ear, the other gripping the dagger for dear life. The thud of a shoulder against the bedroom door out on the landing brought a whimper to her lips. *Bang!* A shot fired at the door caused her to jerk, jolted by adrenaline. The gruff voice of the scar-faced terrorist barked at his companion to push the door open.

The dresser in front of the bedroom door seemed to give way. Libby could tell by the sounds alone that Salim and Nasrallah were pushing against it, fighting to keep the door closed.

Another gruff order preceded a barrage of gunfire, and a body hit the floor.

Salim gave an anguished cry. "Nasrallah!"

Libby echoed his dismay with a sob as she pictured Salim falling to his knees beside his brother.

The door was pushed again, and the feet of the wardrobe screeched noisily over the tiles. An answering volley came from inside the room, suggesting Salim was both defending himself and avenging Nasrallah.

Please, God. Libby prayed for Salim to vanquish the evil that closed in on them.

The sound of a body falling down the stairs told her Salim had hit at least one mark, giving her hope that he might just succeed in stopping his attackers.

But the scarred warrior started shouting threats from the hall into the bedroom. Salim called back what was clearly a refusal to surrender. Libby's heart thundered into the silence that followed.

With an angry roar from the hall, more gunfire ensued, so loud Libby could only grit her teeth and pray for the altercation to end, for Salim to be the victor. The sounds were all coming from the room now. Something hit the bathroom door and slid down it, and in her mind's eye she pictured her protector, his beautiful eyes wide open, blood sliding from one corner of his mouth as he gasped his final breaths.

This is wrong.

Fury edged aside Libby's terror. With an indrawn breath, she pulled herself together. How dare the Hezbollah volunteers betray their leader, their host! She would *not* let them take her. She would *not* become a hostage of Hezbollah!

Adrenaline galvanized her rigid muscles. Over her thundering heart, she could hear ceramic shards from what must have been the bedside lamp crackling under the assailant's footsteps. Salim's killer stopped before his victim. Hissing ugly words, he shoved him aside, and Salim fell like a sack of potatoes. The doorknob jiggled.

Tucked behind the door in the shower stall, Libby briefly squeezed her eyes shut. *Give me strength, Father.* The door shuddered as the terrorist threw his shoulder into it. The frame gave a crack. Another hit and it would give. Libby tightened her grip on the dagger. *What would Gabe do?* She channeled her inner warrior.

Crack! The door flew open, blocking her view of the intruder. Timing meant everything. She could sense him plumbing the moonlit room with his eyes, searching for her. The snout of his semiautomatic pistol slid past the door. If she waited too long, he would sense her presence right beside him.

Stepping from the shower, Libby seized the barrel of the man's weapon and yanked, pulling her assailant into the room and straight into the dagger she thrust before her with her other hand. The blade met resistance in the form of his clothing, but then it slid with astonishing ease into his abdomen.

Choking on his astonishment, the scarred warrior looked down, then up at her. As Libby leaped back into the shower out of harm's way, bullets spewed the sink and mirror, shattering porcelain and glass, sending sharp-edged pieces flying. The assailant staggered, released the trigger, and stared back down at the dagger poking obscenely from his midsection.

Weaving on his feet, he faced her, raising his weapon to shoot her at point-blank range.

"No, you don't." Her snarl raised the hairs on the back of her own neck. Shoving off the shower wall, Libby struck her heel into his groin, sending him crashing into the opposite wall. Bullets strafed the tiles next to her shoulder, then the ceiling as he lost his balance. With a *click*, he ran abruptly out of ammunition.

Libby didn't wait for him to fall. Darting past his listing form, she squeezed out of the bathroom, only to draw up short at the sight of Salim sprawled across the rug, his torso covered in blood that glistened in the faint light. She dropped onto the debris-strewn tile next to him.

He turned his head, miraculously still alive, and looked at her.

"I'll go get help." Her heart, lodged in her throat, made speaking difficult. "You'll be all right."

He whispered something unintelligible as she sprang up again. Fueled by adrenaline, Libby lurched for the door. *I'm free!* Horror usurped her relief as she ran into Nasrallah, lying face down in a pool of his own blood.

With a sob, she stepped over him and slipped out of the room. Down the stairs she flew, edging around the other Hezbollah recruit, the one who'd fallen down the stairs. He, too, was dead. Pausing for breath, she searched and listened for more threats. A small TV lit the lower level, filling it with wavering light and the discordant sound of canned applause. Disoriented, Libby wasted precious moments locating the exit, which was situated in the kitchen.

She threw herself outside without first looking, running into fresh balmy air, a dark yard, and the arms of a stranger who sprang out of the shadows to grab her.

"It's me! Libby, it's me." Gabe silenced her scream much the way he'd done the night he'd pulled her out of Matamoros—with a gloved hand clamped over her mouth.

She focused wild eyes on him.

Freeing her to breathe, Gabe overheard her gasp of relief before she flung herself into his arms, buried her face against his shoulder, and shook like a leaf in a gale.

"This way." He tugged her quickly away from the dwelling, behind the wall that surrounded it, and tabbed his mike. "Target recovered. I say again, we have the target."

Across the field separating this house from the others, more lights blinked on. The firefight had awakened the distant neighbors. They were bound to draw attention to themselves.

Gabe pulled Libby closer, holding her up as her legs gave out without warning.

"You're okay." Sweeping a palm from her silky hair—she'd ditched the headdress somewhere—all the way down her body, he checked her for injury, finding none. The urge to sob with relief that she'd escaped certain death pressured his chest, but they'd yet to secure the area. "Tell me what you know." He forced himself to speak firmly, even as he set her on her feet and put her at arm's length, using his stare to hold her together.

Visibly shocked, she couldn't speak at first. As she worked her jaw, searching for her voice, he noted a cut on her forehead—collateral damage, nothing to worry about. She wore the same robe she had worn in the ransom video.

"I stabbed the man in the bathroom, but he's not dead yet. The one on the floor under the window needs help. He tried to—to protect me. Please don't hurt him!"

Gabe was about to key his mike to alert his platoon when a spate of semiautomatic gunfire hailed down from the second-story window, peppering the inside of the wall. Putting himself between Libby and the wall—just in case a bullet pierced the dried mud—he waited for the bullets to subside.

Libby had gone rigid in his arms. "He's still alive! The one with the scar!"

"It's okay. Don't worry. We can take him, Libby." Turning his head, he glimpsed Rodeo at the corner of the house, ready to lead an insertion.

Ice stepped out of line, pulled the pin out of a smoke grenade, and rolled it into the yard. As it spewed a violet cloud into the air, the SEALs scurried furtively toward the kitchen door, skirting a swathe of still more bullets. Before they'd all entered the house, a single shot rang out, volleyed from a pistol inside the building, and the semiautomatic gunfire ended abruptly.

What the heck just happened?

In his earpiece, the scuffle of rapid footsteps announced the SEALs' push into the kitchen and up the stairs.

Libby gripped Gabe's uniform. "What's happening?"

"It's almost over." He never wanted to see that look of pure terror on her face again.

"Doc, we need you up here."

Rodeo's grim tone and the summoning of the medic told Gabe that someone was alive, but who? "Sitrep."

"We've got two dead and two wounded, both bleeding out. One is the Hezbollah terrorist with the scar, the other one unknown."

"Salim," Libby whispered, clearly overhearing Rodeo.

"Try to keep them both alive," Gabe urged, recalling Bukowski's orders.

"Not gonna happen, sir. Al-Sadr was shot in the back by the guy we can't identify. Bullet's in his heart."

"What about the guy who shot him?"

"Multiple gunshot wounds to the chest. Weak vitals. He's on his way out."

Demonios. Gabe had wanted to arrest at least one of the terrorists for abducting Libby. The silhouettes of neighbors coming out of their houses wrested his attention toward other matters.

"Zen, call for immediate extraction," he ordered.

Libby swayed against him, causing him to hold her more securely. "You okay, *querida?*" The endearment meaning "beloved" slipped out of him as naturally as breathing.

She took her sweet time answering. "I think so."

Tears of relief flooded his eyes as he beheld her pale, dazed face. "I am never letting you out of my sight again." The spontaneous words popped out of him.

To his surprise Libby didn't protest. "Thank you."

Contentment flooded Gabe. He'd never been happier in his life.

Libby sat hugging herself in her bathtub while the water rained down on her in a steady warm shower.

It's over. She had told herself those words a hundred times, hoping to subdue the shudders that still wracked her. Minute by minute, the horror of her captivity and the shock engendered by the violence she'd witnessed trickled off her limbs, pooling into the water, then swirling down the drain. All the while, she lamented using up such a precious resource.

Half an hour before, Gabe's colleague, the medic with the hypnotic eyes, had checked her over with gentle hands and an even gentler voice. "Name's Doc," he'd told her, declaring her to be in good shape. "You're one lucky lady."

She'd come away with a cut above her left eyebrow and another on the sole of her right foot, but the rest of her had emerged unscathed. And when he'd tactfully inquired whether her captors had hurt her any *other* way, she'd been able to say no because Salim, who'd been dead by the time they slid his stretcher into the back of a Humvee, had kept his word. He'd protected her with his life. With his last breaths, he'd even shot the wanted terrorist trying to hamper her escape.

A wave of grief rolled through Libby. Her face crumpled and hot tears mingled with the water that was slowly turning colder. She would never forget Salim's vision for the future, nor his apology accompanied by the bittersweet kiss he'd planted on her lips.

The memory of Nasrallah, who could not have been a day over twenty, lying in a pool of blood made her sob suddenly. She let herself weep quietly, honoring them both for their willingness to die for a cause they believed in. In that regard, they were kindred spirits, she and the brothers.

By degrees, the low timbre of male voices penetrated Libby's awareness. Gabe and Doc were talking in her living room. With a sharp sniff, Libby pulled herself together. She couldn't let the men think the trauma of her captivity had broken her spirit. Not at all. If anything, Salim's quest to hold Clark Petroleum accountable for the slow poisoning of El Chaco bolstered her own resolve.

Shutting off the water, she pushed to her feet, wondering how long she'd sat in the tub recuperating. It was time to shake off recent horrors and move forward. There was work yet to be done.

After drying off, Libby girded herself in the towel, then dashed across the hall to dress. Putting on her nightgown and wrap, she pondered what to do with the chapan still lying in a heap in her bathroom. Wearing the same night attire she had worn when Gabe snatched her out of Matamoros, she went to join the men. At the sound of her door hinges squeaking, Gabe and Doc both turned to look at her.

"There she is," the medic said. When Gabe and Libby locked gazes and kept quiet, he added, "Well, I'd better head back. Night, sir. Good night, ma'am." As he pulled Libby's door shut behind him, Doc sent Libby an encouraging smile.

The instant he was gone, Gabe came straight toward her and clasped her hands, gripping them securely.

"I called your father." His gaze, both possessive and concerned, never left hers. "Have you ever heard a grown man cry?"

"He does that all the time," she assured him while craving

Gabe's embrace. He had scrubbed all traces of the dark paint that had covered his face and neck earlier. "He's not a tough guy like you."

"Well, I nearly cried myself when you came out of that house alive."

Her recent horror bubbled up. "I had to stab the man with the scar to keep him from grabbing me. They were going to take me back to Lebanon."

At her words, Gabe released her hands to cup her face, his touch warm and gentle. "Listen to me. What you did was incredibly brave, Libby. Don't regret your actions for one second. You stabbed him because you had to. You saved your life doing it, and I couldn't be more impressed with you."

Grief broke her chest wide open. *She had murdered another human being.* But Gabe's words made perfect sense, sweeping away her guilt and allowing her to draw a stabilizing breath. She laid her hands over his. "I think you should get some credit. I was too terrified to move. Then I pretended I was you, and this fighting determination overtook me."

An indulgent smile curled the edges of Gabe's mouth. Removing his hands from her face, he snared her hands against and twined his fingers with hers. "I'll take any credit you want to give me. By the way, your father wants to talk to you, no matter how late it is. You can call him as soon as I leave. Look, there's your company phone." He gestured with his head toward the sat phone charging on her kitchen counter.

Libby gasped. "I was hoping you would find it."

"That was smart thinking, hiding it in the van. Might have worked, too, if they hadn't abandoned it in the middle of nowhere."

Wanting to forget the last seventy-two hours, Libby released his hands to throw her arms around him. Plastered against him, she held on fast. What she needed more than anything was his warmth and his reassurance. Only he could drive away the chill sitting in her chest like a hunk of ice. "I'll call Daddy in the morning."

Gabe held her stiffly against him. "Right. You should rest now."

Weariness wasn't her reason for not calling. Her father would use the incident to demand she come straight home. Tonight, she lacked the strength to stand up to him. But Gabe, who probably felt the same way, didn't need to know that.

"How are you feeling, *querida*?"

She glanced up at the question. What would he say if she'd told him what she'd realized during captivity? That she and he were destined for each other, though God alone knew how *that* was going to work.

"I'm okay, I guess." Survivor's guilt impaled her. Salim and Nasrallah were the reasons she could say that.

Gabe's forehead furrowed suddenly. "I thought I'd never see you again. Libby."

Her name sounded as if it were torn from his chest. Maybe he felt as strongly about her as she did about him.

With a slight tremor in his fingers, he lifted a hand to trace the bandaged cut on her forehead. "Please," His voice went gruff with emotion, "please don't put me through anything like that ever again."

Her heart took flight. He *had* to feel the same way. And if he'd said it any other way, she might have taken exception to his request. But how could she when he begged her so honestly?

"I'll try not to." She had no intention of ever being kidnapped again if that meant anything.

He cleared his throat, visibly pulling himself together. "You must be tired. Do you think you can sleep?"

Envisioning the memories that would assault her the instant she lay down, she shook her head. "No."

A beat of silence ensued, then, "Why don't I lie down with you for a while? Since I might be summoned at any moment, I'll have to lie on top of the covers with my uniform on."

She tried not to smile at how clearly he'd stated his honorable intentions. "Yes, please." Stepping back, she caught up his hand and towed him toward her bedroom, turning off the lights as she went. "You can take that side."

While Gabe went to work untying his boots, Libby shook off her wrap and slipped beneath her comforter on the side where she normally slept. It felt as natural as breathing to be going to bed with him—another sign that they were meant for each other.

Gabe's boots thumped one at a time to the floor and then he lay back on top of the coverlet, issuing a groan of weariness.

The feeling that he had experienced a miraculous reprieve smothered Gabe as he lay along the length of the bed next to Libby, separated by two layers but still conscious of her warmth and the scent of her clean, damp hair. God had answered his fervent prayer. Amazement filled him. *Thank You, Señor.*

Libby's long sigh was a balm to his senses.

"You know," he heard himself say, "I think you're right, *querida.*"

"'Bout what?" Her words slurred, betraying her exhaustion.

"God watches over you."

"Mm-hmm, just like I said."

"I prayed for your safety, you know," he confessed.

A surprised silence answered his admission, then, "Thank you. I didn't know you believed in God."

"I always have. But I haven't prayed since I was a boy. I used to pray all the time back then."

"Oh? For what?"

Memories rushed in on him. Should he tell her what his seven-year-old self used to pray? She might think worse of him. Then again—his pride asserted itself—why should he be ashamed of his background? "I used to pray for my mother—that my father wouldn't hurt her too much or kill her by accident in one of his drunken rages."

Startled silence followed this time. "Oh, Gabe." She rose on one elbow to gaze down at him in consternation. In the dark room, he could just make out the damp hair framing her face and her glistening eyes.

"My father was a mean drunk," he added. "I was afraid I might have to kill him before he killed my mother."

"But that didn't happen." She sounded so certain.

"How do you know?"

"Because you prayed. God always listens to the prayers of a child."

"He never listened to my prayers. That's why I stopped praying."

His words clearly shocked her, for she paused as if confused, then shook her head. "No, I'm sure He listened. Think back. What happened to your father?"

Gabe blew out a breath and focused on his memories. "He went to jail," he recollected, "for something like four years. When he got out, he packed up his bags and abandoned us."

Libby drew an audible breath. "And he never came back?"

"Nope. My mother met Felix and later they got married."

"How was that for you?"

Happier memories played in his mind. "Good. Felix treated my mother with respect. My sister adored him. Me, I never really warmed up to him until—" He cut himself off, unwilling to bring up his stint in jail. Nothing would highlight his and Libby's differences more than that. She'd probably never gone near a jail, let alone spent time in one—or even associated with anyone who had. "—until I was older, and I realized how much he'd done for us."

Her silence struck him as thoughtful. "Sounds like God gave you a better father, Gabe. I'm glad to hear that."

With a pat on his chest, she lay back, leaving him to consider her words. *"Sounds like God gave you a better father, Gabe."*

An image of Felix formed in his mind—bald head, liquid brown eyes filled with gentleness, and a sturdy frame that never stopped working in all the years that Gabe had known him. The man had attended every one of Gabe's high school baseball games. He'd treated Isiris like his own daughter and Gabe like his own son. And he'd cherished Gabe's mother—and still did—with his every word and action.

Warmth flooded Gabe. Libby was right! Here Gabe had thought that God had turned a deaf ear to his childhood prayers when, in fact, He had answered them in an unexpected way. Felix had been more of a father to him than his own father ever was.

Stunned, Gabe lay there feeling like the universe had just expanded, rolling back the heavens and revealing the glory of a Creator who not only knew who Gabe was but had stretched out His hand to comfort him.

Basking in a warm glow, it took only seconds for fresh worries to lap at the shore of his contentment. "You still awake?" As much as he didn't want to wake Libby, he had questions only she could answer.

"Mm-hmm."

"So… I'm not going to be here much longer."

"You're not?" She sounded much more lucid now.

"No, now that the Hezbollah threat's been eliminated, we're going to write our reports and head home. The CO wants us gone before the media finds us."

"Oh." The single syllable, filled with both disappointment and uncertainty, pleased him for some reason. She enjoyed his company.

Gabe chose his words carefully, not wanting to offend her by suggesting she should go home. "Have you thought about what you're going to do now?"

"Well, I guess I'll go back to McLean."

Relief filled him, only to be snatched away by her subsequent words.

"But first I need to take some samples in a specific location and run some tests."

He rebelled at the thought. "Can't IWI find someone else to take your place?"

She huffed out a breath of disillusionment. "No, sadly I can't trust my employer to take samples from the right area. Salim showed me photos from a part of El Chaco I've never visited. There were dead cattle everywhere. If IWI's been taking bribes from Clark Petroleum to ignore the poisoning of cattle, then I have to be the one to run the tests. Otherwise, Salim died for no reason."

The emotion that entered her voice when she mentioned Salim brought an unpleasant realization. "You had feelings for him." The words popped right out of Gabe's mouth, sounding more jealous than he meant them to; after all, the leader of the NLB was dead, killed by his Hezbollah volunteers.

"We were like-minded." As a sob hitched in her throat, she lifted a hand to wipe a tear away. "I would have happily helped him get what he was looking for. He didn't have to kidnap me."

Gabe's chest clutched with betrayal. Had she fallen in love with the NLB leader? He'd heard of that happening with some kidnapping victims. "How would you have helped him?" Again, his tone was harsher than he intended.

Libby turned her head to frown at him. "By persuading my uncle to keep Clark Petroleum's promise to the Paraguayan people." Her voice took on a firmer note. "Forty percent of the corporation's stock is supposed to be owned by Paraguayan investors, and that's not the case anymore. Plus, if I prove that the oil wells are contaminating the water, I will force him to make remediations and repairs."

"Your uncle." An unpleasant feeling washed over Gabe. "Van Slyke is your uncle?" No wonder the man's eyes had reminded him of Libby's.

"On my mother's side." Libby eyed him in the darkness. "You make it sound like you've met him before."

Gabe fought to conceal his contempt for the man. "He met with my task unit about the oil rig explosion. You know, he's living in the big house on the hill here in Mariscal Estigarribia."

"Seriously?"

She clearly had no idea her uncle was even in Paraguay. "Yeah. Maybe you should stay with him." Gabe warmed to the idea as soon as it occurred to him. "Especially if you're still here after we pull out. I don't like the thought of you living alone."

"Well, I'm not alone. Jaime should be out of the hospital soon if he's not already. Plus, I won't be here for long, maybe a week at the most."

Gabe didn't know what else to say. Persuading Libby to abandon a task she'd set her heart on was impossible—he already knew that. What he didn't know was whether she might want to stay in touch. Feeling for her hand, he found it resting atop the coverlet. As he went to clasp it, she threaded her fingers trustingly through his. The sense that they were made for each other washed over him, forcing him to scrounge up the courage to mention the future.

"So when you do go home… what do you say I drive up to see you?" There. That sounded casual enough.

"Sure." Her answer was equally nonchalant, except that he could hear a smile in her voice.

"Good." A grin tugged at his own lips. Not only was God looking out for the both of them, but Libby Clark wanted to spend more time with him.

Her next words stopped his heart.

"I actually like you, Gabe Villalobos. Except when you annoy me." Her declaration ended with a great big yawn, after which she heaved a weary sigh. "Now let me sleep."

He squeezed her hand. "Me let *you* sleep! I haven't slept in three days because of you."

"Shhh. You're keeping me up."

He loved how she had to have the last word. Sassy woman.

Careful. His heart cautioned him even as it basked in content-ment. *You're falling head over heels for a woman whose father you can't trust, a woman used to having everything she wants. Don't forget the lesson you learned from Wendie Pheifer.*

Vowing to keep his eyes peeled for the least sign of manipula-tion, Gabe kept a hold of Libby's hand and let exhaustion claim him. *Now this is paradise.*

Paradise in El Chaco Boreal. If Libby could hold Clark Petroleum accountable for the waste it was probably spilling, it might remain a paradise forever.

CHAPTER 14

"Libby!" Gabe waited for a car to streak past him before darting across the street to where she was helping Jaime out of the Jeep.

Swiveling toward his call, she sent him a smile that put the subequatorial sun to shame while flooding him with giddy warmth.

"Hey, you're still here!" Her delight upon seeing him banished the lingering concern that she'd given her heart to the man identified that morning as Salim Ghazal, leader of the NLB. She wouldn't be beaming at *him* if that were the case.

"We're on our way out now."

Her smile immediately faded, making him regret more than ever the SEALs' sudden departure. Sensing Jaime's observant gaze, Gabe turned toward the man who was using the door of the Jeep to hold himself upright. "Need a hand?"

Jaime waved him off.

Libby frowned, her gaze swinging between them. "You know, I never did hear how you two know each other."

Lucía saved Gabe from having to answer as she rushed out of the house to assist her husband. Ignoring Libby's question, Gabe gestured toward her front stoop. "Can we talk?"

"Sure." With a searching look, she pivoted and led the way.

The stoop's eave cast a blessedly cool shadow over them as they stepped beneath it. Now that they were alone, Libby offered him a heartfelt hug, resting her head briefly on his chest. "I'm going to miss you." She stepped back far enough to meet his gaze while clinging to her smile, though he could tell it was wavering.

Falling into her lagoon-like eyes, Gabe considered all that she had been through. No question, God had protected her. "Have you gone out and run your tests yet?"

"Not yet. I need Jaime's help to find the Guaraní village. They're the ones who can lead us to the right place. He's handy with a gun, too." She wet her lips in a way that jolted his pulse and diminished his ability to think.

"Good. Hopefully, you can get that done soon."

"My uncle asked me to dinner tonight," she volunteered. "I'm going to take up Salim's complaints with him."

Gabe envisioned Paul Van Slyke's charismatic smile with inexplicable reservation. On the one hand, he was glad Libby had family in this region, someone influential enough to turn to if she needed help. "Something tells me he won't be very receptive." The man's presumption for thinking the SEALs were here to protect his interests still rankled.

She shrugged. "Probably not, but when did a little resistance ever stop me?" She lifted her chin.

"True." Resistance tended to double Libby's determination. It was time he told her what he'd regretted not telling her earlier. "Hey, remember when we were on the bridge in your father's backyard, and you told me we were both warriors? I want you to know you were right."

She play-punched him in the stomach. "Now you admit it!"

He caught her wrist as she went to hit him again.

Their gazes locked, communicating unspoken desires. If only he didn't have to leave her here alone.

"I wish you didn't have to go." Her smile gave way to a frown. "Seems like you just got here."

To Gabe, it felt like an eternity—especially those three days in which she'd been Hezbollah's hostage. Which reminded him— "My CO wants me to tell you not to talk to the press if they request an interview. Think you can avoid them?"

She gave a quick shrug. "Sure. I'd rather not relive my experience anyway."

"Thanks." Gabe admired the pattern of blues and grays in her irises. The cut above her eyebrow—it might leave a scar. Her freckle-dusted nose with its piquant tilt was adorable. The curve of her irreverent mouth was irresistible. He would miss every little thing about her. "Well, I guess I need to get back. Didn't want to leave without saying good-bye."

What he really wanted was another kiss—which Libby seemed all too willing to give him as she went up on her toes suddenly, looping both arms around his neck. Crushing her lips to his, she seemed to be telling him that her feelings were just as strong as his were.

The kiss took on an energy of its own, going from innocent to steamy in under five seconds. Gabe's heart began to gallop. His blood heated, and desire rolled through him like a freight train. Why did she have to be so impossibly irresistible? Leaving her felt like torture. With a growl in his throat, he severed the kiss and set her at arm's length. "You're still dangerous."

Her eyes widened with mock indignation. "How dare you. Go. Get out."

She gave him a little shove, dredging up a smile for him as he backed down the stoop, loath to take his eyes off her. "I'll see you around, Libby."

Her smile wobbled and a hint of tears shone in her eyes. "See you around, Lieutenant."

Gabe forced himself to turn away and march blindly toward the installation across the street. He loved how brave Libby was, how independent. She didn't cling to him like other women he'd dated— women who'd probably only liked him for being a Navy SEAL. Libby didn't give a hoot about status—perhaps because she already had it.

The reminder of her family's wealth tempered his heightened emotions. *Careful,* his brain cautioned. *Don't give her your heart just yet.*

Letting herself inside her rental, Libby fell back against her door and sighed. As her heart plummeted to her toes, tears rushed into her eyes. No wonder she'd never ventured into relationships with the opposite sex. Her heart ached with loss, and Gabe wasn't even out of the country yet.

"Lord, are You sure I should be falling for a man right now?"

The words coming out of her mouth drove home how perilously close she was to giving her heart to Gabe. While overjoyed that he planned to see her again, a relationship would hamper her work as an environmentalist. She would have to think twice about taking off for the places where she was needed. Being a SEAL, Gabe would be doing that already. When would they even see each other?

With an indrawn breath, Libby straightened away from the door. "With God all things are possible," she reminded herself.

So, there it was. She could leave it up to God to figure out the logistics of dating a Navy SEAL. In the meantime, she had a great deal of work to accomplish before she would allow herself to go home and see Gabe again. Fortunately, her uncle, who'd answered her phone call that morning, had invited her to dine with him in the big house on top of the hill. She would express her concerns about the oil wells and lay the groundwork for the reparations Clark Petroleum needed to make.

Pulling the sat phone from her pocket, Libby saw she had a message waiting. While listening to it, she gasped and checked the time. Uncle Paul's bodyguard would be picking her up in less than an hour, and she'd yet to decide what she was wearing.

"Master Chief, what time did we tell the liaison officer we wanted the bus here?"

At Mad Max's question for Bukowski, Gabe tore his gaze from the Paraguayan Special Forces training outside and looked to Bukowski for his response.

Thirty-three members of the task unit stood waiting in the installation's cafeteria to be taken by bus to the runway. The room was packed with bodies and gear, and not nearly enough air came through the open windows.

Bukowski stole a peek at his watch. "Half an hour ago, sir, but we're on South American time, remember?"

In South America, any scheduled event would run about an hour late. As Mad Max muttered an oath and resumed his pacing, Gabe went back to watching the training taking place outside. But he wasn't really watching the Paraguayan Special Forces. He was pondering the odds of Libby coming to harm before they got together again.

Someone stepped alongside him. "You okay, sir?"

Gabe slanted Doc a dry look. And here he'd thought he was fooling everyone, even himself, by behaving outwardly cavalier about leaving her behind. "Yeah, sure."

Doc's weird eyes, one denim blue and the other golden brown, studied his face with empathy that only magnified Gabe's despondency. They both looked over as the cafeteria door squeaked open. Instead of the liaison officer they were expecting, Bam-Bam rushed into the room, a barely contained grin on his face. The CO and Bukowski regarded him with confusion, then looked over at Gabe, who headed in Bam-Bam's direction under the guise of chewing him out. Poor kid, he'd only been doing what his platoon leader had instructed—to make sure Libby got safely into her uncle's car when he came to pick her up.

"Sir!" Bam-Bam's gray eyes shone with excitement.

"Dial it down, Caleb." Gabe blocked the CO and Master Chief's view by standing between them and the young SEAL. Rodeo joined them to reinforce Gabe's words.

"But you won't believe it." Bam-Bam bounced on the balls of his feet, too excited to be still.

Rodeo threw an arm around Caleb's shoulders to constrain his exuberance. "Believe what?"

"The guy driving the car—her uncle's bodyguard. He's The Annihilator!"

"The what?" Gabe and his chief asked simultaneously.

"The 2017 World Wrestling Federation champion!" Bam-Bam practically bellowed the words. "Elliot Bauer, The Annihilator."

Gabe frowned at him. Okay, so maybe *that* was why Van Slyke's bodyguard had looked familiar. He used to be on TV.

"I know it was him because I saw his championship ring—the size of an egg—right there on his right hand."

A vision of the bejeweled fist arcing toward Gabe's jaw had him sucking in a gasp of astonishment. "What'd the ring look like?"

But he didn't really need Bam-Bam's description of a thick gold band topped with a topaz the size of a boulder to be certain Van Slyke's bodyguard was Kyle Clark's would-be assassin. *That* was why he'd looked familiar. And—oh, crap—Libby was having dinner with the man who'd probably ordered Elliot Bauer to shoot her father. But that couldn't be right. Why would a member of Kyle Clark's family want him dead?

"Sir?" Rodeo studied him with a wary look in his eyes.

Gabe dragged his fingers through his hair while considering his options. With no time to explain himself to Rodeo, he broke away and hurried up to his CO and Bukowski. "Sir, there's a situation."

Rodeo fell into place immediately to his left, lending moral support.

Mad Max's glower conveyed an unwillingness to acknowledge any situation that potentially delayed their departure. "Like what?"

"You remember the assassination attempt on Kyle Clark?"

The CO frowned. "You're talking about this past summer when the FBI called me to verify your identity because you'd thwarted an assassination attempt on the man?"

"Yes, exactly, sir. I just realized who the shooter was—the man I wrestled with in the woods who nearly broke my cheekbone. It's Van Slyke's bodyguard. I knew he looked familiar, but I didn't know why until Bam-Bam mentioned he used to be a famous wrestler. That's how he flipped me over and got the better of me. And now Libby's alone with him and the uncle, who wants her father out of the picture so he can run Clark Petroleum from here on out. At least, I think that's his motive."

"Slow down, Gabe." The CO's deep-set eyes had narrowed into slits. "You're telling me that the new CEO of Clark Petroleum, that pompous cowboy we met the other night, wants the old CEO, Libby Clark's father, dead? Am I tracking with you?"

"Yes, sir. That's exactly what I'm saying. She can't be safe with him."

Mad Max stroked his walrus-like mustache, saying nothing. In desperation, Gabe appealed to Bukowski. "I can't leave her with her uncle, Master Chief. I have a really bad feeling about this. Please." He looked back at the CO. "Just give me permission to stay behind."

"Denied," said the CO flatly. "How would you get back?"

Gabe thought fast. "Through our CIA contact, Jaime Ramirez. I'm sure he's got connections."

Mad Max shook his head. "Forget it. We don't leave men behind."

"Unless they're on leave," Bukowski finished.

The CO slanted him a funny look.

"And I have your leave-chit application on my iPad."

My application? Gabe exchanged a puzzled glance with Rodeo but kept his mouth shut as Master Chief picked up the briefcase at his feet, laid it on a nearby table, and popped it open. His poker face betrayed no deliberations whatsoever as he pulled out an iPad that only needed to be roused before he went to work finding the application in question.

"All it requires is your signature and the CO's." He passed the iPad to Gabe, who skimmed the application with rising astonishment. Bukowski had filled in his name and all the pertinent information, like where he was taking his vacation. How could he have guessed Gabe would want to stay in Mariscal Estigarribia?

Swallowing his questions, he signed the application with the stylus Master Chief was holding out to him, then passed the iPad wordlessly to the CO, who looked as taken aback as Gabe felt. As the CO scrutinized the form, reading it over carefully, Gabe pictured Libby in the clutches of her uncle and his heart began to trot. *Just sign it already!*

"Says here that you're taking five days of leave." The CO's squinty eyes jumped up from the iPad. "You'd better get your affairs in order in that time, Lieutenant. You work for the United States Navy, not for Kyle Clark."

"Yes, sir." Beads of sweat formed on Gabe's forehead. How awful it would be for Libby, who'd survived kidnapping at the hands of Hezbollah terrorists to come to harm at the hands of a family member?

"Fine." Using the stylus, the CO scrawled his signature before he handed the iPad back to Bukowski, who signed his own name, then fixed his black-brown eyes on Gabe.

"Maybe in your free time you could look into that little matter you were wondering about last week."

Gabe regarded him blankly before realizing what Bukowski meant—oh, yeah, the extent to which USSOUTHCOM resided in Clark Petroleum's back pocket.

"Yes, Master Chief. I'll look into that."

"You need a copy?" Bukowski glanced around for a printer.

"Uh, no, let me just…" Gabe pulled the iPad closer, searching for the date and hour he was due back at the Team building. Then, with a grateful nod at Bukowski, he saluted the CO and waited with years melting off his life for Mad Max to set him free.

The commander finally acknowledged him with a tossed-off salute. "I want you back in one piece, Lieutenant."

"Yes, sir!" Gabe had already slung his backpack over his shoulder.

Rodeo followed him all the way to the exit. "You're going without us?" He sounded incredulous, like they were Siamese twins recently separated.

"Look, I don't have a choice. Just keep the guys in line for me, and I'll see you in six days." He backed out the door, making eye contact with Doc next, then sending a nod at Bam-Bam, who might have just saved Libby's life. Whirling away, he let the door slam behind him as he took off running for Libby's little house.

A knock at her door confirmed what he already knew: Libby wasn't here. Letting himself in with his credit card, Gabe's gaze went straight to where he'd left her sat phone charging the other day. To his dismay, it was still there. She hadn't taken it with her, which meant there wasn't any way to call her and warn her of her uncle's likely duplicity. He could, however, use her phone for his own purposes.

Snatching it up, he tapped out the passcode Jaime had shared with the SEALs back when they'd found the phone in the abandoned van. Then he accessed Libby's call history, noting a half-hour phone call placed just that morning to a number with an Austin, Texas, area code. That had to belong to her father. Blowing out a calming breath, he thumbed that number and waited with his heart racing for the call to go through.

"Libby, twice in one day?" Kyle Clark's deep voice conveyed pleasure.

"Sorry, no. This is Lieutenant Villalobos."

"Gabe? Oh, God. Is something wrong with Libby?"

So much for pleasantries, but then there wasn't any time for small talk. "Nothing's happened yet, at least I don't think so. She's having dinner with her uncle tonight."

"Oh yes. I was just on the phone with Paul, and he told me he was having her over."

Well, that news didn't jibe with Gabe's vision of Paul and his would-be assassin. "Sir, there's something you don't know, something I just realized. The man who tried to shoot you at your party, the one I wrestled with—he's Paul Van Slyke's bodyguard."

Silence. Then, "What?"

"It took me a while to realize why he looked familiar. One of my junior SEALs recognized him as Elliot Bauer, a former WWF wrestler who went by the name—"

"The Annihilator." Clark cut him off, his voice heavy with disillusionment. "Are you *sure* it's the same man?"

"Yes, sir, I'm sure."

A long, drawn-out sigh sounded on the other end. "I can't believe this."

Gabe couldn't blame the man for his denial. After all, his long-time friend and brother-in-law had sent an assassin to *murder* him. "Sir, I promise you, Elliot Bauer was the man who tried to shoot you, which means Van Slyke had to have put him up to it."

"Well, he certainly stands to gain quite a bit with me out of the picture." Kyle sounded reflective.

"What about Libby? Would he gain anything from taking her out of the picture?"

Her father went quiet "Oh no. I mean, yes." Kyle's voice was barely audible. "Libby is my heir. Then Paul after her. Gabe, you need to get her away from him!"

Gabe agreed with that statement completely. What he didn't like was the way it was delivered: like he had no choice but to jump at the oil tycoon's command. What if he wasn't presently on leave and couldn't get away? "Yes, sir." He said the words through his teeth.

"Do you have the time? I know you're busy down there."

Everything the man knew had probably come from General DePuy. "I'm on leave for the next five days. What do you need me to do?"

"Oh, thank God. Well, let's see. The first thing would be to get Libby away from Paul. I'll fly down there myself and face the man, but the closest place I can land is Asunción. Can you bring her to Asunción? I'll meet you there, and I'll bring the FBI with me if I can."

At least Kyle had faith in Gabe's abilities, but getting her to Asunción wouldn't be easy. "I'll do my best, sir." Maybe Jaime Ramirez knew a way.

"I can't believe this is happening. I'm supposed to be on the campaign trail, not protecting my daughter from her own uncle."

If Gabe didn't know Libby was the center of Clark's universe, the statement might have sounded self-centered.

"I'll do my best to protect her, sir. I need to get going, but I'll bring this phone with me."

"Yes, yes, go. Once she's safe, would you let me know? You may have to leave a message if I'm flying."

"Will do, sir. Out." After hanging up, Gabe slipped the sat phone into the pocket of his cammies. Looking around, he could tell Libby had left her home in a hurry. The place was nowhere near as tidy as the other day. A couple of unwashed dishes sat in the sink. A pair of sandals littered the hallway, nearly tripping him as he made his way to her bedroom to collect what she might need for their escape to Asunción.

Finding a canvas tote bag in the closet, Gabe proceeded to fill it, first with her work boots, then with a few changes of clothing from her dresser, including socks and underwear. At the last minute, he snatched up her mother's diary, having seen for himself how attached to it she was. The thought of Libby dying young, as her mother had done, lit a fire under his feet.

With one last look at the bed where they'd slept holding hands, Gabe wheeled away and left the house, locking it behind him. He sure hoped Jaime had recuperated enough from his surgery to help him out tonight.

CHAPTER 15

"I'm telling you," Libby insisted, carving into her steak with a dull steak knife, "the proof is out there, and I'm going to find it this week."

She had thought her uncle would object to her insistence that Clark Petroleum's waste barrels and containment walls weren't doing their job and that the flora and fauna of El Chaco were being adversely affected as a result. To her surprise, he'd listened intently while forking up bites of his entrée, a rib-eye steak deliciously prepared by an unseen cook, while two young servers scurried about filling their water glasses and bringing in the next course.

Sitting back in his heavy, ornately carved chair, Uncle Paul stifled a burp and reached for his wine. "You should do whatever your heart dictates, Libby. Whether you succeed in proving your mother's objections to drilling or not, she would be proud of you."

Libby basked in his compliment. "Well, thank you." She liked her uncle for one reason only. It wasn't because she fell for his insincere smiles and zest for the good life. It was because he could talk about her mother without plunging into grief the way her father did.

He tacked on a ponderous sigh. "I miss her, your mother."

A lump formed in Libby's throat, keeping her from taking another bite. A vision of her mother's sweet countenance formed in her mind. "Me, too."

A faraway look entered Uncle Paul's eyes before he loosed a reflective laugh. "Funny how we take people for granted until they're gone. Have you tried the wine?" He held up his glass and swirled it. The burgundy liquid caught and held the light of the gaudy chandelier.

Everything about the mansion her uncle admitted to purchasing was heavy and ornate, including the long table at which they sat, hewn from dense, gleaming quebracho wood. "This is Screaming Eagle Cabernet from Napa Valley," he informed her on a proud note. "One bottle cost me over three grand."

Libby stared in astonishment at her uncle's proud statement. "Three thousand dollars for a bottle of wine?"

"Thirty-four hundred." He set down his goblet.

Her opinion of his character sank to a new low. "You *do* realize that a well can be dug in Somalia for three thousand dollars— providing fresh water to mothers and children, keeping them from having to walk miles and miles in either direction, toting jugs on their heads?" She fought to keep her tone even.

Her observation had him throwing back his own head in a spate of laughter. After a moment, he wiped a tear of mirth from one corner of his eye. "Ah, now, *that's* why I enjoy having you around, Libby. That's exactly something your mother would have said."

The compliment caught her off guard, mitigating her condemnation of his values.

The urge to hear more about her mother had her asking, "What was it like growing up together? Will you share some memories with me?"

Uncle Paul pursed his full lips as he thought back. "Okay, I'll tell you, but first try the wine since I went to the trouble of opening it for you."

She pointed her fork at the young man hovering near them. "Actually, your serving boy opened it."

Uncle Paul wagged a finger at her. "She would have said that, too." Then he gestured at her goblet. "How is it?"

Lifting the long-stemmed glass to her lips, Libby took an obligatory sip. Yes, the wine was good, but no better, in her estimation, than her favorite nine-dollar bottle of Chilean malbec. "Lovely." She set down the glass and eyed him expectantly.

Her uncle drummed his fingers on the tabletop. "A memory, huh?" He took another bite, chewing slowly as he thought. "Okay, when I was eight and she was about six, she used to follow me everywhere—very annoying from a brother's perspective. I remember one day I was hanging out with my buddies up in a tree—a huge oak tree in our front yard in Austin—and she joined us. She didn't say anything, mind you, but I could tell my friends didn't like her there, so I gave her a nudge."

Libby gasped in horror. "You pushed her out of the tree?"

He held up a hand to ward off her dismay. "She wasn't that high up, and she survived the fall with just a sprained wrist. What impressed me, however, was that she never told on me. Most little sisters would have told, don't you think?"

"Definitely." Privately horrified, Libby pictured her blonde mother clutching her injured wrist and marching stoically away. "What about when you were older?"

"Hmm. Our relationship remained strained. You know what it's like in high school, how important it is to be one of the popular kids?"

Libby nodded as her uncle clearly expected, though, in her case, coping with her mother's death had been her biggest preoccupation back in high school.

"I was a junior when your mother was a freshman. There I was, trying my best to look cool and maintain the status I'd earned as an upperclassman. Your mother joined me at the high school, and it nearly ruined me."

"How so?"

He gave a self-deprecating laugh. "She didn't play the games everyone else played. Didn't give a fig for social norms. Instead, she collected misfits. Every new kid, every fat kid, every foreign kid or immigrant became her friend. I had to pretend we weren't related."

While offended on her mother's behalf, Libby had to smile at her uncle's quandary. Poor Uncle Paul. But her mother had it right and had raised her to believe likewise, that all people were God's beloved children. To Melinda Clark, there were no distinctions based on race or appearance, no judgments based on popularity. Admiration toward her mother for defying peer pressure made Libby yearn more than ever for her loving presence. If only her mother were still alive! She would tell her how greatly she admired her. And she would introduce her to Gabe.

The sudden appearance of Uncle Paul's bodyguard kept her from asking for another of her uncle's memories. The taciturn giant who entered the room with a scowl hadn't bothered to introduce himself when he'd knocked on her door two hours earlier and escorted her to her uncle's rented Mercedes. Throughout the ten-minute ride to the mansion at the top of the hill, he'd kept silent, ignoring her questions and observations. It wasn't until her uncle greeted her in the foyer that she'd learned the bodyguard's name—Elliot.

He'd been a former wrestling champion. And the reason he didn't speak, her uncle had explained, was because he'd bitten his tongue so badly in a wrestling match that he couldn't talk without a lisp.

Libby might have pitied the man if Elliot's flat gaze didn't unsettle her. Gabe would have told the man to stop staring. Gosh, she missed him already.

"What is it, Elliot?" Her uncle's reaction to being interrupted was nothing short of petulant.

By way of an answer, Elliot handed him a scrap of paper. As her uncle scanned the message, his expression grew shuttered.

"Well, let him in, then." As Elliot spun away, Uncle Paul sent Libby a forced smile.

Curiosity got the better of her. "Let who in?"

"Someone by the name of Jaime is here. He has a message for you, apparently."

"Jaime." Concerned, Libby swung a look at the door. "Something must be wrong."

"I'm sure everything's fine. Don't you like the wine?" He directed her attention back to her glass.

She was too distracted by the sound of the heavy front door opening in the foyer to answer him. Hearing footsteps, she kept her gaze glued to the doorway until Jaime walked gingerly into the room followed by Elliot.

Her colleague's intent brown gaze had her gripping the arms of her chair, preparing to rise. But then she glimpsed the pistol Elliot aimed at Jaime's back, and her mouth fell open. "Oh!"

"Elliot, put that away!" Her uncle heaved a long-suffering sigh. "I'm so sorry, sir." He stood belatedly to greet the newcomer. "My bodyguard is overzealous in his duties. Please, join us." He beckoned Jaime closer to the table. "Have a seat. I'll have a servant bring you a plate."

"Thank you, but that won't be necessary."

As Jaime approached Libby's chair, the light of the chandelier fell on his taut features. Libby didn't know if it was pain bracketing the edges of his mouth—after all, he was barely out of the hospital—or whether he conveyed bad news. "Libby, IWI is trying to get a message to you."

She started to look for her phone only to remember that she'd left it at her rental.

"Your father has suffered a stroke," Jaime added gently.

Shock slid over her with the feel of cold oil. "No."

"I volunteered to get word to you, then to fly you to Asunción immediately so you can return to him as soon as possible."

Through her shock Libby heard her uncle protest, "But that's impossible! I just spoke with Kyle less than two hours ago. He sounded perfectly fine."

"He suffered a massive stroke about an hour ago. His state is critical. Libby needs to move quickly."

Jaime's urgency drove home the seriousness of her father's condition. Pushing her chair back, Libby came unsteadily to her feet.

Jaime caught her elbow and drew her swiftly toward the exit.

Her uncle remained seated and silent.

"I'm so sorry, Uncle Paul." With a backward glance, Libby caught him scowling. "I have to go."

He sent her a curt nod, watching wordlessly as Jaime ushered her out of the room.

Jaime limped faster as they entered the hallway and headed for the home's enormous double doors. Hearing footsteps behind them, Libby looked back to see the pistol back in Elliot's hand and pointed in their direction. Not waiting for Elliot to open the door, Jaime pulled it open himself and practically pushed her outside, where the sky had already darkened to a bruised hue.

"This way." Shutting the door in Elliot's face, he tugged Libby across the cool, semi-lit yard toward the exterior wall and a pedestrian gate. It stood open, with the Jeep parked just beyond it. Someone was sitting in the driver's seat.

Behind them, the door they'd just exited creaked open. Jaime pulled Libby into a trot. "Run!"

Her mind swam in confusion. Why was Elliot pursuing them?

When they reached the Jeep, Jaime snatched open the passenger door and trundled her into the rear seat before hopping in up front.

As she settled into the back seat, Libby gaped at the man wearing a uniform and sitting behind the wheel. "Gabe!" Mystification undermined her delight at coming upon him so unexpectedly. "What are you doing here?"

His eyes flashed with urgency as he reached back and pushed her lower. "Keep your head down!"

Jaime hadn't even shut the door behind himself before the engine whined and the Jeep flew forward, spinning up gravel as it carried them away.

Libby groped for her seat belt. Why on earth was Gabe even here? And why were both men behaving like their collective lives were in danger?

Keeping her head low, Libby braved a peek through the rear window and spotted Elliot at the gate as they sped away from him, pistol raised as if to shoot.

But they were safely out of range now, barreling down the winding dirt road she'd traversed in her uncle's car just two hours earlier.

∾

"What is it, Elliot?" Paul sat at the table, cell phone pressed to his ear, willing Kyle to answer his call. Something about Libby's abrupt departure smacked of a conspiracy.

Elliot stood over him, trying to tell him something, only his pen had run out of ink. Giving up on scribbling a note, the giant tossed the implement onto the table and spoke with his impediment. "I daw dat navy deaw in da caw."

For once, Paul understood right away what his bodyguard said. "You saw the Navy SEAL? The one I recognized from the party photos on Facebook?"

They'd shared a similar conversation the night Paul had met with the SEAL task unit about the plight of Well 36. Elliot grunted his assent.

"The devil take it!" With the phone still ringing in his ear, Paul pointed an accusing finger at the former wrestler's face. "This is your fault. I should have known your fame would be a liability. What if he remembers you?"

Giving up on getting through, Paul jabbed the call to a close and pushed to his feet. "Why are you just standing there? Go get the car ready. We have to stop them before that man's testimony ruins everything!"

Elliot gave a nod and bolted in the direction of the five-car garage.

Huffing out a breath, Paul planted his hands on the long table and let it hold his weight. His thoughts raced before him. Had the SEAL already conveyed his suspicions to Kyle? Was that why Kyle wasn't taking his call, or had he really suffered a stroke? They'd been best friends decades earlier before their interests took them in different directions. Heck, they would have been equal partners but for the fact that Kyle had taken out the loan needed to start their business.

Paul, however, had been the one to find the most lucrative areas for drilling, including the untapped energy reserves of El Chaco Boreal. Without Paul's instincts, Clark Petroleum would never have prospered and flourished the way it had. Still, Paul had never complained about Kyle getting all the credit. In the back of his mind, he had known Kyle would pursue his political aspirations and leave Paul in charge.

Sure enough, he had. Yet now that Paul's power and wealth were unparalleled, he could never go back to being just a share-holder. Relinquishing the reins of control back to Kyle one day was unthinkable, just as the notion of *not* drilling in El Chaco because his sister opposed it was unthinkable. Who cared about the stinking environment?

Some things had to be done, regardless of the hardship it placed on others, especially if a profit could be made. Now Libby, like her mother, wanted to meddle in Paul's affairs.

He growled in his throat. *Nobody is going to tell me what to do.*

"What is going on?" Libby demanded. Her father suffering a stroke didn't explain why Gabe was driving the company Jeep and speeding them pell-mell down the dark and winding road. "I thought you would be gone already."

Before Gabe could answer, Jaime craned his neck to look back at her. "Libby, I'm sorry to mislead you. Your father didn't have a stroke."

Relief mingled with confusion, putting her thoughts in a tail-spin. "He didn't? So, why—why did you tell Uncle Paul that?"

Gabe replied before Jaime could. "To get you away from him."

"From my uncle? What's wrong with him?"

Tension radiated from Gabe's stiffly held body as he guided the Jeep down the hill in the direction of town. "Remember the assassin who tried shooting your father at his party?"

"Of course." How could she forget?

"He's your uncle's bodyguard."

Libby struggled to associate Elliot with the shadowy figure Gabe had wrestled with in the woods.

Gabe was still talking. "I thought he looked familiar when your uncle visited my task unit last week—asking us to protect his wells, basically. But it took some extra intel for me to make the connection."

They all braced themselves as he took a sharp turn on two tires.

Goose bumps stitched over every inch of Libby's skin. Gabe's dire words could only mean one thing: That her family had turned against itself. That wasn't possible. "I don't believe you."

He shot a frown at her through the rearview mirror. "I wouldn't make this up, Libby." Exasperation and pity underscored his words.

"No." She shook her head, unwilling to accept what he was suggesting. "My uncle would never harm my father. They were friends even before my parents met. And he's my mother's brother! He was just telling me how much he misses her. Why would Uncle Paul want my father dead when Daddy's given him everything he has?"

"Why do you think?" Gabe spared her another glance. "With your father out of the picture, he could be CEO of Clark Petroleum forever unless the shareholders oust him."

Jaime turned his head to ask her, "How much stock in Clark Petroleum does your father own?"

Libby thought for a moment. "I have no idea. Why?"

"Because you would inherit that stock when he dies, giving you a big say-so as to who the CEO should be. You could vote your uncle right out of the position. On the other hand, if *you* were out of the picture, your uncle would inherit your father's shares."

Another rash of goose bumps sprouted on Libby's skin. In denial of Jaime's words, she clung to what she knew. "Uncle Paul would never hurt my father. And he would certainly *never* hurt me."

"How do you know?" Gabe was losing patience with her.

"Because we're family!"

A weighty silence followed her declaration, alleviated only by the sound of wind whistling through the cracked windows as they careened toward the brightly lit town.

"What does my father say about all this?" Surely Daddy didn't believe Gabe's ridiculous allegations.

"Let's just say he wasn't willing to risk your life tonight." Frustration clipped Gabe's words. "Unlike you, he didn't dismiss my suspicions out of hand. He's bringing the FBI with him, and we're meeting him in Asunción tomorrow to discuss Van Slyke's motives."

"You seriously think my uncle was going to harm me tonight?" Libby couldn't fathom it. "*You* knew I was having dinner with him. My *father* knew it. If my uncle had tried to kill me, he'd go straight to jail and end up with nothing. Besides, I wasn't in any danger whatsoever. I was enjoying myself!"

Gabe set his jaw and fell silent. Slowing at an intersection, he ignored the stop sign and swung them out onto the town's main road.

Libby noted where they were. "Where are we going?"

It was Jaime who answered. "To the airport. I'm flying you to Asunción tonight."

Libby sat forward, her blood flashing to a boil as she divided a glare between the two men. "You know what? I've had it up to here with being told where I'm going next!"

Her words prompted Gabe to grip the wheel so hard his knuckles shone white in the deepening gloom. "And I've had it up to here with you resisting what's in your best interest."

Jaime chuckled. "You two crack me up."

Libby threw herself back in her seat and folded her arms across her chest. She glowered at the back of Gabe's head while the sweet memories of their last encounter raked her heart. "I don't *want* to leave the area. I have critical work to do here."

"You can come back after the FBI investigates your uncle."

With growing disappointment, she watched the lights of Mariscal Estigarribia brighten as they approached the city limits. Elliot couldn't possibly be the shooter in McLean. What had led him to that conclusion, apart from the man's size? And now Gabe's confusion was leading to her premature departure when there was work yet to be done.

It was like Matamoros all over again.

"*Aye, demonios*, what's this?"

Gabe's dismayed exclamation drew Libby's attention back to the road. It was clogged with traffic, mostly with vans painted with the logos of news stations.

"It looks like the press just arrived," Jaime concluded.

Word of her abduction had apparently reached the world at large.

Gabe glanced back at Libby. "Keep your head down, *querida*. Don't let them see you."

The endearment slipping out of him convinced her to cooperate. Libby ducked her head below the window.

Jaime took the company phone from the clip on the dash and accessed its map application. "I'll find a way around this mess. In the meantime, turn right."

"Can't I go home first?" Libby wanted to call her father in private to discuss the situation. Who knew? Daddy might relent and let her stay another week.

Ignoring her question, Gabe turned down the street Jaime indicated, speeding them away from the press.

Sitting up again, Libby looked on in sullen silence as they turned down alleys more fit for foot traffic than for cars. As Jaime placed the phone back in the clip, she could see the map routing them toward the airport. How bizarre that she was being plucked out of Mariscal Estigarribia against her will. But what if Gabe was right, and her uncle *was* behind the shooting in McLean? Doubt pricked her briefly. *No way.* Uncle Paul would have to be utterly without a conscience to turn on his best friend and brother-in-law.

All at once her heart accelerated, pounding like pistons in a high-octane engine.

Libby clapped a hand over her jumping breastbone. *What on earth?* It had to be a belated adrenaline rush. Or maybe this disagreement with Gabe was taking a toll on her emotional health. If they were going to attempt a relationship, they were going to have to reconcile their differences. Given the way Gabe was behaving now, refusing to listen to her point of view, their long-distance relationship would never even get off the ground.

CHAPTER 16

Avoiding the downtown area, it took them ten minutes to reach the other side of town. By the time Gabe merged back onto the highway, they were still two miles from the airfield where his task unit had landed—was that really just ten days ago? Given all that had happened, it felt more like a month had passed since then.

Jaime pointed out the lumpy silhouette two football fields away. "There's the hangar."

Gabe sped toward it. The sooner he got Libby in the air, the safer she would be.

"No one's here," she commented from the back seat. Her resentful tone made it clear she considered Gabe's allegations about her uncle completely bogus. She sure as heck resented having to leave Paraguay before her work was done.

While he could understand that, he didn't question for a second what his gut was telling him. And even though Libby was safely in his and Jaime's clutches, he couldn't shake the uneasiness banding his chest. Scanning the dark, flat terrain, he wished he'd thought to stuff a pair of NVGs in his pack. Anyone could be lying in wait, hidden in the shadows.

A few stunted palm trees and tufts of coarse savannah grass grew on either side of the runway. As they sped toward the hangar, a spotted ocelot darted across the tarmac in front of them, betrayed by its light-reflecting eyes. Gabe veered around it. At least the airport looked deserted.

But he wasn't willing to bet on it. "You two stay put." Parking the Jeep next to the hangar, he set the brake and cracked open his door. "Let me take a look around."

"I'll go," Jaime volunteered, snatching the key ring out from the ignition and jingling it. "I've got the key to get us in."

Reluctant to let Libby out of his sight, Gabe deferred to Jaime's wishes. The case officer climbed stiffly out of the passenger seat, a reminder to Gabe that he was still recovering from surgery. With a prick of guilt, Gabe watched him hobble toward the door at the side of the hangar and unlock it. Silence filled the interior of the Jeep, stretched to the snapping point as Libby continued to simmer in the back seat.

Plucking the sat phone out of the clip on the dash, Gabe stowed it in his front pocket. That comment Libby had made about Uncle Paul being family had set off sirens in Gabe's head. It reminded him exactly what kind of family Libby came from: a rich and powerful family who used their influence to control other people's lives—people like him.

Her refusal to believe Elliot was the shooter with whom Gabe had wrestled rankled. She had chosen loyalty to her family over him. How well did that bode for a future relationship?

The noise of one of the bay doors rumbling open gave Gabe an excuse to bolt from the vehicle in order to help Jaime push open the other side. Returning for Libby, he found her already out of the car, standing in her high heels with her arms folded mutinously across her chest. Not trusting her not to take off running back to town, Gabe grabbed his pack and her tote up in one hand while seizing Libby's arm with the other and towing her toward the hangar. She pulled free of his grip, still clearly reluctant but playing along.

The *tack-tack-tack* of her heels echoing off the concrete floor stirred an uneasiness in Gabe. The suspicion that they weren't alone assailed him suddenly. His free hand reached for the pistol holstered to his belt. Every nerve in his body twitched in anticipation of trouble, but he could see no immediate cause for his concern.

"This way." Jaime urged them to follow him toward a plane on the left side of the enormous metal shelter. "The place has electricity, but I say we keep the lights off."

"Agreed." With his ears open, his eyes peeled for danger, Gabe escorted Libby past two midsized, privately owned aircraft to an even smaller one.

A faint crackling sound had him drawing his pistol with the speed of a Western gunslinger while swiveling toward the noise. "Did you hear that?"

The whites of the case officer's eyes shone in the shadows as he peered around. "A bird, perhaps? There are several nests in the rafters."

It could have been a bird. Gabe holstered his pistol while keeping his hand on the grip. At least Libby was cooperating now, unlike in Matamoros when she'd broken his nose.

"This is it." The ghostly outline of a Cessna 182 took shape before them. Jaime walked around it, inspecting it for readiness.

With relief, Gabe recognized the four-seater, single-engine aircraft as one commonly used by skydivers. Its respectable safety record helped to ease his jitters. The flight to Asunción was only 530 kilometers—330 miles—or so. How dangerous could it be?

Jaime unlocked the door for them, and Gabe tossed in his pack and Libby's tote before helping her climb from the strut into the cabin. She went right in, her acquiescence relieving him, as she sank down on the bench seat in the rear.

Gabe went looking for Jaime. "Need help?"

"No, I've got it." The case officer waved him inside.

With one foot in the plane, Gabe hesitated. *Do I sit up front, brooding over Libby's lack of faith in me, or sit in the back with her?* Like a moth drawn to a flame, he chose the back. The royal blue dress she'd worn to her uncle's dinner was cut similarly to the red cocktail dress she had worn at her father's soiree. It hugged her curves and showed her long legs to advantage.

He focused on her high heels. Good thing they wouldn't have to run.

A minute later, Jaime joined them, leaving Gabe to shut the door as he dropped into the pilot's seat.

"You know how to fly this, Jaime?" Libby's anxious question suggested that the fight had gone out of her.

Jaime reached back, putting a friendly hand on her knee. "Libby, once again, I've misled you and I'm sorry. My job with IWI is just a cover for me. I'm *not* an environmentalist, which you already questioned. I work for the government. And, yes, I can fly this plane."

Libby's wide eyes swung in Gabe's direction. "So that's how you two know each other. You didn't meet at *La Cantina*."

Chuckling in lieu of answering, Jaime faced forward again. The evening's adventures seemed highly entertaining to him. He flipped the master switch, lighting up the panel, then hit the auxiliary fuel switch. After several seconds, he turned the ignition handle to start.

The plane's single engine roared to life, sounding inordinately loud inside the hangar. Under normal circumstances, they would have wheeled the plane through the doors and out onto the tarmac before starting the engine, but they were in too much of a hurry for that.

With a lurch, they rolled forward, turning slightly to avoid clipping the other planes and then straightening to sweep through the bay doors. The wings cleared the opening with room to spare. They were easing onto the moonlit tarmac when a metallic *plink* and a faint flicker of light drew Gabe's eye to the window beyond Libby.

"What was that?" It sounded like something hard had struck the wing of the plane, but Jaime, who was wearing a radio headset, looked back at him blankly and shook his head, and Libby merely shrugged.

Gabe's heart beat faster as Jaime lined them up with the long runway. Without waiting for the oil temperature to rise, he pushed the throttle forward, causing the little plane to accelerate. Faster and faster, they rolled until the tarmac streamed under them like a dark river. Then, without warning, they were weightless, climbing up, up, up into the star-dusted sky.

Directing his gaze out the large window next to him, Gabe watched the town's lights shrink to pin-sized specks of illumination in an otherwise pitch-black void. He could see no reason for the tension still gripping the muscles where his neck met his shoulders. It had to be Libby's earlier assertion—*"Because we're family!"*—keeping him so agitated.

If it wasn't bad enough that her work consistently put her in harm's way, she was and would always be the daughter of a billionaire who thought nothing of asking Gabe to rescue her yet again. And that was more than Gabe could stomach.

Paul Van Slyke watched the lights of the Cessna rise higher and higher, headed toward the stars twinkling in the night sky. Then he lowered his gaze to where Elliot was making his way back to where Paul sat in his Mercedes, hidden in a grove of quebracho trees.

He'd instructed Elliot to fire a single shot into the plane's gas tank, and minutes earlier, he'd thought he heard the suppressed shot being fired. It was done, then. The plane would run out of fuel in thirty minutes to an hour, too far away to allow for a quick turn-around. The pilot would be forced to land on rugged terrain where the plane would break into hundreds of pieces, the way Melinda's plane had done in the Pantanal region of Brazil. And everyone on board would die.

A peculiar taste lingered on Paul's tongue.

He hadn't planned on sacrificing his niece in the same way he had dispatched his sister. The coincidence worried him. What if someone made a connection and started to investigate? Not that he regretted having to kill Libby. If she'd drunk enough of that poison-laced wine, she would die eventually, anyway. He could not afford for her to inherit what rightfully belonged to him. Still, he hadn't meant for her to perish in an ugly plane crash.

Luckily, he wasn't burdened with what others called a conscience. But Libby, who had provided Paul with countless hours of entertainment over the course of her life, deserved a painless death. She'd reminded Paul so often of his sister that he'd scarcely even mourned Melinda's passing. Life would be dull without Libby.

He heaved a sigh that his plans had veered off course, if only slightly. His consolation was the SEAL's death. With that man out of the picture, Kyle Clark would eventually forget about the SEAL's allegations—if he'd even heard them in the first place. Besides, Kyle would be so distraught over his daughter's death that he'd have no choice but to lean on Paul as he'd done in the past. Paul would surely remain at the helm and continue as CEO indefinitely.

The heavy tread of Elliot's feet reminded him of the last loose end that required snipping. His bodyguard had proven to be nothing but a liability. And now he had outlived his usefulness.

Glancing over at Libby, Gabe did a double-take. Not only was she hugging herself hard, but her chin was tucked to her chest in an attitude of uncharacteristic terror. "Hey." He laid a hand on her shoulder. "What's wrong?"

When she didn't answer him, he wondered whether she was playing games—acting terrified to break through the barrier between them. Except he could feel her trembling, which suggested this wasn't an act. Cupping her chin, he forced her to look over at him. Her panicked gaze sent a shaft of uncertainty through him.

"What's wrong?"

"I don't like small planes." She spoke in a faint, breathless voice.

It took him a second to realize why small planes were a problem. Her mother had gone down in a plane like this. Comprehension and compassion edged aside his lingering annoyance. "You're not going to die." He infused his tone with confidence.

She nodded, clearly just to placate him, as she still looked terrified.

Moving his pack and the tote to the floor, Gabe scooted closer on the bench seat and put an arm around Libby, knowing it would undermine his resentment the instant they touched.

Sure enough, when she leaned into him, laying her head against his chest, he had trouble remembering why they'd sparred in the Jeep. Her resentment was understandable. She'd been enjoying her uncle's company, hearing stories about her mother, whom she clearly missed every day of her life. Gabe would have to be a jerk to hold it against her for wanting to stay. With his resentment frittering away, he kissed her temple and called a truce.

"It's going to be all right." *We're going to be all right.*

Just two seconds later, Jaime cursed with virulence, and Libby went rigid in Gabe's embrace.

"What is it?" Gabe sat forward, removing his arm from around her.

The case officer shook his head while staring at the display. "One of the tanks must have a leak. It was full when we took off."

Suspicion wormed its way into Gabe's thoughts. He leaned across Libby's knees to peer out the side of the plane where that strange sound had come from earlier. Cupping a hand to block the light from the cockpit, he spied a thin trail of gasoline weeping from the wing where he knew the fuel bladder to be located.

"It's a leak all right." Foreboding tightened his scalp. Giving Libby's knee a reassuring pat, he rolled forward to lean over Jaime's shoulder so he could discuss the problem without having to shout. He didn't particularly want Libby to overhear him, either.

"I think somebody shot at the plane as we were leaving. Could Van Slyke have beaten us to the airfield?"

"Definitely." Jaime studied the display with a grim expression. "We could turn around," he suggested, "though I don't think we'll make it."

Glancing back at Libby, Gabe found her hugging herself for dear life. In the glow of the cockpit's lights, her face was as pale as a ghost's. She had definitely overheard them. "What other options do we have?"

Jaime sighed. "Well, the second tank is full, but based on the mileage we've gotten so far, we won't make it all the way to Asunción, not with the wind in our face."

"Are there any landing strips between here and there?"

"No. We'll have to make an emergency landing."

Gabe's stomach knotted. At least the terrain could be worse. They could be flying over a jungle instead of a desert-like savannah. Still, the odds of someone getting hurt were high. He didn't fancy being battered to death in a crash any more than he'd wanted to be buried alive in a tunnel.

"You two could jump," Jaime suggested, "but I've only got one parachute. You'd have to share it somehow."

"No." Gabe had no intention of leaving Jaime to land alone. He watched the man snatch up the radio handset.

"Let me advise air control at Asunción. Maybe someone has a better suggestion."

Gabe listened in as Jaime hailed the air traffic controller in Asunción. The radio crackled and hissed, its reception poor at best. Jaime tried again, speaking in Spanish and receiving a broken reply.

Glancing back at Libby and finding her face in her hands, Gabe sat back down on the bench seat. "Hey, we're going to be okay."

She dragged her fingers from her impossibly wide eyes. "This is exactly what happened to my mother. Except there was water in her tank, not a leak. And no parachute. It makes me wonder…"

"What?" he pressed her when her voice trailed off.

She shook her head. "Nothing. Never mind."

Whatever she was thinking it caused her to shudder visibly.

"I won't let anything bad happen, Libby." *No way.* After the trouble he'd gone to snatching her out of Matamoros, then wresting her from the terrorists, he sure as heck wasn't going to let her die at her uncle's hands. "I've jumped out of a plane dozens of times. If we go that route, we'll be just fine, even sharing a parachute."

"I think I'm going to throw up."

Gabe snatched a vomit bag out of a pocket in front of them and shoved it into her hands. But she didn't throw up. Instead, she fixed her lagoon-like eyes on him and said, "What if Uncle Paul sabotaged my mother's plane, too?"

He considered it a distinct possibility, but he wasn't going to tell her so. "Don't think about that right now. We're not going to die. We've got plenty of fuel left. We can make an emergency landing if we have to."

Only Jaime wasn't having any luck getting through to Asunción.

"Something's wrong with the radio," he called from up front. Ripping off his headset, Jaime tossed it aside with disgust.

They would have to set the plane down without any input from air traffic control, counting on topographical maps to find the best place for a landing. Nor would there be any emergency vehicles waiting on the ground to tend to them if anyone got hurt. At least they had Libby's sat phone. Once they were down, their location pinpointed by AccuTracking, they could summon help.

Gabe resigned himself for a hard landing. "I guess we'll see how good a pilot you really are, Jaime." As a platoon leader, Gabe had learned that needling his men resulted in them giving their best efforts. "Libby, switch seats with me, *querida*." He wanted her farther from the leaking wing.

She slid over wordlessly and buckled herself back in, her movements jerky with fear.

"We'll be all right." Of its own accord, his hand came out to stroke the back of her head. But then his training kicked in, prompting him to take preemptive measures.

Riffling through the cabin, Gabe located a fire extinguisher and a first-aid kit. He laid the single parachute at his feet, just in case, while refusing to dwell on the odds of all three of them arriving back on the ground in one piece. That was something only God knew the answer to—along with whether he and Libby had a shot at a future together, considering their very disparate pasts.

Libby closed her eyes and prayed. The plane was going down—not in the theatrical way she'd envisioned her mother's plane floundering, but a smooth descent disturbed only by occasional air pockets that vaulted her stomach into the air and filled her veins with adrenaline.

Through her haze of panic, she gleaned that Jaime had chosen a place for them to land by studying a map on the cockpit's display. The area lay two hundred kilometers outside of Asunción. After they landed, they could call for help using her sat phone, which Gabe had assured her was tucked inside his pocket.

At least the terrain wasn't marshy here like it was in the Pantanal, where her mother's plane had ripped open when it hit a swamp.

"Two thousand feet."

She appreciated Jaime announcing their altitude so she wouldn't be caught unawares.

"Fifteen hundred," he added minutes later.

She gulped against a dry mouth.

Gabe remained next to her. "Time to hug your legs, *querida*." His instructions were grim but calm. "Keep your head as low as you can."

Obeying, she thought of Lucía and baby Maya and prayed for Jaime's safe return to them.

Is this what it was like for you, Mama? Did you pray for deliverance only to perish the instant your plane struck the trees? Don't let that happen to us, please, God. I have work still to do!

She stole a peek at Gabe. Was this the end for them? Would she never get to hear him say her name again or, for that matter, the words *I love you?*

Unlike her, Gabe wasn't braced yet in a crash position. He watched their descent through the windows, fire extinguisher on his lap, the first-aid kit stashed into the pack at his feet, looking poised for whatever calamity came their way. There wasn't any question he would do everything in his power to get them out of this predicament alive. Her mother hadn't had Gabe to protect her, but Libby did. She drew courage from his presence.

"I see the ground," he stated calmly.

"Roger that. I see it, too." Jaime's tone was as placid as Gabe's was, though he had to be frantic at the thought of leaving his little family back in Mariscal Estigarribia.

Libby forced her body to relax. The impact would hurt more if she was all tensed up.

"We're looking good." Jaime glanced back at them. "I'm going to bank and come around so we're heading into the wind. Two hundred feet."

The little plane abruptly listed, causing Libby to flash out a hand and grope for Gabe. He caught it, holding on to it firmly. The plane slowly righted itself. Even though she couldn't see outside with her head between her knees, Libby could sense their descent. She fancied she could feel the land rising under them, rough and unpre-dictable.

"Any second now," Jaime announced controlling their descent.

Libby squeezed her eyes shut.

"Easy, easy." Gabe's caution was full of warning like he'd caught sight of something in their way.

Ka-BAM!

On her next breath, they slammed into the earth, rebounded into the air, and crashed again. Even buckled into her seat, Libby came off the cushion as their momentum kept them careening forward, bouncing hard and landing a third time. The sound of hydraulic brakes combined with the thunder of wheels reverber-ating over brush and sand.

The wing on Gabe's side struck something unseen—a small tree, perhaps—and the plane spun around abruptly, its back end lifting into the air. Libby screamed. The tail arced through the air, and the entire plane tipped, striking the ground with such force that Libby's world went black.

CHAPTER 17

L ibby roused to the sound of hissing and clicking. Feeling pressure in her skull, she pried her eyes open only to gasp in horror as she found herself still strapped to her seat, hanging virtually upside down. Gabe's dark form lay sprawled below her atop the Plexiglass window. The plane was lying on its side.

"Gabe!" she cried his name, but he didn't stir.

"Gabe, wake up!" Her voice sounded like someone else's. What about Jaime? Peering forward, she realized the darkness obscuring her view through the windscreen was the crumpled nose of the plane. With the plane's front end stoved in, Jaime appeared trapped between the yoke and his seat. Worse still, the engine, which was located in the nose of the plane, was smoldering. Wisps of smoke rose through vents like thin ghosts, conveying a chemical scent that seared her nostrils.

The pilot's dark head lifted. "Jaime!" Libby sobbed in relief when he released his seat belt and slipped out of the death trap, using his hands to catch himself when gravity pulled him down onto the plane's roof. A larger man might have been crushed to death.

Groaning, he righted himself, bracing his feet to take stock of their situation. "Gabe!" Powering his way to the back, Jaime crouched with a grimace, then picked up the fire extinguisher lying across Gabe's chest and gave him a shake.

When Gabe lurched to wakefulness, Libby sucked in a breath. He was alive! *Oh, thank You, merciful Lord!*

His gaze locked on her as he sat up. "Everyone okay?"

"We're fine," Jaime answered for her. "But the engine's smoking, and even though the fuel is in the wings, we should probably get out of here." Straightening, he reached over Libby's seat to unlatch the door next to her, now pointed skyward. He tried to throw it open, then groaned in defeat when it didn't budge.

Libby's heart lurched the way it had in the car earlier, pounding against her breastbone like a jackhammer. What if they were trapped inside this plane and it caught fire?

Gabe rose to stand alongside Jaime. It took both of them to shove the door straight up. With a long moan, it flipped open, falling onto the hull. As cool air wafted in, Libby filled her lungs with the smell of freedom, and her terror subsided.

Jaime handed Gabe the fire extinguisher and clambered past Libby, out onto the side of the plane. After passing the fire extinguisher up to him, Gabe released Libby from the seat belt and then caught her in his arms when she fell. The security of his embrace made her want to weep with gratitude.

Thank You, God, for this chance to find our future.

"Let's get out of here." With that scant warning, Gabe hoisted Libby through the opening where Jaime helped to pull her out.

Finding herself seated on the rounded curve of the Cessna, Libby scanned the dark savannah surrounding them. Apart from the stars above, not one speck of light pierced the desolate wilderness. The smell of engine fuel competed with the wild fragrance of El Chaco Boreal.

"Stay right here." Jaime, still clutching the fire extinguisher in one arm, slipped down the curve of the hull and landed on his feet to look back up at her. "Just like a slide at the park, Libby. Come, I'll catch you."

By the time she found the courage to slip off the plane into Jaime's arms, Gabe had joined them, leaping with agility into ankle-deep sand beside them. As he reached for Libby's hand, she noted the pack on his back. Jaime had rounded the plane with the fire extinguisher and was hosing down the engine with foam.

As Gabe drew Libby to a safe distance, her heels sank into the soft ground with every step. Tough, calf-high grasses whipped her bare calves, but with the steady flow of blood through her veins and the gentle warmth of Gabe's hand cradling hers, she scarcely noticed. What a blessing to be alive!

Fifty feet from the fallen plane, they stopped and looked back. A crescent moon hung low over the horizon, its light glossing the single white wing that jutted upward.

An unexpected peace quilted Libby's heart. Their isolation didn't worry her. Lifting her gaze in gratitude to the brilliant and innumerable stars glittering in the sky, she reveled in the realization that her entire life still lay before her, brimming with possibility, blessed with the potential of love.

God knew what He was doing, after all, by putting Gabe into her life. He had saved her again and again.

She tugged at Gabe's arm to get his attention. "After this, I think we can handle anything that comes our way, don't you?"

Gabe spared her a distracted glance while rubbing a spot on the back of his head. "I like your optimism." As he spoke, he adjusted the straps on his shoulders. "Just remember your words in the hours to come."

Uncertainty slid beneath her skin. "Who can we call for help? Is my father in Asunción yet?"

Gabe's gaze flashed in her direction. "Do you always call your father when the going gets tough?"

The harsh question had her taking a closer look at him. Just mentioning her father had triggered him.

On a gentler note, he added, "I'm sure Jaime knows someone who can help. And I've got the sat phone." He reached into his front pocket and teased it out. "Looks unharmed." As he pressed a button, the screen lit up.

"I do know someone." Jaime approached them. He must have left the empty extinguisher behind. "Marcos lives in Asunción."

Hope fluttered in Libby's chest as Jaime took the phone from Gabe and tapped out a number. When his contact answered, Jaime explained their situation and then relayed their coordinates, visible right there on the sat phone's screen. Silence followed as the contact worked to determine where they were, relative to him.

Jaime had put the phone on speaker mode so Gabe and Libby could hear.

"Okay, so you're four miles from the nearest highway. If you walk due east, you'll run into La Ruta Nacional. Does anybody have a compass?"

Gabe raised his left wrist. "There's one on my watch."

"Good. Walk dead east for about four miles, and you'll run into the highway. I'll look for you at this same latitude in about two hours. It's going to take both of us that long to get there."

"Thank you, my friend." Ending the call, Jaime passed the phone back to Gabe, who put it back into his pocket.

Without a word, they all turned and started walking. After twenty minutes, Libby's feet began to protest. "Of all the nights we had to crash. I hardly ever wear high heels." Then again, who could have guessed how her dinner with her mother's brother would end?

When she stopped to shake sand out of her shoes, Gabe struck his forehead with his palm and groaned. "What is wrong with me? I packed your boots and some clothes for you. They're back in the plane. I'll go back for them."

Jaime shot him an incredulous look. "Seriously?"

Libby regarded the plane, a mere speck in the distance, over her shoulder. "Gabe we've walked half a mile already. I'll just go barefooted."

"No." Jaime and Gabe spoke the word in unison.

Gabe was already shaking the pack off his back. "Look, you two just relax for like ten minutes. I'll run back to the plane and get Libby's tote. It won't take any time at all."

With a gesture of surrender, Jaime eased himself onto the sandy ground. Gabe was already striking out in the direction from which they'd come.

"Be careful!" Watching his silhouette blend into the darkness,

Libby's fears rose in proportion to the distance between them. She peered over at Jaime, who'd laid back on the sand with his hands notched behind his head, his eyes closed. "What if he gets lost?"

"He's the one with the compass on his watch, Libby. He won't get lost."

But Jaime's tone seemed to suggest something else could happen to him. Libby's imagination ran wild. "Are there jaguars out here?"

"Mm, probably just ocelots, like the one we saw at the airport."

That was not encouraging. "Poisonous snakes?"

"Not too many."

She glowered down at Jaime's relaxed form. "You're supposed to be encouraging me."

He gave an evil-sounding chuckle. "Don't forget about venomous cactus thorns."

"Jaime!"

"Relax. Gabe is a Navy SEAL, not a three-year-old lost at the mall."

The reference to a child made her think of Jaime's new baby. She swallowed her fears as she considered the "government" agent. How close Jaime had just come to leaving sweet Maya fatherless, and all for her! Guilt speared her heart. "I'm so sorry, Jaime, for getting you involved in all this."

His eyes opened, reflecting the expanse of stars pulsing over-head. "Stop right there, Libby. Unlike you, I'm not out here for altruistic reasons. You don't owe me an apology."

"If you say so." His words made her realize why he *was* out here, to promote the interests of the United States, which meant protecting U.S.-owned oil wells from Hezbollah terrorists. "Oh my gosh." A thought occurred to her. "Are you the reason we never found contaminants in our water samples? Did you intentionally take me to the wrong locations?"

Jaime heaved a long sigh. "My primary job is to keep tabs on the Lebanese community here. But, as often happens, the interests of America's most powerful men find their way into my agenda, so I won't lie and pretend I didn't steer you away from the problem areas. But I will promise that the next time we go out and take samples, I'll lead you straight to them."

She stared down at him dumbfounded. "So you *know* the wells are leaking contaminants."

"Yes."

A vision of sweet Salim, who had died protecting her, brought a wave of regret crashing over her. If only Jaime had helped her to identify the problems sooner, then Salim might never have been driven to wage war against Clark Petroleum. The Hezbollah volunteers might never have joined his cause.

Regret broke open, morphing into grief. With a fist pressed to her suddenly queasy stomach, Libby sank onto the ground and dropped her face into his hands. *Salim!*

His visage, the way she'd seen it last, with the life draining from his beautiful eyes, returned to her. The horror and finality of his death sickened her, along with the damning realization that the United States was responsible, at least in part, for his and his brother's deaths. Paraguay was their country of birth, yet *her* country had sullied its untarnished beauty.

A sob tore from Libby's chest, followed by another. She kept her face hidden, appalled that she was crying like a child now. Salim's pointless death, the loss of his passion, his intelligence, and his drive struck her as the saddest thing in the universe.

Jaime sat up with a groan. "Libby, you're breaking my heart. Please don't."

She tried to stifle her sorrow but couldn't. Ashamed by her emotional meltdown, she used the three-quarter sleeve of her dress to mop her face. "I'm sorry. Just ignore me." Another upwelling of grief had her sobbing anew. At least Gabe wasn't here to witness her humiliation.

Jaime heaved a sigh and scooted close enough to put a companionable arm around her shoulders. "Perhaps it would help to talk about it?" He sounded like he would rather have all his teeth pulled than hear her woes.

Yet he needed to know Salim's side of the story. Finding her voice, Libby explained the brothers' vision for Paraguay and how devoted they were to protecting their country. "If Clark Petroleum hadn't started drilling here and taking all the profits for itself, Salim would never have raised an army or invited Hezbollah to join him. He wasn't one of them, Jaime. Both he and his brother died trying to protect me."

Jaime studied her profile with a frown. "Well, I have to agree that Clark Petroleum may have started the problem. But I'm deeply sorry if my actions made the situation even worse." Leaning away from her, he produced a napkin from his front pocket and pressed it into her hand. "Here. I carry this in case the baby spits up on me."

His words pulled a watery laugh out of Libby. After shedding a few more tears, she wiped her eyes and blew her nose.

When Jaime pulled abruptly away from her, she looked up to see Gabe's silhouette, backdropped by sandy terrain, running in their direction, clutching what looked like her tote bag.

Watching Jaime distance himself from Libby, Gabe sternly reminded himself that those two were colleagues, even friends. Not for a minute did he believe the case officer had been making moves on his woman while Gabe was away. Even so, jealousy flared in him. While he'd been setting a world record for running a mile in a dark desert, his companions had been sharing confidences.

He'd seen Libby wiping her face like she'd been crying. How grossly unfair. *His* shoulders were the ones she ought to cry on. The fact that she'd turned to Jaime for that had him dropping her bag abruptly at her feet.

"Your boots are in here. They're heavy." He stood catching his breath from what had seemed like an endless run.

"Thank you so much, Gabe. I'm sorry to be such trouble."

Her sincere apology eased his resentment somewhat. As she pawed through the bag, finding both socks and boots, he reclaimed his pack and took out the first-aid kit to pull out some bandages. "Better cover your blisters first, or the boots won't help."

Minutes later, they were on their way again.

"This is so much better. Thank you, Gabe."

"Sure." The air seemed to get colder with every step, reminding him that it was still winter here in the Southern Hemisphere. Glancing at Libby's bare legs, he tried to remember if he'd tossed any long pants in her bag. "You warm enough?"

"Not really." She was gritting her teeth to keep them from chattering.

"We should walk faster. That'll keep us warm."

Jaime, who was visibly limping, gave a groan. "Can't go any faster than this."

The comment drew Libby's worried gaze to the case officer. "Poor Jaime! I feel so bad about getting you involved in all this."

Yes, poor Jaime, having to console Libby while I ran all the way back to the plane.

Jaime shot Gabe a wary glance. "No worries. I'm just happy to be alive."

"Me, too." Libby glanced inquiringly at Gabe. "What about you, Gabe? Are you grateful?"

Instead of answering the question, he asked one of his own. "What were you two talking about while I was gone?"

Libby swung an uncomfortable look at Jaime, then back at Gabe. "I was telling him how Salim and Nasrallah died to save me from the others. I question my timing, but the tragedy just hit me over the head for some reason."

"You can talk to me about that stuff, you know." Maybe she simply didn't know.

"Can I? You seemed... jealous the last time I mentioned Salim.'

He *was* jealous. "Libby, the man held you captive for three nights."

"Technically just two. I was in a closet the first night."

"Well, you talk about him like you were his guest, not his captive."

"Because he made me feel like his guest. He was very apologetic and treated me as a gentleman would."

"Really?"

"Yes, really!" She rounded on him suddenly. "What are you

implying, Gabe? That I fell in love with him? Maybe that's what *he* wanted. He thought we could join forces and purge El Chaco of the oil wells together. But I told him no, Gabe. You want to know *why* I told him no?"

"I think you're about to tell me." The thought of her and Salim having such an intimate discussion while he was out of his mind with worry made his stomach hurt.

"Because I was already in love with you!"

Oh. The ache in Gabe's stomach vanished. But Libby was storming ahead of them, clearly furious for having to justify herself. Hearing that she loved him made all his resentment seem foolish in retrospect.

Jaime had the audacity to roar with laughter. "You two are painted with the same brush."

For once, Gabe didn't take umbrage with the statement. They walked in silence for a minute before Jaime gestured at Libby.

"Don't you know the first thing about women, man? She wants you to go after her. Tell her you're sorry and you love her, too."

Whoa. Gabe had no issue with apologizing, but declaring his feelings was a step he wasn't prepared to make just yet. All the same, he took Jaime's advice and picked up his speed, overtaking Libby just in time to keep her from catching her dress on a thorny cactus.

"Libby, wait." He caught her elbow, tugging her out of harm's way while slowing her down. "Listen, I'm sorry for acting jealous just now. You went through a lot, and Salim didn't deserve to die any more than his younger brother did."

She shot a frown at him. "You shouldn't be jealous. He's *dead*, Gabe. He couldn't have been more than twenty-five years old."

"You're right. I'm stupid for that."

Even in the dark, Gabe could tell Libby had accepted his apology but was still wrestling with the tragedy.

"I feel like it was my fault." Her choked voice tugged at his heartstrings. "He tried so hard to protect me."

"Querida." Throwing an arm around her shoulders, Gabe tugged her closer. Walking hip to hip warded off the cold closing in around them. "That was most definitely not your fault, no more

than it was your fault that they broke into the lab and killed the guard."

She nodded, even though Gabe could see tears glittering in her eyes. His irrational jealousy of the dead man vanished for good. Truth was, he owed Salim a debt he could never repay. He'd given up his life to protect Libby. The realization humbled him.

While pressing a kiss to Libby's temple, Gabe cast Jaime a look of thanks for urging him to make amends. Next, he checked his watch to verify that they were headed in the right direction. Even with the extra mile of running back to the plane for Libby's tote, they ought to be nearing the highway soon. He searched the horizon until he spotted intermittent reflectors spanning the savannah in front of them.

"Look, there's the highway. See it?"

"Thank God." Libby quickened her pace to get the last part of their long trek over with.

It had been around 11:00 P.M. when Jaime used the company sat phone to call his colleague for help, and they'd walked for what felt like an eternity since then. Moreover, a chill had stolen over the land, making her worry that they might freeze to death before Jaime's friend showed up.

Lamentably, not a single car brightened the dark strip of La Ruta Nacional, the only highway cutting straight south across the wilderness, headed for Asunción.

When they finally reached the road, Jaime stifled a groan as he lowered himself gingerly onto it. "Ah, the asphalt's still warm from yesterday."

"Really?" Libby bent to lay a hand on the road. "Oh, it is!" She immediately sat, hoping to warm her bare legs and tugging Gabe down next to her.

"Here." Gabe placed her tote bag on the other side of her. "Use your other clothing to keep you warm."

As she draped a T-shirt and a pair of shorts over her legs, Gabe riffled through his own pack and came up with two bottles of water. He handed one to Jaime, the other to Libby, then scooted close enough to put his arm around her, shielding her from the chilly breeze.

Libby huddled against his warmth and shared the water with him. Catching him feeling the back of his head, she looked up in time to see him wince. "What's wrong?"

"Hit my head pretty hard in the crash. That's probably the reason I forgot your tote in the first place."

Concerned, Libby felt the spot he was rubbing and encountered a lump behind his ear the size of an egg. "Oh, Gabe. Is there something in your pack for that?"

"Don't worry about me. I'm hardheaded."

"There's got to be Tylenol in the first-aid kit." She started to reach for the kit in Gabe's pack when he stopped her.

"Trust me, I'll be fine. If you want to make me feel better, you'll agree with me that your uncle tried to kill us all tonight."

Libby leveled a frown at him. Remarkably, her first impulse was to defend her uncle, yet she couldn't ignore what they'd experienced firsthand. "It appears you may be right." She swallowed a lump forming in her throat. "I just don't understand how my own flesh and blood could do that."

"Well, he has a motive. You have to admit that."

Libby nodded, still unable to articulate the depth of the betrayal biting into her. If Uncle Paul could undermine his best friend and brother-in-law, then why not her? For that matter, why not his own sister? The gross horror of her uncle causing them such loss broke Libby's heart in two. Dropping her face into her hands, she submitted to a fresh wave of tears.

Gabe's hold tightened. "Some people have no conscience, Libby. Your uncle is obviously a psychopath."

Gabe was probably right. Uncle Paul had admitted to pushing his sister out of a tree when they were younger. And he'd expressed no remorse in telling that story.

Exhausted and overwhelmed, Libby pressed her face into the crook of Gabe's neck and wallowed in sorrow. To her gratification, he rocked her gently while sweeping a comforting hand up and down her spine.

His low voice murmured in her ear, "It's okay. It's over now."

Was it okay? He hadn't returned her confession of love earlier— a circumstance that compounded her grief. But the way he'd behaved in the past two hours, running back to the plane to get her tote, exhibiting jealousy, then apologizing, then comforting her—it all gave her hope that Gabe was simply being cautious. She knew him well enough at this juncture to guess that vulnerability was something he actively avoided.

Once she earned his trust, he would tell her he loved her. Libby was counting on it.

CHAPTER 18

L ibby cringed, turning her head instinctively from the bright light that accompanied the sound of a curtain being whisked open. Memories of the plane crash chased a pleasant dream from her head and brought her fully awake. Lifting her head, she looked around, disoriented for a moment. Oh yes, at the crack of dawn, two hours after Jaime's contact had picked them up and driven them to Asunción, Gabe had tucked her into this queen-sized bed in a hotel room.

"Rise and shine, *querida*."

Going by Gabe's voice, he had fully recovered from their ordeal. As he came to stand over her, she noticed he'd swapped his military attire for a pair of jeans and a green T-shirt that matched the color of his eyes. Given his tolerant smile, their disagreement the previous day was water under the bridge now.

He sent her a grimace. "Bet you're feeling a little sore."

Libby stretched tentatively, which prompted a groan. "Ugh. Every inch of my body hurts."

"That's normal considering what we went through."

"Yet you look recovered. How's your head?"

He probed the back of his head. "Almost back to normal. Told you I'd be fine."

She stifled a yawn. "Why can't I sleep in?"

"Your father's meeting us in the lobby in half an hour."

"Oh." She sat up stiffly. She wore the T-shirt she'd used to cover her legs with the night before. "When did you talk to him?"

"He called your sat phone this morning. That's what woke me up."

"Really? I never even heard it ring."

"I know. I have breakfast waiting—well, more like brunch."

Glimpsing the tray to which he gestured, Libby's eyes fastened on the waffles and omelets. A whiff of maple syrup made her mouth water. "I'm ravenous!" She tossed back the bedding, relieved to see she wore her shorts, too, though she couldn't recall putting them on. Bolting off the bed, she darted into the bathroom to relieve herself.

A minute later, she joined Gabe at the desk, where he'd pushed the recliner alongside the desk chair and was sitting in it.

"Have a seat." He'd left the desk chair for her to sit in.

As she sat down, she noticed the sat phone lying next to the ample fare. "This food looks delicious. Where's Jaime right now?" She picked up the silverware rolled in a cloth napkin.

"His friend's driving him back to his wife and baby as we speak. He said you could keep the sat phone since you need it more than he does."

Envy pinched Libby as she imagined how long it might take before she herself could return to Mariscal Estigarribia. If the cattle by Río Verde were dying and the Guaraní there were falling sick, then time was of the essence. She freed her fork and knife and started cutting into the waffles, hunger making her movements hasty.

On the other hand, why rush into another separation from Gabe when she could use this time to get to know him better? Her forehead furrowed as she realized how very little she actually did know. "Do you have siblings, Gabe, or are you an only child like me?"

A smile touched the edges of his mouth as he carved out a bite of omelet. "I have a kid sister, Isiris, who's two years younger. She's married with a baby boy and lives close to my mom and stepdad in Miami."

"So you're an uncle." Picturing him holding his nephew, Libby chewed her first bite and smiled. "What's that like?"

"Rodrigo's great. He takes after me."

She snorted at the egotistical assertion and forked up another bite. "Do you get to see him often?"

"Not as much as I would like to."

The same would be true for him and her, she realized, her smile fading. As a SEAL, Gabe would be deployed more often than not. Then there was her own work requiring stints abroad.

The ringing of the sat phone kept her doubts from taking hold. Recognizing the number of the caller, she sent Gabe an apologetic grimace before picking it up. "Hi, Daddy."

"Hi, sweetheart. I'm down in the lobby. But take your time coming down to see me. I think I'll just shut my eyes and rest for a moment. I've been up all night."

Guilt rose to the forefront of her mixed emotions. "Rest then, Daddy. We'll finish our breakfast and then come down. Did you get something to eat yet?"

"Oh, yes. Don't worry about me. I'll see you shortly."

He sounded so tired! "Okay. Bye."

Libby sifted through her feelings as she severed the call. Already, the time she and Gabe could spend alone together was dwindling. What was she thinking, believing they might have a future together? Either God knew something neither of them had realized, or she was setting herself up for a long and lonely life.

Loving a Navy SEAL might be more than she could do.

Searching Libby's face, Gabe could tell that, despite her stoic expression, her present predicament was taking its toll. "You didn't tell your dad we crash-landed," he pointed out.

Her shoulders rose and fell in a quick shrug. Picking up her fork, she stabbed at another sector of her waffle. "There's time for that later."

She was keeping thoughts to herself, a circumstance that secretly worried him. Even so, he dared to broach the topic he'd tried touching on before. "I hope you can see now why returning to your work would be a bad idea."

Even though he kept his tone light, Libby's eyes met his, then narrowed as she held his gaze defiantly. "I don't see why I can't. Once Uncle Paul realizes he's a suspect in my father's shooting, he'll vanish. The man is a coward at the core. I should have realized that before."

Gabe's blood pressure rose, giving him an instant headache. "He tried to kill you, Libby—tried to kill *all* of us. Until he's arrested, you shouldn't go anywhere but home to McLean."

Pursing her lips, she drew a sharp breath, then pushed her chair back, taking her tote bag with her. "I'm going to take a shower and wash my hair."

Gabe shook his head as he watched her march back into the bathroom. It was suddenly apparent that nothing he said would keep Libby away from her work. How was he going to protect her when his leave was good for only four more days after today? A larger question overshadowed that one: How were they going to date each other if they weren't even on the same continent?

As he finished his meal, then the rest of hers, he listened to her shower, then blow-dry her hair. The dryer finally switched off, and she emerged from the bathroom with her blonde mane looking soft and silky and a grudging smile on her face.

"Thanks for putting my mother's diary in my bag."

Pleased she'd noticed, Gabe wiped his mouth with his napkin. Hope beat back the doubts plaguing him. "I know it means a lot to you."

Her smile softened. In five steps she closed the space between them, bent over him, and pressed a kiss on his lips that tasted of the complimentary toothpaste. As always, his desire for her surged, underscoring his determination to make a relationship work despite the obstacles of time and distance.

Reaching past him for the sat phone, Libby plucked it up and slipped it into her pocket while withdrawing from Gabe's embrace. "Daddy's waiting."

Right. And keeping Kyle Clark waiting another ten minutes was out of the question, apparently. Swallowing down his resentment, Gabe tossed back his coffee. "Let me go brush my teeth."

Three minutes later, they rode the elevator in silence to the lobby. Gabe started to reach for Libby's hand, then thought better of it as the elevator doors swept open. There on the far side of the lobby, tucked into an overstuffed armchair, Libby's father dozed. His expensive navy-blue suit was creased, his head of silver hair mussed. He must not have slept much on his overnight flight, though his three new bodyguards, standing at a discreet distance in the company of an older man, looked on alertly as Libby and Gabe approached their employer.

"Daddy!" Libby roused her father by shaking him gently, then lowering herself onto his lap when he awoke with an exclamation of delight.

Gabe felt like a third wheel as Clark folded his daughter into a bear hug. From the corner of his eye, Gabe sized up the man's watchdogs. These weren't the rent-a-cops that had protected Clark's party in McLean. Their casual polo shirts and slacks didn't disguise the fact that they were probably former Special Forces. All three wore pistols at their hips while the older man wore a suit. Van Slyke didn't stand much of a chance of killing his brother-in-law now.

"Sweetheart, I'm so grateful you're alive!"

The fervent words drew Gabe's attention back to Libby's father, whose bloodshot gaze finally took note of Gabe standing before him with his hands in his pockets.

"Lieutenant Villalobos!" Without releasing his daughter, Clark stood up, causing Libby's feet to slide to the floor. Keeping her anchored to his side, he offered Gabe a forceful handshake that showed no sign of easing up. "Son, looks like I owe you again." His voice throbbed with emotion.

Gabe waved off any mention of a debt. "Not at all." He shot a meaningful look at Libby while tugging his hand free. *Well, are you going to tell him?*

She wet her lips. "Um, Daddy, we have some really bad news to share with you."

"Oh?" Her father divided an anxious glance between them.

"We believe Uncle Paul sabotaged our plane last night." Both her tone and her expression downplayed the terror they had all felt at the time.

Clark's light-brown eyes widened in horror. "What?"

Gabe took over. "Somebody—probably his bodyguard—put a bullet in one of the wings, causing us to lose fuel. We had to crash-land four miles from the closest highway."

"But we're fine," Libby added, "thanks to my colleague Jaime, who piloted the plane and found us a ride to this hotel."

Her father turned to the man Gabe had recognized but hadn't identified. "Did you hear that, Harry? My brother-in-law tried to kill my daughter. With a plane crash!" His ruddy complexion had gone pale.

"Sit down, Daddy," Libby urged.

The man named Harry moved closer. As Libby's father released her and collapsed back into the overstuffed chair, the agent introduced himself to Gabe and Libby. "Special Agent Harry Hodges. FBI. We met the night of the shooting in McLean."

How could Gabe have forgotten? Hodges had tried suggesting Gabe was in cahoots with the shooter. His pale-blue eyes remained fixed on Gabe's face.

"Mr. Clark tells me you've identified the shooter at his party as Van Slyke's bodyguard?"

"Yes." Gabe nodded. "I didn't recognize him at first—just thought he looked familiar, but then a teammate mentioned he was a former wrestler with a championship ring on his finger, and it all came together for me."

"And you believe his employer, Paul Van Slyke, sabotaged your plane last night?"

"Yes. I heard something hit the wing, and a little while later, we were losing fuel too quickly to make it to another airport. Van Slyke must have reached the airport before we did—not impossible since we ran into the media and had to go around them."

Kyle Clark was rubbing his forehead, clearly processing how close he'd come to losing his daughter.

"There's something else." Libby's announcement wrested everyone's attention to her. She bit her lower lip as if deliberating whether to say anything. "While I was dining with Uncle Paul, he kept trying to foist some wine on me. I think it might have been poisoned or something."

The words yanked Gabe's scalp tight. "What? Why didn't you mention this earlier?"

"Because I didn't drink more than a sip, but even that made me feel funny."

"What were your symptoms?" Hodges wanted to know.

"My heart started to pound really fast."

Hodges seemed skeptical, which eased Gabe's apprehension.

"And I think maybe..." Libby eyed her father as if unsure whether he was ready to hear what she'd realized. "When we had to crash-land last night, it occurred to me that my uncle might have been responsible for my mother's death, as well."

Horror bleached her father's face. "Libby!"

"Just let me finish." She laid a calming hand on his shoulder. "We know the cause of her crash was water in the fuel tanks, correct?"

"Yes, it was an unfortunate circumstance caused by a downpour the day before and someone leaving the fuel cap open."

"But what if it wasn't an unfortunate mistake? I've read Mom's diary, Daddy, the one recovered from the wreck. I know you haven't read it because it's too painful for you. So maybe you never knew how much she opposed drilling in El Chaco. She logged all of her objections and intended to beg you to stop the prospecting, except she never made it home. Only Uncle Paul knew how opposed she was. He could have easily kept her from dissuading you."

Clark's brown eyes went into a long stare before he sank back into his chair as though the life had been sucked out of him.

Libby bent down to embrace him. "I'm so sorry, Daddy."

Worry dropped like a stone into the pit of Gabe's stomach. It was never more apparent that until Libby's uncle was apprehended, her life would remain in danger. And he'd be helpless to protect her.

Clark sought Agent Hodge's attention. "He might have killed my wife, Harry—his own sister! Can you prove that after all this time?"

Hodges hesitated. "Finding evidence will be challenging, but I'll do my best. Luckily, there's no statute of limitations for murder."

Libby straightened while fixing an anxious gaze on the special agent. "So, what happens now? I need to go back. I've got important work to finish."

Her words compounded Gabe's distress.

"No." Her father shook his head implacably. "Until your uncle is in custody and denied bond, you're staying as far away from him as possible."

The words eased a portion of Gabe's fears.

But, as he'd already concluded, Libby could not be dissuaded from her work. "You could come with me to Mariscal Estigarribia, Daddy. Who's going to run Clark Petroleum if Uncle Paul's incarcerated?"

"Oh, I'm going there, all right, but until your uncle's arrested, you're not going anywhere near him."

She swung a desperate look at the FBI investigator. "How long is that going to take?"

Hodges shrugged. "Might not take so long. If the bodyguard cops a plea to save his own hide, it could be just a matter of days."

"So, I'm just supposed to stay in Asunción and do nothing?" Libby cast an exasperated look around the tasteful lobby.

"Wait." Her father roused from his thoughts to pat down his pockets. "I knew you'd hate the idea of not working, so I planned a trip for you." He pulled a folded piece of paper from his breast pocket and handed it to her. "Gabe just told me that he had some time off, so I planned a getaway you can both enjoy."

Gabe's thoughts ground to a halt at the unexpected offer.

"A getaway?" With an expression of abhorrence, Libby took the paper and scanned it.

"Honey, you need it." Her father leveled her with a benign yet firm stare. "You've risked your safety for others. It's time you took care of yourself."

"I do that every time I visit you in McLean, Daddy. I don't *need* a vacation. People are getting sick. They're going to start dying if Clark Petroleum isn't held accountable for its actions!"

"Four days won't make any difference. Please, I need you to be safe while I deal with Paul's betrayal. Read the itinerary." He nodded at the paper she was holding.

A frown puckered Libby's smooth brow as she scanned the document. "You booked a vacation at an all-inclusive resort in Curaçao?"

"Yes, and it's right on the beach. There's horseback riding, golf, a spa, tennis—all the recreation you can imagine. And, best of all, it's next to a forward-operating base for the U.S. military. Gabe can hop a flight back to Virginia Beach with just his military ID."

Clearly torn, Libby studied the paperwork before lifting an inquiring look at Gabe. "What do you think?"

Gabe couldn't find his tongue. A vacation with Libby at a resort on a Netherland-owned island just off the coast of Venezuela sounded like paradise. Still, for her father to assume Gabe would jump at the opportunity—that annoyed him. Taking Libby on an island vacation was something he wanted to offer Libby himself one day, like on a honeymoon. The thought caused a little thrill as it popped into his head. Yet it didn't hold nearly the same appeal when it was her father's idea.

He searched for a flaw in Clark's planning. "What happens when my leave runs out? I just fly off and leave Libby by herself?"

"I'll take your place in Curaçao when that happens. Or perhaps Paul will have been arrested by then, and Libby can fly back to Paraguay."

"To finish my research." She sounded more open to the prospect. Even so, she turned toward Gabe. "What do you think?"

At least she was asking his opinion rather than assuming, as her father had, that he would do whatever was asked of him. So he shrugged. "Why not?" A trace of resentment crept into his tone betraying his true feelings. *If this is how it's going to be with her father controlling our lives, we're never going to make it.*

Libby searched his face. "It can't be that bad." Whether she was trying to convince herself of that or him, he wasn't sure.

"True." He would have to be an idiot to turn it down. Any other man would be thrilled to have a girlfriend whose rich father was sending them on vacation to an all-inclusive resort. Rodeo and Doc would be sick with envy when they heard where Gabe had spent his leave. He shrugged, accepting her father's solution. "Should be fine. When do we take off?"

CHAPTER 19

I t was a first for Gabe, not being in the lead as his horse trailed Libby's to the height of a cliff overlooking the Southern Caribbean Ocean. Unlike Libby who'd been raised riding horses, Gabe had never mounted a horse before. And while he experimented with the reins, nothing compelled his gelding to go any faster. He watched helplessly as Libby pulled away from him, her long hair flowing in the wind, making riding a horse look effortless.

My beautiful Libby. Just watching her stirred feelings in his chest. Unable to catch up to her, he applied himself to memorizing every detail of this moment—the heat of the sun on his tan forearms, the crisp tang of the nearby ocean, the sound of his gelding's hooves clip-clopping beneath him across the semiarid terrain of Curaçao. Memories of the last few days filtered through his mind, filling his heart to overflowing.

Visiting the sea aquarium, spelunking in the Hato caves, and swimming with dolphins. Any of those activities might have been fun without Libby, but doing them with her made him happy in a way he'd never been before.

When they weren't exploring, they had talked—in a way he

hadn't talked with anybody, let alone a woman. He'd shared memories of his childhood—all except for his nine days in jail. Compared to her idyllic childhood, his younger years had been far tougher, yet surprisingly, they'd shared more similar experiences than Gabe would have thought.

Evenings had brought dishes to die for, romantic strolls on a moonlit beach, and kisses that made him feel like, in Libby, he had found a place he never wished to leave. They'd talked about their aspirations, their hopes for the future, daring to believe they would spend time again together—and what they'd discovered in each other would never end.

And then there were the nights when he'd lain in his own bed in the room next to hers and ached for her company. Intimacy would be so natural, so fulfilling. But it would also forge their bond into something permanent. And, in the face of their uncertain future, Gabe lacked the faith it took to give his heart to Libby's care and keeping—not when the occasional look in her eyes told him she was chafing to get back to her work.

Seeing her waiting for him at the height of the bluff while their guide proceeded down a path to the beach, Gabe approached her with a self-conscious grimace. "Sorry, I can't make him go any faster," he shouted.

She raised her voice in return. "Kick your heels into his belly, but not too hard."

He did as she said, and, with a jolt, this gelding began to trot. In seconds, it brought him alongside Libby's mare. When she stretched out a hand to him, he took it, loving the sense of completion that filled him whenever their hands were linked.

"Just look at this view, Gabe." With her chin, she gestured to the endless expanse of ocean. In every shade of blue—teal, turquoise, and aquamarine—the South Caribbean Sea stretched from the beach below to the distant horizon.

But he couldn't take his eyes off her long enough to admire it. "I've got the best view right here."

Looking back at him, she caught his meaning and smiled self-consciously. Her grip tightened. Even before she wet her lips,

Gabe knew what she was going to say. His gut tightened reflexively.

Her blue-gray gaze seemed to plumb the very depths of his soul. "I love you, Gabe."

Even anticipating her words, they stripped the air from his lungs while vaulting his heart into the stratosphere. Not since she'd raged at him about why she'd rejected Salim's offer had she mentioned her feelings for him. Her declaration both elated and terrified him. He knew she expected him to answer in kind, but the words seemed to tangle in his throat, stymied by a decade-old mistrust.

Instead of speaking, he stood up in his stirrups, leaned out over his horse, and crushed his lips to hers. Maybe she would sense his feelings in his touch. But when he released her a moment later, the expectant look in her wide eyes told him she was still waiting. He scrounged for the words, *I love you, too, Libby*, only his lips refused to form them. He cleared his throat. Still nothing.

Libby's slim eyebrows pulled together. "Hah!" Without warning, she jabbed her heels into her mare, wheeling it away from him.

"Careful!"

Heedless of his call for caution, she headed at a trot for the path their guide had descended moments earlier.

Gabe urged his gelding to follow suit, but the horse had a mind of its own, proceeding down the narrow, sandy path to the beach at a leisurely pace. Gabe kept one eye on Libby as her horse all but galloped for the beach below them.

"Libby, slow down!" His request was drowned out by the rushing of the waves and the pounding of her mare's hooves.

Clearly, she was upset with him, and honestly, he couldn't blame her. Even in his dense male mind, Gabe recognized he'd missed the perfect time and place to share his feelings. For that matter, he should have told her he loved her after she'd given him a scare at the Dolphin Academy two days before, going pale and clapping a hand to her heart. If she hadn't immediately recovered, he might have feared her uncle had poisoned her, like she'd suggested back in Asunción. It must have been the thrill of being led around by a thousand-pound mammal that had made her heart race.

Jabbing his heels into the gelding's flanks, Gabe coerced it into picking up its pace. Maybe it wasn't too late to overtake Libby and articulate the words he'd failed to say earlier.

It had to be heartbreak causing Libby's heart to beat so erratically. The same thing had happened at the Dolphin Academy, only to subside after a minute or two. It would pass this time.

Directing her mare straight into the waves, they plowed through the water. But that exhilaration couldn't begin to dispel the anguish of not knowing whether Gabe loved her the way she loved him. Given the months at a stretch that they were bound to be apart, all they would have to hold on to were words. If Gabe couldn't articulate his feelings toward her, this beautiful, blossoming relationship was doomed to wither and die. The tenderness of his kisses wasn't enough.

Spumes of saltwater drenched Libby as her mare barreled a second time through thigh-high waves. Her heart still palpitated wildly. Worse, a peculiar numbness was settling on her tongue, making it feel swollen. Maybe she was dehydrated. She tugged the bottle of water from her saddlebag. As she twisted off the cap, a razor-sharp pain shot up her fingers to her wrists. Growing increasingly concerned, she tossed back a quick sip, only to sputter and cough when swallowing proved difficult. The bottle slipped out of her hand, tumbling into the waves.

Not one to pollute—ever—Libby hauled on the reins to slow her mare, only to notice an implacable numbness stealing over her like the water rushing over the sand.

What's wrong with me?

The mare, perhaps conscious of her plight, slowed from a gallop to a trot, upsetting Libby's balance. Having shifted on the saddle, Libby fought to right herself, but neither her arms nor her legs responded.

She listed toward the water, hoping to jump clear of her horse in lieu of falling, but her body refused to answer her brain's commands. Gravity caught hold of her, dragging her off her mare. However, her right boot was still caught firmly in the stirrup, sending her head and shoulders plunging into the warm water while she was still attached to her horse.

~

"Libby!"

One minute, she was galloping far ahead of him, her hair flowing in the breeze. The next she was being dragged through the water upside down. He wouldn't have believed it if it wasn't happening right in front of his eyes.

"Hah!" Jabbing his horse repeatedly, Gabe coerced it to break into a canter.

Beyond Libby, their guide glanced back. With a shout of consternation, he wheeled himself around.

Libby's horse, realizing something was amiss, started hobbling out of the waves, dragging Libby's head on the sand as it went.

The vision of Libby dangling lifelessly from her horse was a whole new level of horrific, and Gabe had seen his fair share of horrors. He and the guide converged on her at the same time, both of them vaulting off their animals in tandem. As Gabe hit his knees to scoop Libby's head and shoulders off the sand, the guide worked to free her foot caught in the stirrup.

"Libby!" Her wide, staring eyes shocked Gabe. Frantic to get a response, he lightly tapped her cheek. Nothing. Her irises reflected the blue of the sky above them.

With her shoe finally freed, the guide lowered her body onto the sand while Gabe cradled her torso.

"Libby, can you breathe?" He inclined his ear to her mouth and detected a wheezing that partially relieved him. "She's breathing. She must have had the air knocked out of her." A glance at the guide told Gabe nothing like this had ever happened to the kid before.

Leery of moving her, Gabe carefully tipped Libby's head back just enough to help her breathe. Her staring disconcerted him. "Are you just stunned, *querida?*" He searched her impassive face for clues. "Blink your eyes if you're just stunned."

She stared, not blinking.

Demonios. "Libby, blink your eyes if something's really wrong." His voice sounded like a stranger's.

She gave a fluttering blink, and every possibility occurred to him at once, from a broken spine to an epileptic seizure. He glanced helplessly up at the tour guide who was fetching something from his horse. "We have to get her to a hospital now!"

The kid nodded and showed him the cell phone he'd taken from his saddlebag. "I'll call the ranch," he said in Spanish—thankfully not in Dutch, which many of the white islanders spoke. "They'll bring an ATV to pick us up."

Gabe nodded and returned his attention to Libby, whose expression hadn't changed. "*Querida*, what's wrong?" He was dismayed to hear his voice crack; after all, he had kept a level head under worse conditions. At least there wasn't any blood pouring out of her, no gaping bullet wounds, no limbs ripped off her body. He'd seen all that and never been as shaken as he was now.

Her tongue moved slightly as if she was trying to talk, but the roar and retreat of the waves and the cry of a seabird were the only answers he got.

Libby roused by degrees. With her eyelids seemingly glued shut, she listened to the rhythmic beat of a heart monitor, the low-pitched murmur of many voices. Someone not too far away from her seemed to be moaning in pain. Beneath the thin blanket covering her chilled limbs, she sensed she was wearing a hospital gown. The tangy-sweet smell of betadine and the pinching sensation on the top of her right hand had her prying her eyelids open. *Where am I?*

She found herself in a cubicle of sorts, surrounded on three sides by sheer curtains.

"Gabe?" The ability to speak was a relief. She prayed for the footsteps coming closer to be his, but when the curtain swept open, it was a bright-eyed nurse who marched over and smiled down at her. "You're awake and talking!"

Her amazement told Libby this was marvelous news.

"Doctor Troost!" The nurse raised her voice to be heard over the background noises. "Miss Clark is conscious and speaking."

A lean, balding doctor swept into her cubical and regarded her over his spectacles. "How are you feeling, Miss Clark?" His faint accent suggested he was Dutch.

Libby queried her body. "My ankle hurts a little."

"Because it's sprained, nothing serious. We were more concerned with your paralysis and with stabilizing your vitals." He flicked a glance at the heart monitor. Then, taking a penlight from his pocket, he shone it into her eyes. "Good. Good. Make a fist for me?"

Libby did as he requested, using the hand that wasn't attached to the IV tube. "What happened to me? Where's Gabe?"

The doctor looked up. "Your boyfriend's in the waiting room. Only family are permitted in the ER. After we transfer you to a regular room, he may join you." His grave, puzzled expression kept her from drawing a full breath as she waited for him to answer her first question. "It appears that you were poisoned, Miss Clark."

The words were no surprise, but they still shocked her. So, her instincts had been right. Uncle Paul was a snake in the grass.

"By a plant that grows in the Amazon," the doctor added. "*Cojungali*. When consumed, *cojungali* blocks the neurotransmitter acetylcholine, which is required by the nerve cells to control the actions of one's muscles. You're extremely fortunate that I am familiar with this poison from the time I've spent with the Amazon Conservation Team."

Interest licked over Libby—she would love to ask him more about that experience.

"And even luckier for you, I also know the antidote, an enzyme that destroys the protein blocking the neurotransmitter. In a North American hospital, your symptoms would have gone untreated. The poison would have continued to attack your nervous system, eventually killing you."

Libby pictured the scenario in her mind's eye, along with her father's bottomless grief. Thank God she hadn't put him through that! "Luck has nothing to do with it." God had looked out for Libby—and possibly her very own guardian angel, keeping her alive and putting her in the care of the *one* doctor who recognized her symptoms and suspected the true cause. Tears of gratitude stung Libby's eyes.

Troost grimaced apologetically. "Even so, I'm required by law to inform the police."

His addendum had her huffing out a bitter laugh. "The FBI's already investigating the man responsible." She sketched for the doctor an account of her family drama, adding information her father had shared by phone two days prior: Uncle Paul had vanished from Paraguay by the time the FBI arrived at his house in Mariscal Estigarribia. "Interpol intercepted him in Switzerland, but without any direct evidence and no confession on my uncle's part, Interpol had to let him go. Last I heard, the FBI was still looking for his bodyguard, hoping he'll turn informant."

By the time Libby finished her explanation, Dr. Troost's eyebrows had risen well above the rims of his spectacles. "I see. I'm afraid you'll have to explain all this to the police when they come to visit you."

"I understand."

"Good luck finding your uncle. Oh, and here's my card." He took a business card from the pocket of his white coat. "You may share it with the FBI. Should they require proof of your poisoning, I would be happy to provide the medical evidence and even testify on your behalf."

Libby skimmed the card, making a note of his email address. "Thank you, Doctor. I'd love to hear about your work with the Amazon Conservation Team. I'm a conservationist myself, working with International Water Institute."

"Are you, now?" His formal stiffness was fast giving way to friendliness.

They chatted for several more minutes until the doctor excused himself. Libby waited another hour before an orderly appeared to wheel her out of the ER and down a hall toward an elevator. As they turned into it, she caught a glimpse of Gabe behind a wall of glass. "Oh, there's my... boyfriend." The word didn't come close to describing her attachment toward him. One thing this getaway to Curaçao had made clear: Libby needed Gabe in her life. But did Gabe need Libby?

She pointed him out to the orderly. "Can you get that man for me?"

The orderly shot her an indulgent smile. "I will, lady. But first I must take you to your room."

"Lieutenant!"

Gabe lifted his face out of his hands. Was he hearing voices? He'd been lost in thought, praying like he hadn't done since childhood and reliving the shock of seeing Libby dragged along by her horse. The owner of the horse-riding tour had helped him transfer Libby's limp body into a four-wheel drive vehicle. As they'd sped toward the only hospital on the island, seven miles away, Gabe had clung to Libby's hand, begging her to hang on.

"I love you, *querida*." The words had flowed from him then without effort, making him loathe himself for withholding them earlier. Who knew? This travesty might never have occurred if he'd spoken the words then.

A vision of Kyle Clark striding into the waiting area brought Gabe sharply to the present. Libby's father looked every bit as careworn and rumpled as the last time Gabe had seen him in the lobby at the Marriott in Asunción. The tail of his lightweight cotton shirt was untucked. His fair skin was ruddy from sunburn, his silver hair windblown. Gabe pushed to his feet to greet him. "Sir."

"Where is she?" Clark seized both of Gabe's arms in lieu of a handshake.

Gabe glanced out the window at the pink sunset. "She's still in the ER. I brought her in about five hours ago. They won't let me see her."

"Well, that's about to change."

As Clark turned toward the information desk, a gaunt doctor with blue eyes and spectacles emerged from the ER doors, intercepting his path. "You're both here for Elizabeth Clark?" He divided his gaze between them.

Clark answered before Gabe could speak. "Yes. How is she?"

"Recovered."

That one word banished Gabe's despair. His knees went weak with relief. *Oh, thank You, Señor!* God had protected Libby, just as she'd asserted. Gabe marveled at what had to be a miracle.

"At first I thought her to be a victim of sarin poisoning, but the symptoms were slightly different. I'd seen something similar in my work in the Amazon."

As the doctor explained about the obscure plant, indigenous to South America, Gabe's incredulity rose. Even the smallest dose extracted from its leaf resulted in the destruction of the nervous system. Yet, the antidote was a simple enzyme, one that reversed the poison's effects immediately and permanently.

Clark clapped a hand to his weathered brow. "Then she was right. Paul did poison her." Remorse widened his brown eyes as he turned to Gabe. "She mentioned that possibility back in Asunción, remember? Only we didn't take her seriously."

"Because she only had a sip," Gabe recalled.

Troost grimaced. "And that's all it takes. Still, without the antidote, her heart would have eventually stopped beating. She is lucky to be alive."

As Libby's father pulled the doctor into an unsolicited bear hug and professed his deepest thanks, Gabe thought back to the episode in the dolphin pool and berated himself for not taking it more seriously.

Dr. Troost managed to extricate himself. "Well, short of any complications, she ought to be discharged tomorrow. You'll find her in room 215." He backed away while pointing toward the elevator.

Clark wheeled immediately toward the elevator, counting on Gabe to follow him. The doctor's words kept playing in his head, keeping his knees spongy with shock: *"Still, without the antidote, her heart would have eventually stopped beating. She is lucky to be alive."*

He had to lean against the elevator wall as his head spun and his stomach roiled. Over the ringing in his ears, he could hear Kyle Clark's ragged breathing. The man was having as hard a time digesting the news as he was. "I'm sorry, sir—"

"This should never have happened." Clark's assertion cut him off.

Libby's poisoning by her uncle wasn't Gabe's fault. Even so, Clark's comment seemed to insinuate that Gabe had been lax in his protection. He lapsed into brooding silence, then followed Clark out of the elevator as it opened. A short trek down the hallway brought them to room 213. Following a brief knock on the door, Clark pushed his way inside, leaving Gabe to catch the closing door as he trailed him.

"Daddy!"

Hanging back, Gabe remained on the fringes while father and daughter reunited—*again*. He was starting to see a pattern here.

Taking in Libby's teary-eyed smile, it was hard to believe she'd nearly died that morning. Over the swimsuit she'd been wearing, she wore a pale hospital gown. There were probably nodes stuck to her chest as he could see her heartbeat blipping on a wheeled device next to her bed. Her tangled hair appeared to be sprinkled with sand still, making him picture her limp as a ragdoll being dragged by her horse.

She patted her father consolingly as he hugged her, clearly fighting to keep his composure and unwilling to let her go.

"It's okay, Daddy. I'm okay."

Over her father's shoulder she sent Gabe a wry smile. He felt it clear to his toes and shuffled closer. "Gabe, I'm so sorry to scare you like that."

Though her father hadn't let her go, she held out a hand to him. As their hands connected, the depth of their bond steamrolled him. *I love you, Libby.* The words hovered on his lips. If her father wasn't still embracing his daughter, he'd have said them.

"It had to have been the wine at Uncle Paul's," she added. "He kept pushing it on me. Thank God I only had a sip."

Clark released her abruptly. "That monster! I swear he'll regret betraying me."

It was the first time Gabe had heard Kyle Clark sound angry.

"Easy, Daddy." Libby eyed her father with concern. "Let God and the FBI seek judgment. My poisoning might turn out to be a good thing. Dr. Troost said he'd testify on my behalf."

Clark gripped her bed rail with white-knuckled hands. But then he shook his head. "Now's not the time to talk about Paul. You've just been through the wringer, darling. The doctor said your heart could have stopped."

"It's been beating funny for days now."

Gabe gulped. Maybe it *was* his fault that she'd come so close to dying.

Libby's astute gaze swung between them. "Why don't you both have a seat and take a breath?"

As Clark collapsed into the armchair, Gabe eased onto the side of Libby's bed, unwilling to release her hand and still marveling at God's faithfulness. To think that all these years he could have leaned on God for support the way Libby did. Instead, he'd clawed his way through life, trying to make it on his own and probably making a mess of things.

At the earliest opportunity, he would tell Libby how much he admired and loved her, but not now, with her father around.

Just then Clark's phone chimed. Gabe and Libby looked over to see him frowning at the text he'd just received.

He lifted a startled look at them. "Elliot Bauer's body was found just this morning."

"Body. Then he's dead." Libby turned a stunned look at Gabe.

"Where?" He wanted to know.

Clark looked back at his phone. "In an alley behind a bar called *La Cantina*. No evidence of foul play. The coroner thinks he had a heart attack."

"That's terrible." Libby managed to sound sorry for the massive man.

"Terrible for us," her father agreed. "The FBI was counting on him to inform against Paul, and now he can't." Clark scanned his text again. "Witnesses at the bar said he'd been cursing his employer for giving him the sack."

"Why would Uncle Paul fire him now?"

Clark looked up, straight at Gabe. "Maybe he figured you'd recognized Elliot as the man who tried to assassinate me."

"Maybe." A thought dropped into Gabe's head. "Wait." He shook his head. "No, Elliot was as fit as they come. He didn't die of a heart attack."

With a gasp, Libby seemed to arrive at the same conclusion. "You think Uncle Paul poisoned him! Yes, that makes sense. It might have looked like a heart attack since *cojungali* affects the heart."

An electric silence filled the hospital room.

Clark recovered first, looking more revived. "Well, if Elliot was poisoned, then an autopsy can prove it. That might be all the FBI needs to charge your uncle. He's the only one with a motive."

Libby smiled grimly. "I knew my poisoning would be a good thing in the long run. Here." She released Gabe's hand to reach for the business card lying on her bedside table, then passed it to her father. "Dr. Troost gave me his card. Have the medical examiner in Paraguay call Dr. Troost so he knows what to look for in the autopsy."

Her father studied the card for a moment before he slid it into the pocket of his button-up shirt. "Let's hope this works." Optimism had him sitting taller.

"Well."

Libby's cheerful tone drew Gabe's attention back to her eager expression. She'd made a point not to reach for his hand again.

"With Elliot and Uncle Paul out of the way, I can return to Paraguay."

Her assertion resulted in silence as her father gaped and Gabe's heart fell. In that moment, he pitied Kyle Clark as much as he pitied himself. Letting Libby take off to other continents would be the hardest part about being in a relationship with her, especially since his own job had him doing the same thing—on a slightly more dangerous scale.

Dismay wreathed Clark's face. "Libby." He stood suddenly and grabbed up his daughter's other hand. "You don't need to finish your work. I'll send my own people to take a closer look at the effect of the wells on the environment. Any leakage will be addressed and contained for good, I swear it on your mother's grave."

Libby smiled sadly. "Daddy, you're not the CEO anymore. You're not even in charge of the board of directors. You can't guarantee that they'll agree to that expenditure."

"Of course they will. They're still loyal to me."

"Even if they will, this is something that I *have* to do. I promised the man who gave his life for me. If not for Salim, I would have been taken to Lebanon to be used as a political prisoner."

Resentment nipped at Gabe anew. Even dead, that man was standing between him and time alone with Libby.

Her father, dropping his chin to his chest, drew a thoughtful breath and slowly let it out. "Fine. But you're not going back to Paraguay until your uncle is arrested."

Gabe agreed 100 percent but kept his mouth shut when Libby's eyes began to flash.

She threw her hands into the air. "What's Uncle Paul going to do to me from Switzerland? Nothing. He knows the jig is up and killing me now won't make a lick of difference. Just let me go, Daddy."

Kyle Clark folded his arms across his chest and frowned. "We'll talk about this later."

Libby glowered. Gabe could tell by the set of her jaw that she was going back soon, regardless of her father's wishes. An empty feeling expanded in his chest. He himself had to return to Virginia Beach tomorrow. Soon his task unit would take off to Alaska to train for their next big op.

Maybe he'd see her again after that? As hard as he tried to envision what their future looked like, an image failed to form. Could they hold on to their feelings for each other while spending so much time apart?

As if reading his thoughts, Kyle Clark considered him gravely. "When do you have to head home, Gabe?"

"Tomorrow by 1200 hours." Stating the deadline out loud wrested Libby's attention from her own preoccupations. Her mouth drooped, causing his emotions to free fall.

Too bad Kyle Clark hadn't stayed in Paraguay one more day. Then he and Libby would still have twenty-four hours together, even if it was spent in a hospital. Gabe would get to tell her—finally— how deeply he had fallen for her.

As if privy to Gabe's thoughts, Clark bent over to drop a kiss on his daughter's forehead. "Well, I'll leave you two alone while I go find a bite to eat. I'm famished." Backing toward the door, he added, "Could I speak to you for a minute in the hall, Gabe?"

The request turned Gabe wary. He glanced at Libby for her permission.

"Go." She waved him away, though the line between her eyebrows suggested she was also worried about what her father might say.

Trailing Clark into the hallway, Gabe found the taller man clenching and unclenching his hands, looking totally overwrought. "Gabe, I have a proposition for you, and I hope you'll give it some serious consideration."

Gabe suffered the certainty that he wasn't going to like what he was about to hear. "What is it?"

Clark blew out a breath and nodded. "I know my daughter's work means a lot to her, the same way it did to her mother. But the stress is killing me. I can't focus on my platform when I'm worried about her welfare." The harsh lighting over their heads made him look more haggard than ever.

Gabe slid his hands into his pockets. *Tell me about it.* "What do you want me to do?"

"I'd like you to convince her to stay in the States for a while, maybe get a job in Virginia, close to you. You seem to have a strong pull on her. Maybe if you got engaged or something." He averted his eyes, not seeing Gabe's incredulous reaction. "If she still won't quit—" Clark paused as if weighing the impact of his words.

"Well, I'd like to make you an offer." He met Gabe's eyes. 'If you would leave the Teams and guard my daughter full time, I'll pay you twice your current salary. I know that sounds presumptuous. I just—" His voice cracked with emotion. "I can't *stand* the thought of anything happening to her."

A ten-ton tank might as well have rolled over Gabe. Presumptuous? Heck, yes, it was presumptuous. It smacked of elitism and superiority and all those disgusting attributes he associated with the filthy rich. "You want me to give up my career to be your daughter's security detail?"

A stricken look entered Clark's brown eyes as it occurred to him that he'd gone too far. "No, no, of course not." He swept aside the offer with a wave of his hands. "I'm sorry. I'm so overcome with fears and doubts right now that I don't know what I'm saying."

"But you said the words." Gabe's heart hardened to the man's obvious distress. "Can I ask you something?"

"Of course." Clark sounded eager to make amends.

"Did you lean on General DePuy and therefore USSOUTHCOM to get the SEALs sent to Paraguay to defend your oil wells?"

Clark's eyes widened with guilt. "Well, I might have suggested it. But DePuy told me USSOUTHCOM has no say-so over Special Operations. That was strictly up to the Joint Special Operations Something or Other."

"Task Force." And so it was. But there was no telling how much influence USSOUTHCOM had in JSOTF's decision-making.

An awkward silence fell between them. Gabe stood taller to counteract the feelings of inferiority and indignation sluicing through him. Here was this man thinking he could be bought, thinking he had a right to sway the U.S. military to protect his interests. This wasn't only about Libby and her safety. This was about Kyle Clark believing that his wealth gave him the right to manipulate others, even to the point of suggesting Gabe get engaged to Libby and give up his career for her sake.

Not today. Not ever.

Clark sighed. "I think I've said enough." He turned away with a nod. "I'll go get some food."

In a tumultuous frame of mind, Gabe watched Libby's father slump away until he disappeared into the elevator. And then Gabe turned and looked at Libby's door.

The sick feeling in his gut was the same one he'd carried for the nine days he'd stewed in jail wondering why nobody believed his story and everyone believed Wendie's.

And now Libby's father thought he could manipulate Gabe's future just because his wealth made that possible. Sure, his intentions were noble. But Kyle treated Gabe like his own life, his own dreams, didn't matter as much as his and Libby's did. Assuming Gabe would give up his hard-won status as a Navy SEAL was every bit as arrogant as the law assuming Gabe was guilty of rape just because he was Hispanic.

Bottom line: In Clark's eyes, Gabe would never be seen as Libby's equal. He was nothing more than a tool to be manipulated, an insurance policy for keeping her safe. And it had been that way from the moment Clark clapped eyes on him.

Well, guess what, Mr. Billionaire? This is one man who can't be bought. I may never make the kind of money you do, but I'm my own man. No one manipulates me.

With a deep inhale, Gabe sought to harness his runaway temper.

And what about Libby? Did she have any inkling of what her father had just offered him? Surely not. She'd never once hinted he should quit his job and shadow her for the rest of their lives. Gabe, on the other hand, had suggested she quit *her* job. That probably made him a hypocrite, but it didn't change the fact that her father had pressured General DePuy into suggesting the SEALs should guard Clark's Petroleum's wells. And, just now, he'd asked Gabe to give up everything he'd accomplished and marry his daughter, instead.

Hah! Like Clark had any say-so in whom Gabe chose to marry.

That man had had *zero* say-so. None at all. And there would *be* no future plans because Gabe would sooner face a lifetime of looking for a woman who made him feel the way Libby did than bow to another man's dictates.

CHAPTER 20

Libby regarded the door with mounting concern. Gabe had been out of the room for more than five minutes. She'd overheard her father's voice at first, then the sound of him walking away. Still no Gabe. She needed him to pass her the big mug of water on the tray she couldn't reach, and she was hoping he might persuade the nurse to remove the little stickers on her chest so she could get up and wash her hair. Maybe Gabe could help her with that? She didn't want to spend the last night of her vacation looking like something the tide had washed in.

At last, the door opened—slowly. As Gabe edged into the room, the anger and resentment emanating off his stiffly held figure hit Libby like a slap across the face. Approaching the foot of her bed, he stuck his hands into his pockets. His dark green eyes were as inscrutable as the first time she'd ever looked into them.

"What's wrong?" Her heart blipped perceptibly faster on the monitor behind her. "What did he say to you?"

Gabe's jaw muscles jumped. She knew whatever it was, it had changed something for the worse.

"It doesn't matter what he said." His rich baritone voice had turned monotone, emotionless. "Libby, I've realized something about us."

A weight fell on her chest. Here it came. Nothing as good as what they'd shared could last forever. "What?"

"I'm not the man you need me to be."

She hadn't expected him to say that. "What do you mean? What did my father say to you?"

"You need a man who's going to be there for you—to protect you in all the hot spots you'll be visiting." With every word, his tone grew more brittle. "You need a man who wants to follow in your father's footsteps and do everything he says—a trained monkey, basically, but not a Navy SEAL."

Stunned by his vehemence, she could only stare at him in distress.

"I've enjoyed *every* minute of my leave with you." His voice turned gravelly with emotion she was only just beginning to glimpse in the depths of his eyes. "And you are a remarkable and beautiful woman, both inside and out. But I *can't* give up my honor and my identity for you."

Dismay pegged Libby to the bed. Where on earth had he gotten the idea he needed to give up anything to be with her? "Look, whatever my father said—"

"It doesn't matter what he said. I knew this would happen. I'm not from your world, Libby. I've fought for everything I have and everything that I am. I won't give that up for anyone. Not even you." The words sounded like they were being dragged out of him.

A knot had lodged in Libby's throat, preventing her from saying more as he stepped alongside her bed, bent over, and brushed her cheek with a remote kiss.

He straightened. "Now that your father's here, I don't need to stay."

"Gabe." Helpless tears flooded her eyes. "Why are you doing this to us? We were fine before he came."

The firm line of his mouth softened at her protest. He reached for her hand, seeming to waver as he gave it a regret-filled squeeze. "I have to go." Pivoting, he stalked to the door.

With a gasp of despair, Libby watched him pull it ajar. He sent her one last inscrutable look before slipping soundlessly through it. The door shut a second later with a *click* that seemed to echo the snapping of her heart in two.

Just like that, Gabe was gone, possibly forever.

Libby fell back against her pillow and covered her mouth to stifle the sob that escaped her tight throat. How could this have happened? Only this morning they'd been on horseback, looking forward to another wonderful day. He hadn't said, "I love you, too," but at least she'd sensed emotion in the kiss he'd crushed to her lips. Or had she just been deluding herself?

Her father must have stated something awful to drive Gabe away.

Battling the urge to leap out of bed—she'd been told it would set off some kind of alarm—Libby hit the call button summoning the nurse. It was either that or scream for her father at the top of her lungs. Tears of frustration flowed freely from her eyes. She didn't bother to wipe them away. Her father needed to see what his controlling behavior was doing to her. She was going to lose Gabe forever if Daddy didn't make this right.

A nurse pushed into her room and drew up short. "Is everything okay, dear?"

"Please, I need you to find my father. He went to find food. His name is Kyle Clark."

"I'll have him paged. Is there anything I can do for you myself?"

"No, thank you. Just find him, please."

Minutes dragged by, feeling more like hours as Libby waited for her father to reappear. When he pushed into the room, bearing a tray of dishes for them to share, he wore a distinctly uncomfortable expression. "Where's Gabe?" His gaze darted toward the bathroom.

"Gone!" She tamped down the impulse to berate him. "What did you *say* to him?"

Her father kept quiet, taking care not to spill anything as he laid the tray on her raised table, a guilty expression on his face.

"What did you *say* to him, Daddy?" Her voice wobbled with the urge to yell.

He hung his head, staring down at the food he'd brought in. "Oh, Libby, I was out of my head with worry." He had the grace to look ashamed. "I offered to pay him a salary if he quit his job and stayed with you."

"What?"

"I wasn't thinking." He spread his hands in a gesture of helplessness. "I'm just… exhausted with trying to keep you safe and running for Senate while chasing down my brother-in-law, who wants me and the rest of my family dead."

"Daddy!" She interrupted him sharply. "This is not about *you*. Gabe took off, do you understand? You insulted his pride by making him an offer like that. How could you *do* such a thing?"

He looked down at his expensive shoes. "I'm so sorry."

"Not everyone can be bought." Not since she was a teenager had she railed at him like this. "Especially not Gabe. You should have realized that!"

"Yes, yes, I should have realized. That was—" He shook his head. "That was bad form on my part. I'll go find him and apologize." He moved abruptly toward the door.

Libby let him go while knowing in her heart he wouldn't be able to find Gabe. Not only did the love of her life have a ten-minute lead, but he'd probably fled the hospital like there was a fire under his feet.

In despair, she lay back against her pillow and wallowed in her misery. *Merciful Father, You know Gabe's the one for me. Please bring him back into my life.*

Forty minutes later, Kyle Clark slipped quietly into his daughter's hospital room. He'd involved the entire hospital staff in scouring the halls and grounds for an athletic, swarthy man named Gabe. Finally, a witness reported seeing someone fitting that description catching a taxi just outside the hospital's main doors. Kyle had immediately called Gabe's cell phone having gotten that number way back on the night of the assassination attempt, but, of course, the SEAL didn't carry his phone overseas. After leaving a lengthy and heartfelt apology on Gabe's voicemail, Kyle called the hotel where he'd made reservations and left a message on his room's phone, also.

But something told him Gabe would never see the flashing red light. He would have stopped by his room long enough to collect his stuff, then headed straight for the forward-operating base to find a military hop that would take him to Virginia Beach. Maybe then he would check the voicemail on his cell phone.

Bottom line, Kyle had done all he could do to rectify his mistake, and he suffered a sinking feeling it wouldn't be enough.

Wallowing in guilt, he neared Libby's bed, relieved to find her sound asleep. Her puffy, red-rimmed eyes forced him to acknowledge he was responsible for her heartbreak. He'd gotten so accustomed to "fixing" problems with his wealth that he'd forgotten some things couldn't be bought—like a man's pride.

Ironically, he respected Gabe hugely for turning him down the way he had. What had he been thinking about making such a ridiculous offer anyway? He'd been too preoccupied with Libby's welfare to think clearly. But Libby had nearly died today! And Kyle had every right to be concerned since she insisted on fulfilling her contract with IWI, even with her crazed uncle on the loose.

And now there wouldn't be any Navy SEALs in Mariscal Estigarribia to rescue her if she got herself into trouble again. At least the terrorist threat had been dealt with, according to General DePuy. With Paul in Switzerland, how much trouble could she really get into?

Knowing Libby? Plenty.

Gabe's breath fogged the window on the C-123 Provider as he watched his plane descend toward Virginia Beach, specifically Naval Air Station Oceana, where the airport for all the local bases was located. He'd been away for less than three weeks, so why did it feel like a lifetime since he'd lived here?

Picking out the boardwalk by the bright hotel lights, he

distracted himself from the ache in his chest by remembering those late nights he had cruised the strip as an enlisted Navy man. Those days were long over. As the officer he had made himself by getting a degree and attending officer candidate school, he was expected to comport himself with restraint and dignity. And now, at thirty-two, he had no interest whatsoever in the kind of woman who would let herself be picked up in a bar by a military man. He preferred a woman who was too busy making the world a better place to hang out on the strip.

Thoughts of Libby weighed Gabe's chest.

Who was he kidding? Libby was one in eight billion. He would never find another woman like her. Remembering how good it felt just to hold her hand brought tears to his eyes.

Maybe he should have taken up her father's offer and run with it. How many times had he asked himself in the last several hours if he'd made a huge mistake? Double the salary, huh? Making twice the money he earned now, he could buy himself and Libby a house wherever she desired to have a home base. He could follow her from one site to the next. Under his vigilant watch, he wouldn't have to fret so much about her safety. That sounded like paradise, except for one thing: He wasn't made that way. He was his own man. He charted his own seas. His goals didn't come second to Libby's.

I made the right decision. Maybe if he said it enough times, he could convince himself.

Libby looked over at the driver's seat. "Thanks for doing this, Jaime." She dredged up a smile for the man maneuvering the Jeep down a rutted track that cut through South Chaco. Riddled with holes and gullies created by a recent downpour, the route would have been impossible in a two-wheel-drive vehicle. "I appreciate your willingness to put the environment first despite your employer's instructions to do the opposite."

He cast her an enigmatic glance. "I don't know what you're talking about."

"Uh-huh." She was sure he worked for the CIA, but she wasn't going to make him say it.

"Besides, I'm only driving you because it goes against my code of ethics to let you venture into the wilderness alone."

"Oh, you have a code of ethics. That's good to know."

"Don't get cocky, miss, or you'll be walking back to Mariscal Estigarribia." Laughter underlaid his threat.

Libby's answering laugh was brief. Her smile faded as she regarded the isolated landscape, marveling at how it reflected the desolation in her heart. Ever since Gabe had walked out on her at the hospital in Curaçao, she had struggled to return to who she was before knowing him. Just as she'd known it would happen, her father hadn't caught up to Gabe in time to make amends for his meddling.

Knowing she and Gabe would never have a future ought to relieve her, in part. What with their demanding careers and the distance between them, the odds had always been against them. This way, she could focus on her and her mother's dream of protecting indigenous populations—in this case, by restoring the purity of their water sources. Yet the passion that had fueled her before had dimmed to a gasping flame. Without Gabe in her life, her labor of love felt more like a grim duty.

Jaime's gaze turned to pity as he glanced her way again. "Maybe he wants you to go after him this time."

She didn't bother to pretend she had no idea what he was talking about. "I don't think so."

From the corner of her eye, she could see Jaime shaking his head. "I've never met two more stubborn people in my life. You two are meant for each other, Libby. Find a way, or you'll regret it for the rest of your life."

For a moment, she dared to picture herself tracking Gabe down and knocking on his door. It wasn't just her pride that balked as she pictured the torn look on his face. Gabe had said being with her would entail giving up his honor and his identity. She didn't want to take anything like that away from him.

"I can't do that," she replied.

CHAPTER 21

Feeling like Scrooge, Gabe slipped unnoticed from the Christmas party in the Shifting Sands Club and dropped onto a cold, wrought-iron chair on the balcony out back to listen to the drumbeat of the Atlantic Ocean as it pounded the nearby shore.

More than three months had passed since he'd walked away from Libby. He'd thought for sure he would have stopped obsessing about her by now, stopped spying on her Facebook page and hunting for her name on the Internet while also following her father's political career. Kyle Clark had won the Senate seat, just as Gabe had expected. But Gabe was still as caught up in Libby as the day he'd seen her topple off her horse into the water. Not even his renewed faith could mend his broken heart. *Are You trying to tell me something, Señor?*

"There you are."

Startled by the deep voice behind him, Gabe looked over to see Rodeo and Doc slipping out of the brightly lit door to join him. The throb of a bass guitar emanated from the nightclub on the lower level, telling Gabe that the Christmas party was well underway. Unless something unexpected happened in the world, zero work would occur at the Team building until after the New Year. Gabe ought to be celebrating his time off with the rest of his platoon.

His teammates plunked down in the two chairs across from him, their backs to the ocean, drinks in hands. They behaved as if this was what they wanted to do: sit and stare at Gabe's long face. He met their pointed stares. "Why are you here?"

The blaze shining through the windows behind him lit up Rodeo's blue eyes. "Sir, we need to talk." He made an elaborate show of balancing his bottle on the grooved tabletop.

Gabe rubbed his eyes. This moment had been coming for some time. There was a limit to how long his top NCOs could put up with his pathetic and distracted leadership. "I know." He forced himself to sit up straighter and not slouch. "I've been a lousy platoon leader."

He'd pretty much continuously snarled at every man in his platoon for three months straight. He'd even leveled a punishment on Bam-Bam this morning for a violation he couldn't now recall, forgetting that the young SEAL had saved Libby's life by identifying Elliot Bauer as The Annihilator. "I've been a total jerk."

Rodeo pointed at him. "You said it, not me. And Mad Max has started taking note."

Which was never a good thing.

Gabe sighed. "All right. I hear you. I'll take some time over the holiday to get myself together."

"We think you should talk about it."

Gabe frowned at Doc, who'd offered up this morsel of wisdom. "Talk to whom?" Were they implying he needed professional help?

"To us." Rodeo caught his bottle as it started to tip. "We're the guys who have to work with you, and we deserve an explanation."

Gabe glowered at him. "You know what's eating me."

"Of course we do." Doc's soothing assurance kept Gabe's frustration from climbing. "What we want to know is what you're going to do about it."

"Because we can't put up with your crap much longer." Rodeo softened his statement with a crooked smile before he tossed back a swig.

Gabe nodded several times while digesting their request. "So you're here to counsel me." How ironic. As platoon leader, he was supposed to be the one advising *them*. "Okay, fire away."

Rodeo elbowed Doc. "You tell him."

Doc widened his eyes at Rodeo before facing Gabe resolutely. "Well, we think you should forgive Libby's father. He did apologize, remember?"

It had taken Gabe two months to even listen to Clark's message. He'd done it at the Veterans Day picnic at Little Creek Park, the last time all of SEAL Team Six had gotten together for a barbecue. Clark's apology had thrown Gabe into such a confused state that Doc had driven him home before he lost points with the upper brass.

"What exactly did he say in his apology?" Rodeo wanted to know.

Gabe had to think to remember. In a fit of disgust, he'd deleted the voicemail before he could listen to it again, and now he regretted his haste. "He said he should never have asked me to quit the Teams. He'd been so upset about Libby almost dying that he'd spoken in haste. Blah, blah, blah."

"That sounds pretty sincere, though." Doc's steady gaze invited Gabe to reconsider.

"Why don't you believe him?" Rodeo demanded.

"I do. It's just—" The fact that his teammates were siding with Kyle Clark ratcheted Gabe's annoyance to new heights. "What he asked me to do was insulting. I'm supposed to give up my career for his daughter?" His anger simmered anew. "How could he even suggest such a thing?"

Rodeo frowned. "What? You've never said anything in haste that you've regretted? He already apologized. What more can he do?"

Doc laced his long fingers together. "I heard him give a speech on TV the other night about healing our deep divisions and finding common ground."

"That has nothing to do with me and Libby. Yes, he's a great guy. It's rich people in general that I don't like."

"Wait." One of Doc's fingers rose above the others. "You know he wasn't born into money, don't you? He grew up dirt poor in Waco, Texas. He put himself through college and built Clark Petroleum, literally, from the ground up."

Rodeo piggybacked on Doc's information. "Not liking someone just because they're rich sounds like stereotyping."

Gabe hated stereotyping and Rodeo knew it. The impulse to bite off his NCOs' heads morphed into reluctant self-reflection.

Even if Kyle Clark were destitute, he might have made the same request about Gabe protecting his daughter. Maybe it wasn't that he viewed Gabe's career as unimportant. He'd simply been over-wrought with concern for his daughter's safety, just like Felix had been for his stepson when Gabe was stuck in jail. Wealthy or poor, it was a father's job to protect his offspring.

Gabe swiped a hand over his eyes. *"Demonios."* Was it too late to make amends?

A comfortable silence fell over the table, filled with the roar of the ocean and the lulling throb of the bass guitar.

"So, you're going to call him?"

Gabe lifted a wry gaze to Rodeo's expectant stare.

"You should call him tonight," Doc seconded. "See how Libby's doing."

Gabe threw both his hands into the air. "All right. You've made your point. I'll call him tonight." A weight seemed to lift off his shoulders, pulling an apology out of him. "Thanks, guys. I'm sorry I've been such a jerk."

Rodeo flashed him an evil grin. "Any time you need a kick in the butt, LT, I'm here for you." He pushed his chair back, taking his bottle with him.

Doc rose after him, and the two went back inside, leaving Gabe stewing in a whole new cauldron of emotions.

If he called Kyle Clark after all these months, would the man even answer? What if Libby had given up on waiting for him and gotten on with her life? She ought to have finished taking samples in El Chaco Boreal by now. Was she still analyzing them or already hard at work on another assignment? Assuming Gabe even secured her father's blessing, would she be open to forgiving him after he'd behaved like a moronic idiot?

With the frigid air chasing the fog of misery from his brain, Gabe teased his cell phone out of his pocket and accessed his contact list, relieved to find he hadn't deleted Clark's number. As he hit the call button, a bolt of lightning, unusual this time of year, jagged out over the ocean, forking into half a dozen branches that sizzled across the sky. Warmth pulsed through Gabe's heart. God was applauding him.

"Where've you been?"

Looking harried, Libby's father greeted her at the door of the garage where she'd just parked. It was quarter to ten in the morning. Where did he think she'd been on a Sunday? "I went to the early service at church like I always do."

"Oh, that's right." His confusion gave way to a self-deprecating smile. "Silly me. I forgot what day of the week it was."

Libby searched her father's expression as she shut her car door. There was something different about him this morning. He seemed to be harboring news he wasn't sharing. But with her thoughts still hung up on the sermon she'd heard an hour earlier, she was too distracted to guess what it might be. Needing more time to herself to think, she kept her coat buttoned up. "I think I'll go outside for a while."

"Oh? Is there anything I can help you with, honey?"

She mustered a smile as she approached him. "No thanks, Daddy. I've got to figure this out on my own."

Brushing past her father, she hurried through the lower level toward the great room at the rear of the house and out the French doors that led to the veranda.

The flagstone path edged with flower beds of purple and white cabbages, routed her toward the tree line and the little bridge she hadn't visited since the night Elliot Bauer had targeted her father.

Thoughts of Uncle Paul's upcoming trial flitted into her head. Libby's idea to implicate him in his bodyguard's poisoning had worked, thank God. Paul was arrested, charged, and extradited from Switzerland to face trial in Paraguay at the end of January. Justice would prevail, just as it had in El Chaco Boreal. Both her presentation to Clark Petroleum's board of directors showing them the appalling damage done to the area and her father's lingering influence in the corporation had persuaded the board to make immediate reparations, not just to the wells but to both the Guaraní and to the people of Paraguay, putting exactly 40 percent of company shares into the hands of the locals. Salim's spirit could rest in peace now.

And yes, Libby's sense of accomplishment felt substantial, but it failed to fill the emptiness in her heart.

The path ended at a fountain, drained for the winter. From there, she crossed a bit of dead, bristly grass to enter the woods. Pine needles crackled underfoot. The crisp December air smelling of firewood filled her nostrils.

Gabe. The memory of the last time she'd been here assailed her without warning, lancing her heart with pain. She could still recall the thrill of holding his hand, of guiding him toward the bridge arching over the creek ahead. She'd wanted so badly for him to understand that her calling was just as real as his was, that they were alike in that regard.

And that had happened, though not until much later. By the time Gabe realized how like-minded they were, Libby was head-over-heels in love with him. Gabe, in turn, seemed to be falling for her, too. If only her father hadn't inserted himself between them.

Her heeled boots struck hollow notes on the bridge's wooden planks as she climbed to its height. Pausing at the railing, she studied the creek, edged in ice, rippling below her, while letting the message of the sermon she had heard that morning filter through her thoughts again. It had been based on the Scripture of Matthew about reconciling differences with loved ones *before* approaching God's altar. Maybe Libby couldn't tell what God wanted from her next because she and Gabe had left things unfinished between them.

She needed to put these feelings of abandonment and bewilderment to rest before she could discern where her next job should take her.

With a deep breath of resolve, she accepted what needed to be done. She needed to clear the air with Gabe. At least she knew he was man enough to face her and not run from her call like a coward. Once they talked things out and ended the beautiful bond they had begun to forge, she would know where God wanted her to go next.

A peaceful hush, filled only by the distant sound of the beltway and the wind stirring the naked branches, reached her ears. God seemed to be whispering His encouragement.

Gabe's stride faltered as he spotted Libby through the naked trees ahead of him. Her father, after greeting him with a brief but firm embrace, had shooed him into the backyard with the assurance that Libby had just gone that way. Instinct guided Gabe across the lawn toward the bridge where she'd led him the night of the soirée. Catching sight of her sad, resolute expression stopped his heart briefly before it started again at double the tempo.

He approached her slowly, determined to make this work. "Libby."

At the sound of his voice, her head turned, and her eyes flared with a look of amazement. She stared at him, saying nothing, not even when he paused at the bottom of the bridge.

"Hey," he ventured.

"What are you doing here?"

That wasn't the warm welcome he was hoping for.

"Did my father send for you?"

He had to chuckle at the familiar line. "No. I came because I wanted to."

Her indignation evaporated. "Oh."

"I should have come a long time ago." He started up the bridge one step at a time until they both stood where they'd been that late summer night before they'd been so abruptly interrupted. Six inches separated them now, but it felt like six miles.

Libby's blue-gray gaze locked with his. The cold teased vapor from her slightly parted lips and painted her cheeks pink. She was the prettiest woman he'd seen in his entire life.

She shook her head. "It's crazy that you're here. I had just decided to call you. We need closure so I can discern where I'm being called next."

Still not the words he was hoping to hear. "I'm not here for closure, *querida*."

The endearment slipped out of its own accord, putting a pained look on her face and forcing him to slow his roll. "Your father caught me up on the situation in Paraguay. All good news." He let his admiration show. "And none of that would have happened without you."

"Thanks," she said more remotely than he wanted.

He pushed bravely to the point of his visit. "I've been a stubborn idiot, Libby. I should never have walked away from you."

She blinked, dropped her gaze, and stiffened. "But you did."

Gabe's hopes faltered. If she didn't forgive him, he had no one besides himself to blame. "I have a story to tell you." He swallowed hard, ready to relinquish his pride.

Her forehead puckered. "Okay."

Gabe slipped his cold hands into his coat pockets. "I went to high school with a beautiful, wealthy girl named Wendie, whose father was in the pharmaceutical industry."

Libby's expression turned quizzical, but she was listening.

"After graduation, Wendie hosted a party at her house—a big, whitewashed house in Miami, right on a lagoon. I saw her go upstairs with two of her male friends. Later, when I was about to leave, I heard her screaming for help. So I ran up the steps and used my debit card to get into a locked room, where I caught her friends raping her."

Libby flinched. "Oh, gosh."

He nodded. "I reacted instinctively. I beat up the boys, and someone called the cops. When they arrived, Wendie told them I'd been the one to rape her. So they arrested me."

Her eyes widened with horror. "What? Why?"

"The boys' parents were close friends of her parents. She didn't want to cause a rift between them."

"Oh, Gabe."

Libby's empathetic tone encouraged him. "Her father convinced the magistrate that I was dangerous, so I spent nine days in jail until my stepdad found a lawyer who could get me out on bond. We beat the charges in court, where Wendie broke down and admitted to her lie."

"Thank God."

"Problem is, she left me with a very negative view of rich people."

Libby studied him, then shook her head. "I'm so sorry."

"It's not your fault, *querida*." He wanted to reach for her but kept his hands firmly in his pockets. "None of this is your fault. It's all mine." He had to clear his throat of the knot forming there. "I just want you to understand why your father's offer offended me so much. Since that experience, I've been carrying a chip on my shoulders and making stereotypes that simply aren't true. But that's no excuse for the way I walked out on you. I was a fool for that, and I wish I hadn't." He swallowed hard. "I'm also sorry for not telling you a long time ago that I love you. I've loved you since the moment I laid eyes on you opening the shutters to your room in Matamoros."

The burble of water was the only sound to fill the sudden silence. Gabe's heart suspended its beat as he waited for Libby to either accept his proclamation or reject it.

While holding his gaze, she lifted a hand and gently stroked the side of his face. "Oh, Gabe."

But she didn't say, *I love you, too*. Had things changed between them? "What are you thinking?" He had to know.

A smile played around the edges of her mouth. "I'm listening for a still, small voice to tell me what's next."

"Oh." He should have expected that his apology wouldn't fix everything.

~

Libby queried her spirit—no easy feat when it had sprouted wings and was soaring above her. Two minutes ago, she'd been lonely and despairing. And now, thanks to a heartfelt apology and a glimpse into Gabe's past, she was flooded with joy.

Yet a relationship with Gabe would not be easy. The world needed her more than ever to protect its most valuable resource. And the world needed Lobo to defend against terrorism and corruption. When would they have time for each other?

Gabe's expression was nothing short of anxious. "What's God telling you?"

Gazing into his beloved features, with the crooked nose caused by hers truly, she rejoiced to know that, regardless of what she said next, Gabe would accept that faith guided her decisions.

The answer occurred to her in that very instant, bringing a surge of confidence and a broad smile. "Matthew 9:26. 'With God, all things are possible.' That's what He's telling me, Gabe. We can do this."

As he closed his eyes in relief, Libby threw her arms around his neck and hugged him hard.

Snatching his hands from his pockets, he wrapped her tightly in his embrace and buried his face in her fragrant hair. How he'd missed her scent! "Yes, we can. We belong together, Libby. Nothing will tear us apart again, I promise."

Turning her head, she sought his lips to seal his prediction with a kiss. Beneath the warmth of his mouth, the broken pieces of her heart melded together, stronger than ever. Yes, there would be separation and sacrifice ahead, but she and Gabe were committed to the world and to each other. What a lovely gift from a benevolent Father.

EPILOGUE

ONE YEAR LATER

Libby sat in the back seat of their SUV, one hand on the baby carrier that doubled as a car seat. "I can't believe how much she looks like my mother." She couldn't take her eyes off their newborn.

Gabe shot her an indulgent smile through the rearview mirror. "That's why you won the name game."

She smiled at the memory of them wrangling over what to name their baby. Gabe had chosen the name Sofia after his mother. But because the baby was a dark-haired clone of Melinda Clark, Libby got her way. Looking up, she realized they were already swinging into the driveway of their updated rancher. A six-foot-tall stork standing in their front yard holding a placard shaped like a bundled baby commanded her attention. "Who put that there?"

"No idea." Gabe's tone suggested he knew but wasn't going to tell.

"Where is everyone?" The empty driveway came as a disappointment. "I thought your family would be here by now." She couldn't wait to show off their baby.

"There must have been traffic. It's a long drive from Miami."

"True." Since her marriage to Gabe, Libby had reveled in the boisterous and close-knit family she had married into.

Before she could unbuckle both herself and the baby carrier, Gabe had parked the SUV and rounded the car to pop the other door open. "I've got her." He flashed Libby a grin as he released the baby carrier.

They'd been sparring over who got to hold Melinda since she came into the world, hiccupping but not crying.

He cast a protective eye at Libby as she slipped out of her own door. "You good over there?"

"Yep." Her labor had been long but without a single complication, and Melinda's small size allowed for a quick recovery.

With the carrier hanging from the crux of his arm, Gabe circled the vehicle to escort Libby toward their front stoop. "Wake up, little one," he urged as he unlocked the door. They had bought the updated rancher, located just three miles from Gabe's home base, a month after marrying. "You're going to miss it."

"Miss what?" Libby hugged herself against the chilly January weather. It had been warmer three days ago when Gabe rushed her to the hospital.

As he pushed open the door and stepped back, she dove with relief into the warm house, only to be hit with the scent of exotic food being cooked.

"Surprise!" People leaped into view from behind the sofa and the island in the open-concept kitchen. The baby's arms flailed as Gabe simultaneously snapped on the lights and shut the door behind them.

Libby loosed a peal of laughter. She grinned at Gabe. "You got me, love."

"It wasn't easy to wrangle their cooperation."

Isiris and Sofia swarmed the baby carrier, gasping in unison. "Oh, she's so beautiful!"

Libby's heart swelled with pride even as she spotted Rodeo and Doc hanging back in the kitchen with Isiris's husband.

Holding Gabe's nephew in her arms, Gabe's mother showed Rodrigo his new cousin.

Melinda, now wide awake, returned their rapt stares with slate-gray eyes that kept them guessing whether they would turn green or blue.

Straightening away from the baby, Sofia kissed both of Libby's cheeks. "*Mija*, you did a beautiful job!"

Libby's heart warmed with pride.

Isiris wiggled her hands at Gabe. "Take her out of the carrier. I want to hold her."

As the baby was passed from the doting aunt to the gushing grandma, Gabe led Libby over to the couch and told her to sit. "Don't you move. Your job is to relax."

She rolled her eyes. Her husband was infernally bossy.

Stealing the baby from his sister, Gabe carried Melinda over to his teammates while Libby looked on.

Rodeo stared like he'd never seen a baby before. "Good thing she doesn't look like you, LT."

Gabe scowled. "What do you mean, she doesn't look like me? Look at all this dark hair."

Libby stuck up for him. "And she has his eyelashes."

Rodeo made a show of comparing Gabe's eyelashes to the baby's. "Yup, okay, I see it now."

"You want to hold her?" Gabe tried to hand the baby to him.

"Nooo." Rodeo behaved like Gabe was passing him a live grenade.

"Can I?" Doc held out his plate-sized hands. "I just used sanitizer."

Libby's smile softened as Doc told Melinda what a special baby she was. Could life get any better than this? True, finding herself pregnant right away had thrown a wrench into her work for IWI, but it had kept her and Gabe from being wrenched apart the way she'd dreaded. God had known what He was doing—as evidenced by the online work Libby had found with the Amazon Conservation Team, thanks to Dr. Troost's referral. The Team's five-year grant meant Libby could work from home for the next few years, ensuring she didn't have to be apart from her family.

As baby Melinda began to mewl, Gabe brought her back to Libby before settling on the sofa next to her and putting an arm around her. Surrounded by lively conversation, Libby nursed their baby under a blanket draped modestly over a shoulder. With her infant sucking rhythmically and mouth-watering fare appearing on the coffee table in front of her and with boisterous conversation all around, Libby marveled at the gifts so freely given.

These memories would sustain her when the time came to travel once again to campaign for the protection of Earth's limited resources. Maybe, by then, Gabe would have retired from the Teams, and he could join her. God surely knew they were better together than they ever were apart.

END

FLEE FROM EVIL

THE LOST ARE FOUND, BOOK 3

As he boarded the gleaming white cruise ship, *Escapade*, Navy SEAL First Class Noah Iversen used his six-foot-three height to observe the events unfolding ahead of him. Crewmembers had formed a line on either side of the gangplank. Some hurled confetti atop the boarding passengers while others shook hands and called out warm welcomes. On a balcony overhead, musicians played upbeat jazz—a fitting choice for the port city of New Orleans.

Combined with the warmth of an April morning, the festive atmosphere brought a smile to Noah's face. A sidelong glance at his teammate showed Rodeo grooving to the music as they made their way through the cheerful reception. This Caribbean cruise was just what they needed after their recent, grueling operation in Africa.

A frisson of alarm skittered up Noah's spine without warning, causing him to miss a step. His gaze darted to the periphery of the crowd, half-expecting to identify a threat. But then he remembered, he wasn't in Sudan anymore. The tingle of alarm he'd felt was just lingering PTS from having witnessed scores of civilians brutally massacred.

On the other hand, having been blessed with the gift of

prophecy, Noah would be foolish to dismiss his foreboding out of hand.

Rodeo, perhaps sensing his disquiet, glanced his way and did a double-take. "You good?" He searched Noah's profile with bright blue eyes.

"Yeah."

Ahead of them, crewmembers were pulling passengers aside to take their boarding photos. The cameraman standing behind his tripod called instructions to his current subjects. "You, pretty lady, turn to the right. Husband, give her a hug. Now, both of you smile!" Peering at them through his camera, the sandy-haired man snapped their photo several times.

Click, click, click.

What Noah saw in place of the camera was a semi-automatic rifle. Bullets punctured the flesh of the young couple, making a sound in Noah's head that sickened him. Blood spattered the canvas backdrop. He blinked, and the vision disappeared. "Dang it!"

Rodeo yanked on his T-shirt. "Dude, what's going on?"

Noah firmed his lips and shook his head. What could he possibly say? *I've got a bad feeling about this?* His teammates took his intuitions seriously, and Noah had little desire to worry Rodeo for no reason— not when they were still shaken by the scale of the genocide they'd witnessed in Africa. Why ruin their vacation when it was just getting started?

"Nothing. Forget it."

As the cameraman waved off the couple and called up the next party, Noah's gaze snagged on the long auburn tresses of a woman around thirty, stepping up for her photo, along with a blonde about her age and a little girl. He stared. Wow, the redhead looked just like...

Heeding the cameraman's instructions, the trio turned to face the cameraman and smiled. The breath tangled in Noah's throat.

It was her—Francesca, his high-school sweetheart, in the company of her younger sister, Juliet, whom he also recognized.

Noah stared, dumbstruck by the odds of running into her here. The young woman he had loved beyond bearing, who had altered the course of his life and remained the ideal of womanly perfection in his mind, had grown even more striking.

Always slender, her tall frame struck him as willowy, now. Her cheekbones were more sculpted, and those rosy lips, which he remembered being curled in skeptical amusement, were now lifted in a genuine smile, as she made bunny ears behind the little girl's head.

She had a daughter, maybe nine or ten years old. Noah gulped. The little girl's heart-shaped face was a replica of her mother's, only her hair was dark brown.

Pain as raw as when Francesca had broken up with him raked Noah's heart. She was married. To someone else. Well, of course she was. What did he expect? That no man would measure up to him?

How bizarre that she was here. More than a decade ago, they'd lived in Northern Virginia and gone to high school together. Yet, here they were in New Orleans, boarding the same cruise ship bound for the Western Caribbean.

Click, click, click.

The camera's digital sounds spawned a similar horrific vision, only this time Francesca was the victim. Blood spattered the screen behind her. Cold swept through Noah as her body crumpled in his mind's eye.

God have mercy! No, not her. Anyone but her.

His horrified stare must have caught her attention—suddenly she was looking back at him. Her long lashes came together as if she struggled to place him. Just as quickly, she turned away, catching up her daughter's hand and walking off with her sister.

With a prick of hurt, Noah watched them disappear into the ship's large foyer. Of course she hadn't recognized him. Twelve years ago, he'd been a lanky eighteen-year-old with a head full of brown curls. The Navy hadn't just shaved off his hair; it had packed fifty pounds of raw muscle onto his frame.

And even if she *had* recognized him, would it make any difference? There were 2,400 passengers aboard this ship. They could travel for the next seven days and never cross paths again. But if

Noah's prescience was right—and it had rarely been wrong—then God help them all.

He needed to find her and protect her from whatever evil was about to be unleashed.

Available at your favorite online retailer or by request at your favorite bookstore.

Scan the QR Code for Buying Options

http://bwlnk.com/9781644578124

ABOUT THE AUTHOR

Rebecca Hartt is the *nom de plume* for an award-winning, best-selling author who, in a different era of her life, wrote strictly romantic suspense. Now Rebecca chooses to showcase the role that faith plays in the lives of Navy SEALS, penning military romantic suspense that is both realistic and heartwarming.

As a child, Rebecca lived all over the world. She has been a military dependent for most of her life, first as a daughter, then as a wife, and knows first-hand the dedication and sacrifice required by those who serve. Living near the military community of Virginia Beach, Rebecca is constantly reminded of the peril and uncertainty faced by US Navy SEALS, many of whom testify to a personal and profound connection with their Creator. Their loved ones, too, rely on God for strength and comfort. These men of courage and women of faith are the subjects of Rebecca Hartt's enthusiastically received *Acts of Valor* series.

RebeccaHartt.com

Sign up for the Rebecca Hartt Newsletter Here

https://rebeccahartt.com/contact